The

Short stories about the search for Mr. Right…

Stories By

Princess F.L. Gooden, Kay Trina Morris, Keleigh Hadley & Gina Johnson, Cherritta L. Smith, Richelle Denise, Patrice Tartt, Victoria Kennedy, Tania Renee Zayid, LaChelle Weaver, Gina Torres, Trenekia Danielle, Natalie Woods Leffall, Cheryl Ashford Daniels, M.C. Walker, Marcena Hooks and Loureva Slade

Houston, Texas * Washington, D.C.

Brown Girls Publishing,
LLC www.browngirlspublishing.com
ISBN: 9781625176745
9781625176738 (ebook)

First Brown Girls Publishing LLC trade printing

Manufactured and Printed in the United States of America

Table of Contents

Letter from the Publishers

Dear Reader,

When we started Brown Girls Books, we wanted to bring you the best in fiction, non-fiction, and everything in between. Our plan had been to introduce you to all these wonderful, full-length stories by amazing writers. And while we did that, we noticed that there were some equally amazing stories that weren't being told. Quickies, as we called them. Short stories that would have you laughing, crying…that were heartwarming, motivating, and inspiring. And so, we decided we needed to bring you those, too.

That's why we are proud to present to you, **The Dating Game**, a collection of short stories about the search for Mr. Right. These stories delve into the topic of love in all of its glory: the quest for love and the celebrations and heartbreak that often come with it.

When we issued the call for submissions, we were stunned at the sheer volume that we received. Out of nearly 400 submissions, it was very difficult to par down the selection. But we did…and boy, do these ladies deliver.

Thank you to all who submitted. We had to eliminate some awesome stories, so, who knows, maybe we'll have to do a Volume 2 next year!

Readers, know that we don't take your support for granted. We work very hard to bring you quality reading material that not only satisfies your hunger for good stories, but also gives talented writers the opportunity to tell their stories and have their voices heard, which is at the very heart of Brown Girls Books' existence.

What you don't see is that behind the scenes, the contributors have created a strong friendship and sisterhood. They came together because of their love of the written word, and they've bonded in their desire to propel each other toward greatness.

Thank you for your support of these amazing authors. We hope you enjoy their stories and visit their websites, blogs and social media pages to discover more!

Sincerely,
Victoria and ReShonda

Man In My Dreams

By Princess F.L. Gooden

First of all, I shouldn't have put on this body wrap and these six-inch heels to meet this man at this mall. Trying to be sexy. But every piece of flesh over the hundred and fifteen pounds that my Facebook picture advertised had to be tucked away.

Okay, so I lied on my page. I'm much bigger now. I took that picture when I was twenty, but my face still looked the same, so I used it. Plus he never asked me if I had gained weight or changed. And I didn't ask him if his picture was current. I could be meeting a monster. Right in the middle of the food court near the Yogurt Bar.

Which led to my second problem. How was I going to sit down at these low tables in this mummified suit? I couldn't breathe standing up.

"Sample ma'am?" The young girl pointed the toothpick at me that had a fat piece of meat hanging off the tip. "We have a dinner special for $4.99. Two meats and fried rice or noodles."

"No, thank you." I definitely didn't need any food. Something was guaranteed to pop.

I looked around to see if Todd had arrived. He hadn't. He was already fifteen minutes late, which gave me a good reason to run to the car to take this fat masher off. I looked around for a seat that would allow me to slide into it. I found one in the corner near the entrance. My mini skirt rode up my thighs and stopped on a roll.

I watched as the young girls passed by with their boyfriends. Holding hands. Appearing to be in love. I couldn't remember the last time I was in love, or in like for that matter. I just knew I was tired of being lonely. Twenty-seven years old and no one to call boo.

Last year, I spent $49.99 on three dating sites. I ended up with a stalker and a relationship with an overbearing mother who tried to set me up with her son. He wasn't interested in me at all, but she thought I was a good match for him. So she invited me to family gatherings and church even after he got a girlfriend. She promised to pray to the almighty God that he would come to his senses and find me to be a "good thang." He got married and she is still praying.

I walked over to the windows near the food court entrance so I could see.

Another ten minutes passed before Todd arrived. I spotted him as he got out of the car on the driver's side. He had a beautiful blue car. I couldn't tell what kind because the car next to his was sticking too far out. He hurried around to the passenger side and opened the door. He reached out his hand to help a very pretty pregnant girl out of the car. I thought it was his daughter until she poked him in his side and pulled his shirt toward her causing his lips to land on hers. He popped her on the butt and closed the door to the car.

My mouth dropped. My first instinct was to get up and head to my car, but my curiosity requested I stick around. Todd held her hand until they reached the sidewalk. I couldn't hear the conversation, but it ended with them going in opposite directions.

Todd took a deep breath, checked his clothes, grabbed the door, and walked in. He headed over to the Yogurt Bar where we discussed meeting. He didn't look like a monster. He was really handsome. I had to admit he looked much better in person. He reminded me of T.I. with the way he dressed and walked.

I let him circle the food court one time around before getting up to meet him. I decided it was better to walk into him, so I headed in the opposite direction and stopped when I arrived in front of the Chick-fil-A. I knew he wouldn't miss me because it was in the corner that led to the mall.

"Shay, yo, ShayBaby." ShayBaby was a nickname he had given me fifteen minutes after we met on Facebook.

I turned around, pretending that I was surprised to see him. "Oh hi, Todd."

"What up, girl? I thought you changed yo mind. Had a brotha walking roun' the track ta get ta ya."

"No. I waited where we discussed meeting. You're late."

"A'ight then. Little Feisty. You mad?"

"No. Just saying."

"Ahhh, look at ya. Pouting. I can make it up to ya. Le's get some nuggets and som' of dis sweet tea. Chitchat a lil bit. You good wit that, lil' mama?"

"I guess."

He grabbed my hand and led me into the Chick-fil-A. "You guess? Well, I guess I will have to order for ya." He looked over to the cashier and pulled out his wallet. "Let me have two numba eight wit' sweet tea. Them jumbo ones."

The young girl smiled and said, "My pleasure," as she reached her hand out for the money.

Todd responded, "Naw, it's my pleasure, lil' mama."

She handed him his change and placed our food on the tray in no time. He looked at her and smiled before saying, "Don't work too hard, baby girl. The world needs for you to keep all that pretty together."

He was flirting and she looked confused because he was doing it while standing next to me.

He didn't see a problem. He grabbed the tray, and started walking all the way to the back, and offered to let me get in the booth first. My body wrap hurt worse as I bent to sit down. I was almost pressed to the wall when he dropped down in his seat and pushed me over. He quickly opened up both boxes of nuggets before looking up at me.

"So, wat up?" he asked as he dipped a nugget in the sauce and threw it into his mouth.

"Who was the girl who got out of the car with you?" I couldn't wait to hear the answer.

"Oh, that's Meka. My baby mama. She work at Macy's." He kept eating and looking at me as if he was ready for the next question.

"I saw you kiss her and pop her on her butt."

"Man, you is tripping hard, baby girl. Eat and I will explain." He placed one of the boxes of nuggets in front of me. "Eat. Okay see, me and old girl don't really kick it no mo' since she got pregnant. I try to help her out ev'ry now and then because she ain't got no car and she carrying my baby. Can't let my baby mama walk. 'Specially since I was coming dis way to meet you. You know what I'm saying?"

"That doesn't explain the kissing and the pop on the butt."

"Whew, little mama, you on a roll. You would think this our third date or sum'n. You got fifty questions and eight nuggets. We ain't even got dat much time. I bought you them nuggets to eat. If you ain't gone eat dem, den I'm gon' take them to my little man. He love him some Chicken- fil-A." He laughed so hard his mouth flew open, revealing two gold teeth and the rest covered in silver.

"You can take them to your son. I ain't hungry."

"Why you ain't say that before I bought them? I ain't got money to waste. I got kids I got to take care of."

"How many kids you got?" I was ready to leave but curious to know what Todd was thinking when he agreed to meet. After I got the answer to that I would say good night.

"I got six and that one you saw on the way. How many you got?" He started packing up all the food that he hadn't eaten.

"None. I have a question."

"Ask."

"I thought you said you were single."

"That ain't no question." He got up and walked over to the counter and asked the cashier for a bag. As he walked back over to me, he shook his head.

I didn't wait for him to continue. I knew this conversation would die a sudden death and I wanted to be the one to kill it. "It was nice meeting you, Todd." I slid out before he could sit back down.

"No problem, shawty. I thought you wanted to get together and have a little fun. You seem to be looking for a husband. You probably need to try one of dem dating sites. Facebook ain't for that."

"I appreciate the suggestion," I said as I walked off. I wished I could twist or walk sexy enough for him to regret letting me get away.

When I turned around to see if he was even looking, he was at the counter laughing with the cashier that had taken our order. I couldn't stop and make a face of disgust. The restroom had to be my next stop. This body wrap was going to end up in the trashcan. On my way to the restroom, I made a promise to update my Facebook picture once I got home. This could not happen again.

I made it to the stall and pressed and pushed until I was free. Within a few seconds, it felt like my feet were screaming, "Help!" I looked down and my feet were red and swollen.

It was time to go home. I had planned to get food on the way out, but I wasn't sure how many steps my feet would allow.

As I turned the corner to head out of the bathroom, I ran right into a stocky man who smelled like he had been working out for days. I tried to make a facial expression that wouldn't be offensive.

"Hey, you, you need to hold your head up. You can't see anything looking down."

I knew the best thing to do was apologize and keep it moving. I looked up, but quickly swallowed my words.

"Hey, I know you," he said. "You use to talk to my brother, Matthew."

"Ummmm yeah. We went to high school together. For a minute I thought you were Matthew. You guys favor a lot."

"I get that all the time. Matthew is my older brother. I was two classes behind him. It's been ten years for you guys."

The smell made me want to cut the conversation short. My mind was telling me no, but my body was telling me yes. I was mesmerized by his eyes and captured by his smile. His teeth were pearly white and his skin rode his muscles like waves. Why did he have to smell so bad? And why was he acting like he didn't know he smelled?

He continued, "Shay Barnes. You really looking good, girl."

"You don't look so bad yourself."

"So what you doing at the mall on a Monday night?" He looked across the room and waved at a custodian who was mopping the floor.

"Had to meet a friend. What are you doing here?"

"I do an exercise class for the special needs kids on Monday nights. I bring them here once a month to walk around because the gym where we practice is closed for routine maintenance. Sorry about the smell. I run on the outside while they walk with their teachers on the inside. Gotta stay in shape."

"Oh, that's nice. How's Matthew?"

"Pretty good. Married with four kids. He just moved back here with my mom. His wife got a job offer in Los Angeles. He will have to tell you about that. Hit him up on Facebook. What you been up to?"

"Oh wow. Matthew got married?" Not that I didn't expect him to. Especially since he asked me to marry him after we had sex for the first time. We were sixteen and I wasn't ready.

"Yeah, he married Danielle. You know her. They dated in high school. Went to the prom together and everything. She got pregnant their senior year."

I looked him up and down again. This time I noticed his height. He was short. Too short. Matthew was the tall brother.

My feet were numb by now. Poor circulation and the fact that he was short made it hard to continue the conversation. "Oh yeah. I remember that. Well, I have to go now. It was nice seeing you again."

"Oh, okay." He looked puzzled, but he stuck his hand out for me to shake. After I did, he walked off.

I hit the corner like Cinderella did the night of the ball when she realized it was almost twelve. As soon as I was out of view, I snatched my shoes off and walked straight to my car. I opened the door and threw them on the passenger side. Cranked the car and drove home.

Loneliness embraced me immediately when I walked in my small one-bedroom condo. Silence kissed me and led me back to the couch where I sat every night and I wondered if I would ever meet anybody. I leaned over to check my voicemail messages.

"You have three new messages. Press one to hear your new messages." I pressed one before it could continue with the prompts. "Message from Elaine Barnes . . . Shay, it's mama. If you're there, pick up. Your dad and I think we know someone you can meet. He's a new guy down at the car wash. He's been in a little trouble, but not much. He goes to church and -- hey, just call me when you get this. I don't want the machine to cut....Beeppppp." She was known for long messages. She was also known for trying to hook me up. I hit delete so it would move on to the next message.

"Message from 555-671-2432. . . Hey, this is Jamal. I know it's getting kind of late, but I was trying to see if I could come over after I dropped my boys off. It shouldn't be no later than twelve. Hit me up and let me know. You know I want to see you."

Jamal was my cuddy-buddy. He never called to take me anywhere. He just called to have one-night stands over and over again. I was usually down with it, but tonight I really wanted to be with someone who wanted more than my booty. I pressed delete to listen to the last message.

"Message from 555-432-1111 . . . Hey, you know who this is. I don't know why I haven't heard from you. Maybe the sex wasn't good or something, which I doubt. Hopefully ain't nothing tragic happen. Anyway, hit me up." I couldn't hit the delete button fast enough to get rid of this one.

I met Jermaine two weeks ago at the grocery store and we hooked up because I was sad, lonely, and horny. Like I am tonight. He is why I am staying put.

We'd gone to the movies and two nights later, we had the worst sex. He was arrogant and sweaty and he kissed all around my mouth. His hands were rough. The only good thing was he was fast and that is all I appreciated about him.

I picked up the remote and figured the reality shows would keep me company. They made matters worse.

My laptop sat next to me on the end table. I decided to check my Facebook page before taking my bath. Sleep would be the next best thing.

I cruised through the timeline and was bored after seeing three couples, two smiling babies, and recipes. I moved on to the messages.

I was surprised to see a message from Matthew already. I opened it quickly.

"My brother said he saw you today. He also said you were still pretty. Add me as a friend so we can chat." I added him and searched his page for about two minutes before a message popped up in the chat box.

"Hey, Shay. I'm glad you added me. What you been up to?"

"Hey, Matthew. Nothing much. You?"

He ignored my question and asked, "What you doing?"

"Sitting here on the sofa, chatting with you. How is your family?"

"They good. Having a few martial problems, but who doesn't."

"Sorry to hear that. It'll work out."

"I don't know. I found out Danielle cheated on me about a year ago so I am staying at my mom's."

"You just found out?"

"No, I found out a year ago. I just haven't been able to be around her."

I didn't know how to respond to that so I didn't say anything.

"You still there?"

"Yeah."

"Hey I know this may sound weird, but you want to hook up tonight? I'm kinda bored here."

I looked at his picture again. He looked better now than he did in high school. I thought for a sec, then answered, "It's kinda late. Everything is closed except for Waffle House and IHOP."

"Well, I was thinking of your place because I really don't want to be seen out right now. Trying to wait till everything is final. Plus, I don't want Danielle to think I've moved on before the divorce."

"You're getting a divorce?"

"Maybe."

"Oh."

"I just don't want anyone spotting me out on a date or with a woman before I figure this all out."

"Oh, well it's been a year. Do you think she's coming back?"

"Yeah, we have kids. Look if you don't want to you don't have to. I just thought it would be good to see you. We always had good conversation."

"Well, okay. There's no harm in conversation." This way I could see if he missed me since we were each other's first. Everyone claims there is something special about the first. Maybe tonight I would feel special.

"Okay. Send me your address."

I sent the address and telephone number before logging off. I hurried to take my shower and straightened the apartment. Twenty minutes later, the bell rang. I looked through the peephole and opened the door. Matthew did not look like his picture. I estimated he had gained over a hundred and fifty pounds. The only way I could tell it was him was by his features. But the rest of him had changed drastically.

"Ummm, Matthew?"

"It's me. In the flesh," he said as he walked in with a bottle of cheap wine.

More flesh than I ever imagined, I said in my head because I didn't want to hurt his feelings.

"It's so good to see you, Shay. Mark told me you had gained a little weight, but it really looks good on you."

"You have gained a little weight yourself." Little was a lie. He was huge.

"Yeah well, this separation has really taken a toll on me. I eat when I get depressed. Danielle moved in with the other guy."

I offered to let him sit down on the couch, but he headed to the kitchen as if I'd given him freedom to walk around.

"You have two glasses for the wine?" he asked.

"It's too late for me to have a glass. I have to go to work in the morning."

"Oh, well, I will have yours. I thought you were okay with me coming over and hanging out."

"I am. I just thought you needed to get out for a little while. You know, since you were bored. Talk a little bit and call it a night."

He chuckled and mumbled, "Women."

Excuse me? I really didn't want to offer him a seat again because he gave off these creepy vibes, but I did anyway. He was a friend. "So Matt, what else have you been doing with yourself?" I asked when we settled in the living room.

"Well. Just breathing what little air I have, trying to make it from day to day. I go to work and back to Mama's. Danielle snatched my heart out. She knows she was the only woman I ever loved," he said as he sipped the wine.

He needed some lessons on what not to say to your ex-girlfriend. "How are the kids?" I asked.

"They're good. I guess. I hardly see them now that Danielle has moved to Los Angeles. She went with that man. I told you that already. She said she wasn't in love with me anymore, and she left."

"Oh. What's going on with the divorce?"

"Well, she's asked for a divorce several times, but I just want to make sure because once I leave, I'm not going back. She may change her mind. She has before."

"Huh?"

"Yeah we went through this a couple of times before."

"Are you serious?"

"I've changed a lot in the last eleven years."

"I'm really sorry you are going through this."

"Oh, it's okay. She got bored with us, but she'll be back. You know how people cheat and they think the grass is greener, but when they find out it's not…."

"Yeah but has she ever moved before? Los Angeles is a long way from Atlanta."

"Well, we'll see. You never know. I just have to find ways for her to love me again."

"Have you talked to her?"

"By email." He kicked his shoes off and folded his feet under his body. "You have any snacks? Talking about Danielle makes me want to eat."

I jumped up to see what I had that he could eat quickly. I passed him the chips and went back to the spot where I was sitting.

I looked at Matthew and wondered what had happened to him. He was extremely cocky in high school. His height, smooth ways, and athletic abilities made it easy for him to have any woman he wanted. He was known as the "hype man." He knew he was all that and a bag of chips. Now he just chewed them and talked about Danielle and how he had failed to keep her excited. He claimed to be the reason why she cheated. As I listened I realized his self-esteem had been shot, killed, and buried. Now he was a glob of nothing. He looked pathetic.

That's what I get. His brother was single, sexy, just smelly, but I didn't like him. Instead I just had to know what Matthew was doing. When his brother told me he was married I should have run.

"So Ms. Shay, why are you single?"

"I'm waiting on the right one."

"Oh, good luck with that. Danielle was the right one. Man, she hurt me bad. I know I will never find anyone like her. She changed me."

"I see. You have changed a lot." I rolled my eyes and scratched my head.

"Love will do that to you." He finished off the chips and laid his head on one of my pillows.

I let him talk for another hour about Danielle before I told him I needed to head to bed. He made suggestions for getting together in the future, but I didn't want to talk about

Danielle anymore, ever. I gave him a pat on the back and closed the door.

I hurried to my Facebook to make changes because this had all started because of that old picture. I took it down and replaced it with a recent one of me at our company picnic. Fat jaws and all.

I had learned a lesson about lying on social media. I was willing to take a chance and see what I could attract with greasy lips and a double neck.

It wasn't three minutes since Matthew had left, when he started sending chat messages to my Facebook from his phone.

"You still up? I thought you were tired. You want me to come back by?"

Instead of typing curse words, I simply said, "No, I'm in the bed."

"I don't mind. You're so easy to talk to. I really would like to spend some more time with you. Maybe even cuddle."

I hesitated before responding, realizing that anything I said to him would and could be held against me. So I typed back, "It was good seeing you, but I'm not ready for something steady."

"No problem. I am not ready either. I really don't know what Danielle will do. We can just be good friends. If things don't work out with Danielle, then maybe more."

I laid my head on the pillow and crossed my eyes at the computer. This had to end quickly. He was literally making me sick and tired.

I typed back, *I'm gay.*

I closed the computer. Being single wasn't so bad after all. I grabbed my pillow, placed it between my legs, and went to sleep.

Since I couldn't have a man in my life right now, maybe I could have a man in my dreams.

Princess F.L. Gooden *was born in Atlanta, Ga. She is the co-author of Touched By An Angel (written with Victoria Christopher Murray). For more about Princess, visit www.princessgooden.com.*

Can You Stand the Rain?

By Kay Trina Morris

It's hard for me to believe that it has been over 20 years since I met her. I had seen her between classes. Her Sophomore English class was next to one of my friend's locker. I did find myself hanging around his locker for no reason, hoping for a chance just to see her again.

The first time I saw her, she nearly took my breath away. She looked like the perfect doll, only she was living and breathing. Her almost-shoulder length hair was in a different style every day. One day, she would wear it straight. The next day, she would wear it curly.

I asked around and found out that that she was a transfer student but no one really knew much about her.

She was mysterious – even at fifteen years old. She was like fire to me, and I was almost scared to touch her. I knew that she was different.

My hanging around paid off when one day after sixth period, I saw her approaching. But before I could make a move, Hurricane Sabrina blew in.

Loudmouth Sabrina Jones had had a crush on me since freshman year and I spent a good deal of my time avoiding her. On this particular day, my luck ran out.

"There he is," she squawked, rushing toward me. "There is the man I am going to marry."

Suddenly, the loud, crowded hallway got eerily silent. Seeing that all eyes were on her, Sabrina continued as she looped her arm around mine. "We are gonna get married, and have some kids. How many children do you want, Sweetheart? I am thinking five or maybe six. And I hope they all look like you, Darling."

By the time I wriggled out of her reach, the object of my attraction had long-gone. All I could do was sigh.

My luck soon changed at a school dance. I am not a big fan of the R & B group, New Edition so I was headed to the bleachers once their song came on.

But then I saw her walk in. She looked nervous as she slid her hands in her pocket and bit her bottom lip. I had to take this chance to get to know her.

I didn't cross my mind that she might reject my invitation to dance. So when she said "Yes," it really didn't matter. I had already pulled her to me. Looking back, I guess it was kind of aggressive, but she didn't seem concerned so we were cool.

In the span of a few seconds, Deana relaxed. She told me that her father was in the Army so they moved around a lot.

"I'm an army brat," she said softly, causing me to laugh. That was my first time hearing that term.

"I've been seeing you around school," I said, pulling her closer as I realized the song was ending. I prayed they played another slow song so that I didn't have to let her go.

"I've been seeing you, seeing me," she said with a sly smile. It wasn't a pretentious smile. It was one that let me know she was interested, too.

A tap on my shoulder snapped me out of my Utopia. "Hey man, we got to go. We are going to be late," my brother, Alan said.

"All right. Give me five seconds," I told him, holding up my hand for emphasis. I looked Deana in the eyes. "Listen, I have to go. My Moms is tripping. Me and my brother are really supposed to be on punishment. But I'm glad I got a chance to meet you. Can I call you sometimes? I don't have any paper but if you give me your number, I will remember it. I promise."

She rattled off her phone number. I repeated it back to her to make sure that I got it right. But really, I just wanted to hear her sweet voice again.

I noticed that I was still holding her hand. I just did not want to let her go. So I brought it to my lips and kissed it just like the old dudes used to do in the movies. Out of the corner of my eye, I could see my brother watching me. I knew he was going to clown me, but I didn't care. I knew Deana would be in my life for a long time.

I turned around and saw Alan staring at me like he was trying hard not to laugh.

"I cannot believe you kissed her hand like that!" he said. "I mean, weren't you scared that those big, crusty lips would scratch her up?"

I ignored him and raced to the parking lot. I wanted to get to the car and find some paper to write down Deana's number before I forgot it.

I never got a chance to call her. My brother and I were on punishment and my mom had unplugged the phones so we couldn't use it. Alana and I weren't "bad" kids; it's just that it was hard for a single mother to raise two mischievous boys.

The only time I could talk to Deana was at school, and even that was hard because we had different classes and different lunch periods.

I wanted to skip to spend time with her, but she was the studious type and wasn't trying to hear it. We did make plans to get together that weekend.

I was supposed to meet Deana at her house on Saturday at three. My buddy, David, who was always doing some borderline-illegal stuff called, and asked me and my brother if we wanted to go for a ride with him. My brother was smart – he didn't go. Me? Well, let's just say I never passed up an opportunity to hang with my boys.

David came from a family of criminals, mostly burglary, so it wasn't like I considered him a hardcore criminal.

"What's up, D?" I asked as I climbed into his car back seat. "Hey, Sean," I said, speaking to his cousin in the front seat.

Sean grumbled what I guess was a reply.

"Nothin' much, man," David said. "We're gonna roll by my aunt's house and pick up something for my moms, then just go get something to eat."

"Well, it's noon. I need to be back by 2:30. I got a hot date," I replied.

David laughed. Sean remained quiet, which should've been clue number one. Sean was never quiet.

We rode for a minute, bumping the new Tupac song, and David pulled into a convenience store.

"You getting out?" David asked. Sean climbed out right behind him.

"Nah, I'm good," I replied. I just wanted to hang a bit then go get ready for my date.

"Leave the gump and let's go," Sean mumbled.

I waited in the back seat of the car, hoping that they would hurry up. David had left the keys in the ignition so I reached up and turned the radio on. The first thing I heard was that bass line and the singer crooning the opening lines. It was that New Edition song that Deana and I danced to. Suddenly, every memory came flooding back to me and I remembered how her hair felt against my chin. How soft her hands were. How her body seemed to meld into mine. I could feel our hearts beating to the same rhythm. I wanted to talk to her. I had to hear her voice at that moment.

I reached up and snatched the keys out of the ignition, climbed out of the car, and walked over to the pay phone. Dialing her phone number from memory, I waited for someone to pick up the line. Just then, I hear a couple of quick, loud pops coming from inside the store. I looked at the store and saw David running out with a gun pointed. He ran out to the car and got frustrated because the door was locked.

"What's going on, D?" I yelled, just as someone picked up the phone at Deana's home.

"Where are the keys? We have to go!"

"Wait a minute. What's going on? Where is Sean?"

"Hello," the voice said. "Terry, is that you?"

"Let's go, man!" David frantically yelled.

I didn't want to, but I hung up the phone and raced over to the car.

"What happened?" I said, fumbling to unlock the car door. I dropped the keys.

"Dammit, man! I should have left your goofy ass at the crib! We have to go!" He snatched up the keys and unlocked the door. We got in the car and raced off just as the police sirens approached.

David proved that adrenaline, an inexperienced driver, and a police chase were not a good combination. He sped through the city streets, running lights and swerving to avoid hitting pedestrians. Soon we saw the cops in the rear-view mirror.

"Man, you gotta tell me what's going on!" I yelled at him. The fear building in his eyes scared me.

David veered left when he should have veered right and we crashed into some parked cars. David was able to jump out of the car and run. Unfortunately for me, my door was caved in from the crash. By the time I was able to climb over the seat and get out,

I was greeted by four cops, all with their guns drawn.

I found out later that David and Sean had tried to rob the convenience store. However, they didn't realize that the same store had been stuck up three times in the past month and that the owner was ready for the next robbery.

Sean had pointed a gun at the owner just to scare him. The owner's son was in the back of the store and fired his own gun at Sean, hitting him in the back, paralyzing him. David was soon caught and charged with being an attempted murder and a bunch of other stuff.

Because I really wasn't involved and had been getting decent grades in school, my public defender was able to negotiate a deal with the court and I got probation. My mother – at her wit's end with me - sent me to Mississippi to live with my aunt to finish high school.

Living in the country wasn't so bad. I became used to the dark and quiet nights. The slower pace. The mosquitos that were as big as your hand. The only thing that I could not get used to was that I had to share a bed with my younger cousin, who was too old to still wet the bed. But all in all, it wasn't so bad. My high school credits transferred and I was able to graduate in two years, like I was expecting. I tried to forget Deana. I wanted to move on and stop thinking about her. But it seemed that every time I would forget about her, that song – our song- would haunt me. Those five simple words – Can. You. Stand. The. Rain. - would take me back to that moment in the gym.

After I graduated from high school, I joined the Navy. My commanding officer had given me three choices of where I wanted to be stationed: San Diego, CA, Norfolk, VA, or Guantanamo Bay, Cuba.

I heard through the grapevine that Deana was headed to Hampton University in Hampton, VA so Norfolk was my first choice. I ended up in San Diego.

San Diego was nice. The weather was perfect. The people were friendly. But I was miserable. I felt that my heart was on the east coast. If I ever had the opportunity to see Deana, I would tell her exactly how I was feeling. As soon as a position opened in Norfolk, I was going to jump on it. It took several months but my prayers were finally answered.

After I arrived in Norfolk, I didn't even take the time to unpack. I headed straight to Hampton's campus, which was about a 30-minute drive. I had never been on a college campus before so I didn't even know what to expect and I had no idea how I was going to find this woman. I didn't know anything about her habits. I didn't know what she did in her free time. I didn't know what dorm she stayed in. I didn't know her favorite place to study. I just knew that I couldn't give up.

I guess I looked frustrated because one of the groundskeepers approached me.

"You need help?" he asked.

"Yes, sir. I'm looking for a friend of mine, it's her first year here, but I don't know where to start," I told him, not caring if I sounded crazy.

"Well, if she has you on this wild goose hunt like this, she must be pretty special," he cackled. "And if she goes to school here, then she is smart. That's a dynamite combination. I can't help you find your friend but I will tell this: See that building right there?" He pointed to a large brick building. "That's Virginia-Cleveland Hall. That's where most of the freshmen women stay. Leave a message for her on the board. If she sees it, she can call you."

I thanked him and was about to leave when I heard him say, "Can you stand the rain?"

"Excuse me?" I asked, confusion all over my face. "What did you say?"

"I said, we need some rain. Look at this grass. It's so dry."

I must be losing it, I thought to myself, as I headed inside the building. I left a message on the board, then I waited. And waited. And waited some more. I was about to give up but three weeks later, she called."

It was so good to hear her voice. She invited me to a birthday party at one of her friend's apartment on Saturday.

"I will definitely come through," I told her, smiling so hard that my cheeks hurt.

I was giddy all week thinking about seeing Deana again. I had decided right then and there that I was going to ask her to be my girl. I knew that it was a big decision, and some would even say it was crazy, but I had not been able to get this girl out of my system.

We had never said 'I love you' to each other – we had never even kissed for thatmatter. But I knew that we had a connection. There were two things that I knew for sure, I didn't want to be apart from her, and I definitely didn't want her to ever date anyone else again.

"Man, you are crazy," my shipmate, Nolan responded when I told him what I was going to do. "That girl don't know you. Y'all were kids when you hooked up."

"It was only a couple of years ago. And don't you believe in love at first sight?"

"Nope. I believe in hittin' it at first sight," he laughed. "And I'm hoping to hit some college girls tonight."

Nolan was a hothead from Brooklyn, New York, but all in all, he was cool dude. That's why I'd invited him to the party with me.

"Here are the reasons why that girl ain't gonna be with you," Nolan continued his rant. "She is probably too pretty for you and once she sees me, she ain't gonna be thinking about you. Me and her are going do it in the bathroom."

We roared in laughter. Nolan was known around the ship for always talking trash. Sometimes his mouth wrote checks that his ass couldn't cash. In those times, somehow cooler heads prevailed and he would get out of it.

I laughed at him as I parked the car. The only thing on my mind was seeing Deana again.

We walked in the apartment and immediately felt the tension. The college boys obviously were not fond of a couple of Navy guys crashing their party. A short dude with an obvious Napoleon complex strutted up to us.

"Y'all need something?" he asked.

"I'm looking for Deana," I replied, not the least bit intimidated.

He sucked his teeth before he led me to one of the bedrooms in the back of the apartment. Deana was napping and she looked so peaceful that I almost didn't want to disturb her. The short dude sat on the bed and gently shook her shoulder. "Your company is here," he said before looking at me and sucking his teeth again.

Her hair was messed up and her makeup was slightly smudged, but she was still beautiful to me.

She told me that she was laying down because she wasn't feeling well – something about "girl problems" - and fell asleep waiting for me.

My heart plunged when she told me that the short guy was really her boyfriend. Still, we sat in the room and talked for a while. I admit that I really wasn't listening to what she was saying. I was concentrating on her. She could have recited the alphabet and I would have been just as happy.

"Hey, do you remember our song," I asked her.

She turned up her nose like she was trying to think.

There went my heart plunging again.

"Oh, yeah, the New Edition song," she finally said, putting me a little more at ease. "Yeah, I think about that night often," she added, giving me her smile.

Our trip down memory lane was interrupted by some commotion from the living room. There was some arguing and sounds like something – or someone – being banged around. I recognized of the voice in the ruckus as Nolan's.

"Damn," I muttered. "I'll be back."

True to his reputation, Nolan had been too aggressive with one of the young ladies at the party. When her boyfriend tried to intervene, Nolan had grabbed him by the collar and had him pushed up against the wall. I heard someone had mentioned calling the cops. Not wanting any trouble, I wrestled Nolan away and pushed him out of the apartment.

"And don't come in here or somebody's gonna get cut," Deana's stocky little boyfriend said.

Nolan was still riled up and I knew we needed to get out of there. I looked up and saw Deana watching us from the window. I put my thumb and pinky to my ear, motioning for her to call me. She nodded.

When we got to the car, I had to remain quiet to keep from going off on Nolan. I couldn't take him anywhere.

A few days later, I received orders to report to Greece for two years. And once again, my chance to be with Deana slipped away.

I was actually enjoying Greece. The food was good and the women loved the American military men. I enjoyed that overseas assignment so much that I signed up for Egypt, and then Japan. I'd finally convinced myself that maybe me and Deana were never meant to be.

I was happy until "it" happened: I was on leave visiting family while I waited for my next assignment. I hadn't seen most of them in a few years. I was meeting my brother for lunch, near his job in downtown Chicago. I was waiting for Alan when I saw a pretty, petite lady smiling at me. I studied her for a minute.

"Deana?" I finally said as recognition set in. She was still beautiful but she gotten very thin. And she was wearing a wig. She looked nice in the wig but I like real hair much better.

She told me that she had graduated from Hampton and was living downtown. I frowned when she told me that she was now engaged to that annoying short guy from the party.

"He's good to me," she said. We made some more small talk then she said, "I'm on my way to a doctor's appointment so I really can't stay. But let me get your phone number."

We exchanged numbers and in typical Deana fashion, she kept me waiting. Or we would schedule a date and she would cancel at the last minute. Finally, she suggested that we meet at the park by her house. I arrived early and waited. I was speechless when she finally arrived.

The first thing I noticed was the cane she was walking with. She looked tired. And thinner than the last time.

"Hi," I said, hugging her gently. She seemed so frail, like a simple hug would crush her bones.

"Surprise," she said, gently easing onto the bench.

"Wh-what's going on?" I asked, even though I knew before she said a word.

"I have cervical cancer. Energy gone." She touched her head. "Hair gone."

I took her hand. "Oh, my, God. I'm so sorry to hear that."

"My doctors are concerned because the cancer is aggressive and isn't responding to the chemotherapy." Her eyes filled with tears. "I have good days and bad days." She looked at me and smiled. "Today is a good day."

I took her in my arms and we cried together.

I spent the next few days in a daze. How could someone so young and beautiful and full of life have such a horrible disease? It had literally sucked the life out of Deana. I tried to spend more time with her. Sometimes she would let me visit her. Sometimes she wouldn't.

One day, she called me. It was Homecoming Weekend at Hampton University and she wanted to go. She was too weak to fly but felt that she could manage a road trip. She figured that way, she could get some fresh air when she needed it.

I didn't ask her where Napoleon was, the name I'd given her boyfriend. I had the feeling that he'd all but abandoned her. She didn't tell and I didn't ask. I just relished the opportunity to finally spend some extended time with her.

The trip to Hampton was rather uneventful. It broke my heart to see her so frail but I could tell that she didn't want to make me feel bad. I made sure she was hydrated and stuck to her schedule for taking her medication.

The weather in Virginia was perfect in late October. I had forgotten how pretty Hampton's campus was. It was Homecoming so the campus was packed. Alumni had taken over. We checked into the hotel and headed over to enjoy the festivities. I could tell that Deana was tired but she really put on a brave face. We met up with some of her sorority sisters. They hugged her and some even cried when they saw how fragile she was. A few of them even kissed me on the cheek, thanking me for taking such good care of their sorority sister.

Deana didn't feel strong enough to go to the game so we headed over to Emancipation Oak. Emancipation Oak is a tree where newly freed slaves gathered to hear President Abraham Lincoln's Emancipation Proclamation. We sat under the shade and listened to the people cheering for the home team. During halftime of the game, we listened to bands for both schools compete for bragging rights.

We were supposed to leave in the morning but Deana said that she had a burst of energy and was ready to head back to Chicago. It would mean me driving all night but I was willing to leave if she was ready. We gassed up the car and headed for the highway. Deana decided to ride in the back seat instead of sitting up front with me like she had done earlier. She wanted to be able to stretch out.

I turned on the radio when we were close enough to be able to pick up a Chicago station. As soon as I turned on the radio, the song's familiar opening filled the car. We listened to the song in silence. I had heard that song so many times over the years, but this time, on that day, I got a different understanding. Every relationship has its peaks and valleys, sunshine and rainy days. Days that you love that person so much that you feel you could just "eat them up" – and days that you wished that you had. I had always thought the song was focusing on the bad days; I thought they were singing about the hardest part of a relationship. I realized, at that moment, that they were actually talking about the good days. They were saying, if we can make it past the rain in our relationship, we will be okay. The rain is the glue that holds us together. If you can tolerate the storm, when things are uncomfortable, we will be fine when it passes. In other words, 'Just hold on, baby. I promise it will get better.'

I turned my head to tell Deana about my revelation. I called her name but she never answered. My love had died peacefully in her sleep.

I know that it is a contradiction, but the funeral was actually nice. Deana looked so tranquil. I was sad to say goodbye but I know that she struggled so much in those final days and I felt blessed that I'd been able to be a part of them. At the cemetery, Deana's boyfriend – I found out his name was Bernard – shook my hand and re-introduced himself. It was weird to stand next to him because we loved the same woman.

Finally, he broke the silence. "I just want to thank you. Thank you for making her last days so special for her. That disease – I can't even say the name – but that disease ate her up so bad. The doctors had given up on her and they were planning to put her in a hospice when she called you. I knew I couldn't talk her out of it. I always knew that that there was a part of her heart that belonged to you. I knew it from the party. I tried to fight it but her love for you was so strong. I couldn't compete with you. So thank you for loving her so much."

That day stayed with me for years. It was with me now as I loaded Taryn, my two-year-old daughter, into the car. Her older sister, Taylor, insisted that she was a big girl and didn't need my help. As soon as I buckled Taryn into her car seat, she went back to sleep. I smiled and kissed her on the forehead.

While I waited for my wife, I turned on the car radio. The first lines shook me. I wasn't expecting that reaction. I hadn't heard that song since Deana and I were leaving Hampton. I listened to the song and saw our entire relationship in my mind. I saw the first time I saw her in the hall back in high school. I saw the dance. The dates that never were. A love that was instant and never had the chance to flourish. By the time we got to the end of the song, a tear was rolling down my face.

My thoughts were interrupted as Taylor said, "Daddy, I don't like this song. It makes you cry."

I forced a smile. "I was thinking about my friend. She used to like this song."

"What's her name? The one who likes this song. Is she nice?"

Getting myself together, I tried to talk to her four-year-old level of understanding. "Yes, she was very nice. Her name is Deana." My voice cracked.

"She has my name! My name is Taylor Deana Miller. Daddy, we have the same name."

Now she was excited. She told my wife as she sat down in the car. "Mommy, I have the same name as Daddy's friend. Deana. That's my name, too!"

Lydia's head whipped to face me. "What? Was that really her name?"

All of my emotions got caught in my throat. I didn't answer her right away. I couldn't. Instead, I concentrated on backing the car out of the driveway. I glanced at Lydia and she was biting her lip, like she does when she is in deep concentration. I had told her bits and pieces of my relationship with Deana and I had never mentioned Deana by name. When Taylor was born, she was so perfect. I felt the name fit her.

I wanted to tell Lydia so many things. I wanted to say that she didn't need to compete with a ghost. Because of Deana, I learned about life. She taught me to dream. Knowing Deana – and loving her – had made me a better man because Deana gave me hope.

I reached over and grabbed Lydia's hand and kissed it and held it to my heart. There was nothing that I could say to her but I promised myself that I would spend the rest of my life showing her that I could, indeed, stand the rain.

Kay Trina Morris *is an author and screenwriter. A graduate of Hampton University, she decided to use her overactive imagination put pen to paper. She currently lives in the Chicago area.*

Cocoa Butter Love

By Keleigh Hadley & Gina Johnson

Mason

The taste of blood filled my palate with the first blow, and the second blow took my breath away. I stumbled to the ground and could hear their drunken laughter as they kicked me simultaneously in the ribs.

What had I gotten myself into? I was always taught to be a gentleman, but tonight being a gentleman was about to send me to the hospital or worse.

Some people have dating disaster stories: getting stood up, greedy dates that order the most expensive thing on the menu, and Catfish dates who look nothing like their picture. My dating story, is the most epic fail of all. If the dating game was an Olympic event, I would win the Fail Gold.

The faint sounds of sirens rang through my ears as everything slowly faded to black.

That's pretty much how my date, the worst date in the history of dates, ended. This is how it began:

Saturday morning. 9:13 am

"I own you!"

My shot sliced through the air, and even though it had the perfect arc, the ball ricocheted off the hoop, and toward the gym door.

"Ha! I win. Now, my dread-locked, friend, you have to go." My boy, Khalid lifted his hands in victory and strutted around the gym floor. "Two in a row, you have to go. A bet is a bet."

I groaned and shook my head. Why had I taken this bet?

"I'm telling you," Khalid slapped me hard on the back, "there are going to be some fine women there. You could meet, Ms. Right Now."

"I'm not trying to meet anybody."

"I'm not trying to meet anybody," Khalid mocked my Trinidadian accent but his sounded more like a drunk Jamaican's. "You're the one telling me, 'He that finds a wife, finds a good thing.' What's wrong with finding her at a speed-dating event? Faster finding is better finding."

"You Americans and your microwave love." I shook my head, knowing I wouldn't win this argument. "What time do I have to be there?"

"Eight, but you are on Trinidadian time so, I'll see you at eight-thirty." He picked up his duffle bag and we headed toward the gym door. "Don't be too late though, or you won't get the tickets." He handed me a flyer with the speed dating information on it.

"I'll be there." I pointed at a highlighted box on the flyer. "I want those tickets. You better be there too."

"Man, I'm your wingman." He raised his right hand and put his left hand over his heart, in a mock promise. "Your back up in case of an emergency. I'll be there."

Charlie

Saturday morning. 9:14 am.

I had been dreading this moment for a week. I really didn't know what to expect and was nervous as all get out.

"You can do this, Charlie. It's okay. Just be prepared for the worst," I whispered to myself. I looked in the mirror and frowned at the sight of the red scarf that adorned my natural mane. "I won't be needing this." I sighed as I snatched the scarf off of my head. Okay, here we go. The moment of truth.

I took a deep breath and stepped on the scale while India Arie sang to me from my iPod:

"Your love is like cocoa butter on my heart
Your touch is like cocoa butter on my heart
Your kiss is like cocoa butter on my heart
Oh, boy, you are like cocoa butter on my heart."

I need a love like that. I thought. *A soothing love; a healing love; cocoa butter love.*

I looked down at the scale and was catapulted back to reality. *I gained another pound?* Before I had a chance to wallow in my misery the doorbell rang.

I'm not home. Whoever it is, I'm not home.

I grabbed my black bathrobe and quickly put it on as I tiptoed into the living room to peer out the window.

"There she is, Mama," I heard my sister say. "Charlie, I see you. Now quit being antisocial and let us in."

This couldn't be happening. I didn't have the energy to deal with Sam and Mama right now.

I opened the door and my mother and younger sister stormed in like a hurricane in September.

"Hey, Mama; Hey, Sam."

"Hay's for horses, Charlie, and it's no way to greet your favorite sister and your mother."

"You're my only sister," I mumbled.

Mama took off her sunglasses as she sat on my crimson sofa and smiled. "What's the matter, Charlene? Aren't you glad to see us?"

"It's not that; it's just--"

"This is your weigh in day, isn't it?" Sam interrupted.

"Is that what's the matter?" Mama asked. "Is Samantha right? Is this the day that you, um...weigh yourself?" Mama said with a look on her face that was similar to someone who'd just drank castor oil.

"No it's not my weigh in day," I lied. "I'm just tired."

Sam chimed in, "Well Charlie, you won't be this tired when you get some of that weight off."

"So, what brings you two here?" I asked, changing the subject.

Sam clasped her slender hands together and smiled. "Can I tell her, Mama?"

"Go ahead, baby," Mama said, grinning.

Something told me that I needed to sit down for this. I eased onto my love seat, and braced myself for a load of crap.

Sam fingered her five-karat diamond wedding ring as she spoke. "Well, with my three-year wedding anniversary approaching, Byron and I have been making plans for our celebration. You know we went to Paris for our honeymoon, and Italy for our one year anniversary, and last year we went to Greece, so this year we're thinking something simple like Hawaii--"

I cut her off before she could finish, because arrogance was dripping from her words and I'm allergic to arrogance. "Um, the point, Sam. Get to the point."

"Right!" Sam giggled. "Because you're a plus-sized woman, I know it's hard finding a man who will look past your...your, girth," she said, with a fake smile.

I raised an eyebrow as she continued.

"So, we think it would be a great idea if you tried speed dating."

Silence.

Mama's voice was filled with genuine concern as she picked up where Sam had left off. "We're worried about you, honey. You'll be thirty-five in a few weeks, and you haven't dated since that Leonard boy broke your heart a year ago."

Sam interjected. "Lorenzo, Mama."

"Was his name Lorenzo?" Mama asked.

"London!" I snapped. "His name is London!"

There was a millisecond of silence, and then Mama continued. "We want to see you happy, Charlene. You've always been a stout girl, but ever since Lionel broke your heart, you've gone from stout to . . . really stout."

Mama didn't have the heart to tell me I had become fat. To her, being fat was a disease like HIV or cancer, and she just couldn't bring herself to admit that her eldest daughter had it.

"If you don't hurry up and get a man," Mama continued, "you may keep getting bigger and soon no one will want you."

More Silence.

"With speed dating you'll get to meet lots of different guys, and who knows," Sam said smiling. "You may even find a man who *likes* big girls."

I cringed at the thought of dating anyone, let alone several guys, but I cringed more at the thought of them hounding me for the next month about not speed dating.

"Fine," I said. "I'm in, now how does this speed dating thing work?"

Mama and Sam clapped their hands in jubilation. Seeing the smiles on their faces almost got me excited until Mama said, "Now we need to go girdle shopping! That Lorenzo will be jealous when he hears that you've moved on."

I sighed. What had I gotten myself into?

Mason

Saturday night. 8:27pm

I was positive that this was the dumbest idea ever. I don't know why I let Khalid convince me to do this speed-dating event. Bet or no bet. I was done with women. I wasn't planning to switch teams, but I was done with women. I wanted to move back to my boyhood home, Trinidad, build a shack and fish for the rest of my life.

The last sista I dated brought her mother with her on every date. I was cool at first because I knew she had trust issues, but then, Mother Lolita started hitting on me, while my date was in the restroom!

Wait, I'm lying, I remember why I decided not to renege on tonight; they were raffling off two tickets to the On The Run tour at the dating event. Beyoncé and Jay-Z. Front row seats. Enough said.

The event was being held at the Downtown Hilton, in one of their ballrooms. I got there late, because all I wanted to do was register for the tickets. When I signed in, an overly caffeinated woman with a tattoo of Kobe Bryant on her forearm, told me that I had to "date" ten women and turn in ten evaluation/match cards, in order to qualify for the Jay-Z/Bey tickets. Khalid never mentioned the ten women part.

She looked me up and down and licked her lips. "The way you're looking, I hope I get to be one of your ten dates."

Slow your roll, sis.

"Sorry, I don't date Laker fans. I'm down with the Clippers, despite Donald Sterling." I tipped my head to her, even though she scowled at me and I made my way into the ballroom.

I'd done speed dating before. Usually, there are eight or nine guys and twenty to thirty females, all vying for your attention. I scanned the room and was pleased to see the ratio of men to women was two to one - less pressure on me.

My boy Khalid was nowhere to be found. Typical. He probably already hooked up with the thirstiest girl in the room and left.

A microphone squealed as a pretty, Asian woman cleared her throat.

"Attention...everyone...we are about to get started. The informal meet and greet portion is over and now it's time to get to the real business. For anyone new to this process, let me go over the rules:

"All of you should have an initial starting number in your hand. Go to that booth number to meet your first date. You will have exactly six minutes; try to keep your introduction to three minutes, and then when you hear this sound," she rang a little silver bell, "the gentleman will get up and move to the next booth. Ladies, you stay where you are. And please remember, you must turn in ten match cards in order to get the tour tickets.... I know that's why we have such a high turnout for men tonight." She laughed hard at her lame joke, and I knew why she was single; she sounded like a seal barking for fish. "Now remember, the maximum number of dates is ten tonight. Sorry, we can't allow more than that because then we'd be here all night. And don't get any funny stalker ideas," she pointed a finger at a few suspects in front of her, "about dating more than ten or harassing anyone after the event is over. We have a top-notch security team in place to prevent that from happening...again. Don't try any funny business. If you find someone you like, write their name on the card. If they like you too, then congratulations, you've made a love match! We will connect you happy lovebirds. But please respect our rules...no more than ten dates."

I looked at the number in my hand, Booth 13. Good thing I don't believe in bad luck or omens.

All right, let's get this over with.

Mason

Saturday night. 8:40 pm

The bell rang and I scrambled to get out of the chair.

"Wait, wait, I wasn't done yet," the blonde with diamond piercings in her top lip, (*yes, lip*), said. She reached over the table and grabbed my shirt. "I didn't get to tell you that my goal in life is to get in the Guinness Book of World records for having the most body piercings."

I shook myself free and hurried over to the next booth. A sigh of relief escaped my mouth when I set eyes on a normal, sweet, looking lady.

No detectable piercings. Hair color doesn't glow in the dark. And she isn't eight months pregnant, like the first girl.

"Hello." She smiled. "Have a seat, I'm Emma." She giggled. "You look like you've just seen a ghost."

I ran my hand over my face. I needed to get my b-boy swag back.

Man, what a brother wouldn't do to get some Jay-Z tickets.

"Naw, I'm good." I let out a breath. "So, Emma...tell me about yourself."

"What did you say?"

"I said, tell-"

"Not you...him." Emma pointed a manicured finger to the right of my head. "That's my best buddy, George, who died when I was eight. He goes everywhere I go."

I was almost scared to turn my head.

Is, "I'm attracted to psycho women" stamped on my forehead? What happened to sane, God-fearing, sane, church-going, Bible-believing, sane, Christian women?

"Okay...sorry for interrupting ...George. I'll just let you...listen to him."

She smiled serenely and her eyes glazed over. I looked over at the large countdown clock on the stage.

Five minutes and eight seconds left!

I let Emma continue her conversation with Casper and surveyed the room. I had three dates down, seven more to go...who's next…

Number Four is too thin.

Number Five's weave is doing too much. High maintenance. She won't want to have real fun.

Number Six is so old, she must have an autographed Bible. I like cougars not dinosaurs.

Number Seven looks like she's trying to be the next Lil' Kim.

Number Eight... has.. .a... good... God Almighty body... but... she's . . .too naked.

Number Nine...is crying...must be her time of the month.

Number Ten...Oh my dear God...she's so ugly...it's affecting my self-esteem.

I glanced at the clock again.

Four minutes and twelve seconds left.

I am never getting out-- Whoa.

I caught a glimpse of number 12.

Number 12.

One of God's favorite numbers.

I leaned way back in my chair to get another look at this goddess.

Wait...wait...Mason. Get it together. You aren't here to meet.... She suddenly turned her head and I got a full shot of her face.

There is a God and she is one of his angels. I have to meet her.

But, just as I realized that she was definitely worth talking to, I did the math in my head. She was two dates out of my reach. I wouldn't get a chance. And with their strict rules in place...I might never get a chance.

I was listening to Number Five talk about her two-thousand-dollar weave, mink eyelashes, and how she is the only one of her friends who knows how to pronounce Christian Louboutins correctly, when my Angel stood up.

Thick.

I could just hear my cousin Kerwin, who still lived in Trinidad exclaim, "Dat girl rel bess. She top-notch sexy, yuh." Bess was Trinidadian slang for hot. And my Angel was bess and beautiful.

"Esscuse me?"

I winced.

"I axed chu a queshon." Number Five snapped her long, acrylic claws in my face. Her voice literally made my testicles draw up. I needed to get out of earshot from her before she did permanent damage to my boys.

I tore my eyes away from my Angel and tried to remember my Trinidadian manners. But every second with Number Five was a second wasted.

Ding!

My six minutes of hell were up. *Saved by the bell.*

I popped out of my seat and looked over at Old Number Six. Old Mother Hubbard. She was asleep. Poor Nana, out way past her normal 6 pm bedtime, but that gave me the chance to find my Angel.

He that findeth a wife, findeth a good thing, right Lord? I don't know if this is my future wife, but I'd appreciate some divine intervention in helping me find my Angel.

Charlie

Saturday night. 8:50 pm

I pinched myself as I scurried to the bathroom. *Don't start crying. Not here. Not now.*

This whole speed dating experience had been a complete disaster, and I couldn't help but blame Mama and Sam. All of this was their stupid idea, along with the waist trainer that was cutting off my circulation.

"Kandi Burruss swears by her waist trainer," Sam had said.

"Isn't Kandi that fat girl on Real Housewives of Atlanta?" Mama asked, while looking at herself in the dressing room mirror.

I had been irritated beyond measure. I would've been content with wearing an outfit in my closet, but leave it to my condescending family to make me feel like everything in my wardrobe looked like a burlap bag.

"Kandi is *not* fat," I said, sucking in my stomach. "Hell, I'd love to have her figure," I mumbled under my breath.

Mama had gasped as she made her way over to me. "Charlene, baby, I'm your mother. Nobody loves you more than me, but you need to listen to me on this. Kandi *is* fat. You've just gotten so big, you can't tell anymore. Breaks my heart," Mama said as her eyes welled up with tears.

"You're crying because I'm fat? Seriously, Mama?"

Sam rushed to Mama's side and rubbed her back. "Charlie, you have no idea how hard it's been for us to just watch you while you let yourself go. Ever since you and London broke up, you've never been the same. You used to be shapely, and now…."

I shot Sam a sharp look.

"I mean, you're still beautiful, but you're just big and beautiful," Sam said, with a half-smile. "Really, really big and beautiful."

"And that hair," Mama said.

I wasn't about to listen to Mama give another one of her natural hair bashing speeches.

"Well I think I'm going to go ahead and get the blue dress," I'd said changing the subject. "I love Maxi dresses and this one is slenderizing."

"It is," Sam said. "But it will look better with a waist trainer."

I had reluctantly gave in, and now here I was in the bathroom, feeling like I was being hugged by a boa constrictor. I looked in the mirror as I wiped a tear from my cheek. Some men could be so cruel. I couldn't believe that date Number One told me that he had a strict policy against dating women who weighed more than him. And date Number Two told me that I had a "pretty face," as if the rest of me was plagued. But date Number Five had topped them all by coming right out and saying: "I don't date plus-sized women; they're not good in bed."

The little inkling of hope that gave me the slightest amount of excitement that I might actually meet a decent guy, was gone. I blew my nose, blinked back the remainder of my tears, and exited the bathroom, only to bump into someone.

"I'm sorry," I said, walking by.

"It's all right," the stranger replied.

I didn't even bother looking to see who I had bumped. I was just trying to hurry up and get outside to my car before I died from asphyxiation. *Can't wait to get this stupid girdle off.*

I made my way out the door and took note of the sky. It was breathtaking. Streaks of purple, orange, and pink were the perfect garnishment to the blue horizon.

Almost to the car. Just keep moving. You're almost there.

With about ten steps to go, I felt it. A pop, and then instant relief. My waist trainer was history.

I wanted to laugh and cry at the same time, but was interrupted by the voice I'd heard just a few minutes ago; the voice of the stranger I had just bumped.

"Excuse me, sis," he said, jogging toward me. "I think you dropped something."

This time I looked up at him and standing in front of me, was a sexy, chestnut complexioned man. His eyes were so alluring I almost forgot how upset I was. His velvety locs were pulled back into a ponytail, and his masculine hands made me yearn to be touched. *Get it together, Charlie. He's fine, but he's more than likely a jerk.*

When he spoke again, my knees weakened. *He has an accent?* Then I looked at what he was holding in his hand and almost fainted.

"You were in such a hurry that I think you dropped this. I noticed it fall from...somewhere; I don't know, probably your purse."

My mouth was dryer than tree bark, as I looked at this perfect specimen of a man holding one of the staves from my waist trainer in his large hand.

My cheeks were hot with embarrassment, and my hands were trembling as I thanked him for this catastrophe.

"Thanks for um...for getting this," I said, looking down and walking to my car.

"You seem like you're in a hurry," he said.

I let out a sarcastic laugh. "You could say that. I have a hot date with my shower and then bed."

He smiled, and my heart turned a flip. "Well I don't want to hold you up, but I just wanted you to know that you were the most angelic woman here tonight." He paused and then said, "I'm being rude. I'm sorry, my name is Mason."

It took me a minute before I remembered how to speak. "I'm Charlene, but my friends call me Charlie."

"That's a great name."

"Thanks," I said, opening my car door. "Well, it was nice meeting you, Mason."

"The pleasure was all mine, Charlene."

I exhaled as I started my car and watched Mason walk away. *He looks just as good from the back as he does from the front!* I gazed at him a bit longer, when suddenly he turned around. I probably got whiplash from looking down so quickly. *I hope he didn't see me looking! Wait! What is he doing?*

With each step that Mason took back to my car, my heart pounded a bit harder. *What does he want?*

I rolled my window down and smiled. "Did I drop something else?" I said with a nervous grin.

Mason chuckled. "No, but I was wondering if you'd like to get together to have dinner sometime."

All I could do was stare.

Mason continued. "Or if you're not in too much of a hurry, maybe we can go somewhere and chat tonight? We could enjoy this sunset."

Don't do it, girl! Remember what happened with London! He probably just wants to get in your pants!

"I'd love to," I said, ignoring my conscience.

Mason smiled. "You'd love to...what? Go to dinner sometime or go watch the sun set tonight?"

Don't do it, girl!

"I actually wouldn't mind grabbing a bite now." *Stop acting like a fat girl!* "Then we can watch the sun set. If you don't mind," I said, sheepishly.

Mason looked like he was as excited as I was. "That sounds great."

I couldn't believe what I had just done. This would be the first time I had dated since London.

I've got nothing to lose, I thought. *It's not like this night could get any worse.*

Mason

Saturday night. 9:02 pm

I pointed back in the direction we had just come from. "Why don't we have a meal back at the hotel. They have a five star restaurant." God, I was thankful that I took that second chance.

She opened the car door, stood up, and exhaled like she had been suffocating all evening. Up close, I could see that she had a faint smattering of freckles across the bridge of her nose. Her skin was refreshingly clean and smooth and she smelled like gardenias and sunshine. And her name was Charlene. She locked her car and we headed back toward the hotel.

"You know, my mother's name is Charlene. Her friends called her Charlie, too."

She stopped walking and punched me in the arm playfully. Our first love tap. "Get out of here!"

"No, no, I'm serious. Look." I pulled out my wallet and showed her the obituary I kept folded in my billfold.

She raised her eyebrows as she held the worn paper gingerly. "Wow. She's breathtaking. You have her soulful eyes." She placed a soft, warm hand on my back. "I'm sorry that she passed away."

"Thanks. She was my best friend, and I miss her every day." I shook my head. "I'm sorry to be such a downer. This isn't exactly the proper discussion for a first date."

"This is a first date?" she said with a giggle. Her laughter sounded like musical instruments.

But before I could answer, two guys that I recognized from the speed dating event approached us. I could smell the alcohol emanating from them and knew this was about to be a problem. Where was Khalid when I needed him? This felt like an emergency. I instinctively stood in front of Charlie.

"Heeeeeeeeeyyyy, it's Big Blue. The one with the pretty face and junk… all over." He elbowed his friend and they almost fell over one another.

"You can't go home with that one, son. She's going to break your bed!" He wiped some drool from the corner of his mouth. "Here's a tip. Do it on the floor."

I felt a surge of heat and adrenaline flow through my body. I balled up my fist and said through gritted teeth, "That's enough. I can see you're drunk, so I'm going to allow you one chance to apologize to this true lady here."

I felt Charlie pull me back a little. "Ignore them, Mason. I'm used to it and I don't want you to get hurt over little ol' me."

"Little?" the one with the reddest eyes said. "Girl, ain't nothing little on you but your pinky toe."

The other one laughed. "Hey Julius, have you ever been with a big girl?" He turned his lustful eyes to Charlie. "I wonder what it's like…"

The air crackled with tension because this suddenly changed from harsh teasing to something far more sinister.

The next few moments were a blur.

Charlie

Saturday, 9:54 pm

I regretted answering the phone as soon as I said, "Hello."

"So how was your date?" Sam giggled.

I was walking so fast that I was out of breath as I tried responding to my sister.

"I can't talk right now, Sam. I don't even know why I answered the phone."

Sam's laugh turned naughty. "Whoa, the date went that good huh?"

A nurse's voice boomed throughout the hospital over the P.A. system, as I walked through the double doors of the emergency room.

"Paging, Dr. Murray…"

"Charlie! You're at the hospital? What happened?"

"I gotta go, Sam!"

When I walked into the room, I didn't know whether to burst into tears or run up to Mason and give him a kiss. He had a black eye, a swollen lip, and was wincing in pain as he held his side. Still he managed to give me a little smile, when he saw me standing in the doorway.

"Hey you," he whispered.

"Mason, I--I don't know, I'm just--"

"Charlie, it's all right."

"No, it's not."

"Come here, Charlie."

I wanted to come closer, but I couldn't move. The lump in my throat was growing and I was so overwhelmed with gratitude toward this man; this gorgeous stranger who had actually fought for me. London wouldn't even have done that. He would've walked away knowing that I, his fiancée, was mortified by the insults. But not Mason. He had defended my honor. He had defended my womanhood as those two jerks made fun of the most sacred parts of me.

"It's okay, Charlie."

As I pulled up a chair next to Mason's bedside, the dam broke, and warm tears spilled onto my cheeks.

"Charlie, please. Don't cry. I'm so sorry."

"You have nothing to be sorry about," I sniffed. "What you did for me out there..." I fought back more tears as I continued. "What you did for me out there was heroic. No one has ever; no one *would* ever; no man has ever thought I was special enough to defend, and you don't even know me."

With one hand Mason held his side, and with the other hand he wiped my tears away.

"Charlie, I know we just met an hour ago, but I know enough about you to know that you're worth fighting for."

My heart raced, and suddenly I felt as shy as a virgin on a honeymoon. "How do you know that?"

"I knew that when I first saw you. It's the way you carry yourself. It's the way you walk, it's the way you smile. You're not like the other girls. I know when I'm in the presence of a lady."

Wow, I guess chivalry isn't dead.

"So what did the doctor say? Sorry I didn't ride in the ambulance with you. I was still talking to the police. It looks like those creeps are going to be charged with assault."

As Mason answered, I took note of his muscular frame underneath his hospital gown.

Oh my....

"No need to apologize. Doc says I have a couple broken ribs, but that's the worst of my injuries. I'd say I'm blessed because it definitely could've been worse. Nowadays cats fight with guns instead of their fists, so I'd say all in all I'm pretty fortunate."

I smiled. "Well I'm glad that you're going to be fine."

Mason chuckled. "Some first date, huh? We were supposed to be having dinner right now, not waiting in the emergency room."

"It's fine, Mason. I'm just glad that you're alright."

"And," Mason said slowly. "I'm sure there will be plenty more dates after this."

I tried not to smile too hard. "I'm counting on it."

What had started out as a horrible evening had turned out to be enchanting and somehow I knew that this was only the beginning.

India Arie sure was on to something. Mason was cocoa butter to my bruised heart, and I was looking forward to being in love again.

Keleigh Crigler Hadley believes faith and fiction is a match made in heaven. She is the award-winning author of the Preacher's Kids series, Revenge, Inc., co-contributor of, The Motherhood Diaries, and the upcoming novel with Brown Girls Books, What You Won't do for Love. Connect with her on social media and at www.keleighcriglerhadley.com

Gina Johnson *is a passionate author who's had the privilege of being co-contributor to the Motherhood Diaries 1&2. Her love of all things literary is the driving force behind her God-given talent to write. She resides in Southwest Michigan with her husband of fourteen years and their three children. Gina is excited about the release of her first novel, Diary of a Homewrecker, coming soon. You can follow her and the comical antics of her children on Facebook's Johnson Family Circus page.*

Sunday Love

By Cherritta L. Smith

I put the music on and even though it was our song, he wouldn't dance with me. He ignored the black mini dress that accentuated the small of my back, and the batting of my hazel eyes. Even my new honey blond highlighted pixie cut didn't faze him.

"Not right now," my man said, and put his hands in between us and gently pushed me away.

He wouldn't hold me . . . he wouldn't caress me. . . no matter how hard I loved him. . . he wouldn't do it. Romell wouldn't love me back.

I closed my eyes and felt the wetness of a teardrop roll down my left cheek. This wasn't his first time doing this, but it was going to be my last time trying. I'd said that before, but this time I meant it. My heart couldn't take any more. I was close to being done. . . and the sad part is that I knew he was, too.

Every since, our son. . . my son, Jamere, turned five years old three months ago, I couldn't sway us back to romance. It wasn't like it used to be . . . a bouquet of white tulips every Sunday morning, with a new dress that just happened to catch his eye, laying out for me before church, or a kiss mid waist after making love. It had been his ritual. But, it just hadn't been that way anymore. We were broken.

We both turned our heads toward the bedroom door when we heard the knocking.

"Wait a minute," I shouted as I blew out the candles and turned on the light, wondering how my son had escaped sleep.

I opened the door, pulled him inside, and bent down, coming face to face with him. "I put you to bed at seven o'clock. What are you doing up?"

Romell interrupted, "Come here, little man," and beckoned the glue that held our relationship together.

Jamere ran over to Romell with bright widened eyes.

At the sight of this, I marched over to the stereo, and twisted the knob bringing Toni Braxton's sultry riff to an all time low - lower than I've ever listened to one of her soulful compositions before.

"My boy," I heard Romell say as he scooped him up into his arms.

Jamere giggled and leaned his head on top of his daddy's shoulder.

I turned around and faced the both of them with my hand on my hip. "You need to go back to bed," I demanded. With Jamere up, I'd never be able to finish what I was trying to start.

Romell took one look at me and then spoke into Jamere's ear. "Tonight is mommy and daddy's special time," he said and then explained further. "You know? Like, how me and you do when I take you to see the Laker's play basketball," Romell said. "That's our time . . . and now this is our time," Romell said, putting Jamere down as he pointed at me and then at himself.

Jamere frowned after Romell took hold of his tiny hand and led him back to his bedroom, with me following behind them.

I stood in the doorway with my arms folded and watched as Romell tucked him underneath his Kobe Bryant themed basketball sheets. "Sleep tight, son," Romell said and kissed Jamere's small rounded forehead. Then, their balled hands touched for the second fist bump of the night.

That was my signal. I walked in, went over to his bed, bent down, and kissed his chubby cheek. "Good night, Jamere," I said, making my tone stern. "I love you. And, don't get up any more tonight." I gave him that 'I mean business' glare and walked out.

Romell was behind me. He'd left an inch of space between Jamere's bedroom door and his door post, before making his way up the hallway.

Romell reentered our bedroom and eased the door shut. "Carmella, when are you going to tell Jamere that I'm not his father?" he asked.

I turned my face away from him.

"I think that it's time." Romell paused for a moment and then gained eye-to-eye contact with me. "He'll be in kindergarten this year . . . and, you messed up so you need to fix it."

I knew better than to say anything. He was right. I messed up but the problem was, I didn't know how to fix it. I wasn't a fixer. But, the one thing that I did know was that I loved Romell more than life itself, and I was willing to do whatever it took to make things right again.

I walked over and sat on the edge of our bed and gazed out into open space. In my opinion, Jamere never had to know.

Finally, I looked at Romell and revealed what I'd been thinking. "I never thought that I would have to," I mumbled, and then lifted my right hand and swept the hair away from my face. . . the piece that covered my right eye.

And, that was probably a pretty silly thing to confess. . . stupid almost, I gathered, after Romell raised his left eyebrow, lowered it, and then shook his head. But, it was true. . . it was what I believed. . . to be more honest. . . it's what I'd hoped.

Romell never wanted to hear any of my explanations or excuses for why I cheated on him. Not then, and probably not now. Back then, I was spun inside the web of our wedding issues, our fighting families, and I had reached out for some comfort.

I reached out for what felt good, which was Jonah, my childhood sweetheart, but he wasn't safe. He lived an undesirable life. Often, making bad decisions and living life on the edge, and I knew that. But, for that moment it didn't stop me from making him my solution, and because of it, Jamere ended up being our result.

Romell never brought it up, talked about it, or dwelled on it, so why now I wondered. Then, I remembered, it was the fifth anniversary of our failed wedding attempt, and the unforgettable remembrance of my official day of shame.

We hadn't discussed it since the incident. Of course, everything was canceled, all the wedding gifts were returned, and Romell moved out as expected. Thanks to his 'something ain't right' sister, Ramona, the sleuth, the whole thing was a wash.

But, there was one thing that couldn't be washed away and that was his love for me. No matter how many pictures she'd shown him of me going inside Jonah's apartment and us coming out hours later, together, holding hands.

The love that Romell had for me, pulled him back into my arms, and led us to that beautiful July, Sunday morning, at Cedar-Sinai Medical Center's maternity ward, where Romell severed Jamere's umbilical cord with the scissors that the doctor handed him, and we were back together. . . a couple. . . again.

Once that happened, I thought he'd cut away my wrong, but, sadly I was mistaken. Here we were five and a half years later and I could see that he was still hanging on to it. He wasn't going to let it slide. And, Romell standing over me at this very moment, while I sat on the edge of our bed, unloosening the straps on my fire red six-inch heels, commanding me to face this head on, was proof of that.

He followed the length of my legs with his eyes, then broke out of his trance. "So, when?" he asked, reminding me that I hadn't answered his question.

I looked up. "Am I'm gonna tell Jamere?" I asked with big eyes.

"Yes."

I shrugged. "I don't know." And, I didn't know. But, he stood there as if he was waiting for me to give him a better answer, and everything within me wanted to do that, so I tried again. "As soon as the time is right. . . I. . . I guess." It was the best that I could come up with. First of all, I never figured that I'd have to do this ever and secondly, that I'd have to do it alone.

Romell paced back and forth. He stopped in front of me.

"The sooner the better, he's bound to find out in the years to come and you don't want that. . . you don't want that hanging over your head," Romell advised.

I just sat there with a blank stare.

"Aren't you going to say something?"

Say, what? I had no comeback. I was stumped. "Babe, I was listening to you."

He gave me the side eye. "If you hadna'..." Then, he stopped mid-sentence, and then started up again. "I can't believe that you let him. . . " he uttered and then cut that one off too.

I sighed. "No, speak." I really didn't have the right to order him to do anything, and the fact that he was coming at me like this, made me nervous. But, I'm a woman about mine's so I squared my shoulders, braced myself, took a deep breath and then let it go, "Say, it. Let him what?" I asked ready to deal with whatever I had to in order for us to get through this.

"Take what belonged to me. I got over everything. . . you having Jamere and him not being my seed, the wedding not happening, but it's hard to erase the thought of another man entering my woman," he blurted. "I felt like I'd been robbed."

There it was. He was ready to talk about it. After all these years, he finally put it out in the air, but the truth is that Jonah hadn't stolen anything from Romell. I gave it to him. . . twice.

"We didn't make love, it was just sex." Then, I added, "I didn't even kiss him." Saying that, I hoped would ease his mind because it was true.

"You're unbelievable. After, all this time that's the best you can come up with."

I smacked my lips. Nothing that I said seemed to be good enough. I had no right answers for my wrong action. "What do you want me to say? I haven't seen or heard from him since. I thought we moved way past that. I love you and you know that." I made my way over to him. I tried to slip my arms around his defined muscled abs. "Please, don't do this," I begged.

He backed away from me. "I need to be by myself."

I threw my arms up in the air. "Okay." I grabbed a pillow from my side of the bed. "I'll sleep on the sofa."

He hesitated, then said, "You don't have to. . . I'm leaving."

I stopped in the middle of our bedroom floor. "Wait. What?" I asked, but what he'd said wasn't unintelligible. I heard those six words and twenty-two letters loud and clear. I was just shocked that he was going this far.

"I can't continue to live with you anymore. Every second, minute, hour, day, month and year it gets worse. It's eating me up inside. I've tolerated it long enough. I love you but marriage is not for us and I don't know that it'll ever be."

I had to catch my breath. “Is there someone else?” I asked with a nervous laugh. “Tell me something.” Tears filled my eyes.

“There’s no one else,” he said and then added, “It’s not a workable situation, Carmella. Things aren’t adding up.”

Romell was dignified when he’d said it, as if he was talking to one of his clients, at his accounting firm. Now, he was handling me like a job.

The combination of his calmness and slow calculated breaths screamed confidence. I could tell that he was comfortable with his decision, but I didn’t let that stop me.

I reached for him...tried to touch his hand. I wanted him to feel me. I was desperate. Now, I had tons of things to say. “You signed his birth certificate and played the role of his father, but you can’t get over how he got here. I’m not understanding this at all.” I understood. . . he was ending it. Everything that I fought to keep was fading and fast.

He moved my hands away. “Jamere will always be a part of my life. I’m his daddy and no one can take that away from me. . . ever. I will be that for him till the day I leave this earth but a boy should know who his father is. It happened to me and I don’t want him growing up unsure about his manhood. Those are his roots. He needs to know where he came from.”

So, Romell wanted Jamere, but he didn’t want me. Now, I had clarification, but it hurt. My redemption had taken place with God, but evidently my man was in his flesh. He hadn't forgiven me at all.

What he'd said made sense, but the truth complicated things and things had been complicated enough. "Just because I admitted to the affair and the paternity test proved you not to be his biological father doesn't mean that we have to open up this can of worms."

He held his hand up. "Carmella, set the record straight. We have lived this lie long enough."

And, that's all Romell had to say. He was a man of few words and seldom got angry. He didn't like to fight, or argue. I knew his limits. So, I backed away, before I pushed him further away.

He left me standing in the middle of the floor by the pillow that I'd dropped. I stooped over to pick it up and felt his brisk breeze as he passed by me and entered the bathroom. He began throwing some toiletries into an overnight bag. I heard each item thump as they hit the bottom.

I threw the pillow onto the bed and stood inside the bathroom. "Where will you be? How can I reach you?"

He stopped adding his belongings to the bag and took a firm a grip of the handle. "Excuse me." That's all Romell said and he was very courteous when he'd said that.

I stepped out of the way and watched him walk over to our dresser. He stuffed the bag with a few shirts, and a couple pair of underwear. I was dealing with this fine, and would continue to do so just as long as his path didn't lead him over to our closet. I couldn't have handled seeing the white zippered bag that secured my wedding dress. . . not right now.

But then, something happened that was much worse than that. Romell stuck his hand inside of his sock drawer, and pulled out the small black box that held my Princess Cut diamond ring. The one that he'd bought to place on my finger. . . it had been there ever since the day that he'd come back to me.

He opened the box, stared at the ring, then pushed it shut, and tossed it into the bag.

A tear dropped from my eye. My stomach quivered. I took a deep breath and counted to ten. At this moment, I couldn't remember if I was supposed to count fast, slow, or breathe into a paper bag to calm my nerves. All I know is that I was about to hyperventilate. This man was leaving me. . . for real.

I stayed behind him.

Romell toted the overnight bag low. It hung close to the carpet. . . kind of like my spirit. . . it almost dragged.

Before he reached the front door, he looked back and focused his eyes on Jamere's bedroom door.

Romell loosened his grip on the bag, but it didn't quite hit the floor.

I dried my tears and became excited inside. Maybe Romell's mind had changed and his heart followed. He was going to stay.

No sooner than I thought that, he squeezed the handle, lifted the bag a little higher, and turned his head. He took one step out the front door. Then another, and another until he took so many steps across our concrete sidewalk that I'd lost count, and was at his car. . . our car.

He pulled out of the driveway.

I stood at the front door, walked out to the curb, stared down the street, and watched until the car disappeared after crossing over the third stop sign.

I walked in the house, shut the front door, and then locked it. There was no one here to keep me and Jamere safe. We were unprotected. My Superman was gone.

I was hollow. I couldn't do a breakdown on it. . . there was no better way for me to explain it, other than I felt more than empty. . . he had deserted me.

I walked slow and lifeless to our bedroom. My head hung low and my shoulders sagged. Misery had found me. I needed a confidante, a friend, or maybe a family member. I yearned for my mother's voice, but instead of picking up the phone, I dropped to my knees, and I prayed.

I talked to God about everything that I'd done wrong and everything that I wanted right. After I'd tarried with my petition, and made my request known, I slid into bed. I tossed and I turned. . . even my dreams were missing him.

I don't know how I did it, don't know what time it happened, but I fell off to sleep on a Saturday night, and woke up to a radiant golden Sunday morning sun.

Out of habit, I turned over, stretched my arm, and felt for Romell. Instead, my fingers touched something that was soft and misted. I drew my hand back, slightly opened my eyes, and saw a bundle of tulips. I no longer squinted and a grin came across my face.

I sat up and opened my eyes wide. I hadn't had any flowers in a month of Sundays. I picked them up. They were fresh, they were white, and they were covered with dew. I held them close to my chest, and inhaled a whiff of his intimacy. My hero was back.

I laid them aside while my eyes veered around the bedroom. I looked for more hints of him. I spotted his overnight bag; it was propped up against our bedroom wall.

I threw the covers off, hurried out of bed, and rushed toward the bathroom. He wasn't there.

I made my way to the kitchen and saw leftover breakfast dishes in the sink, but I hadn't yet laid my eyes on him. And, then I heard voices coming from Jamere's room. I took off in that direction, and what I saw through a small opening in Jamere's door. . . I wouldn't dare interrupt.

All I could do was listen, and watch, as Romell straightened Jamere's white satin bowtie and said, "I love you."

Romell hugged Jamere tight.

"You're special to me." Then, Romell sniffled, and wiped a tear from his eye with Jamere saying, "Daddy, be a big boy." Something that Romell would command Jamere to do when he'd cry.

My eyes watered at the sight of this.

Finally, Romell released our five-year-old bundle of joy. "It's time to make your bed while I go and wake mommy for church."

Jamere nodded as Romell started for the bedroom door, and then turned around, "Do the very best that you can, and pick up these toys, too," he instructed Jamere and then hugged him again.

I darted away from the door, and hurried to our bedroom. Once inside, I dashed toward the bathroom, looked in the mirror, brushed over my hair with my hands, checked my face for overnight flaws, then eased into our bed, and shut my eyes.

I heard his footsteps. I sensed his presence. I smelled his cologne and felt his touch.

He nudged me.

I laid there with my eyes still closed.

He bent down and kissed the bridge of my nose.

My insides fluttered. Everything within me took notice. I was filled by his incredible energy.

He sat down next to me.

I couldn't pretend anymore. I opened my eyes.

He ran his fingers through my hair. “Good morning, Beautiful.”

I yawned and rubbed my eyes. “Good morning,” I said and stretched.

Romell reached over me. He grabbed the bouquet of tulips, pulled one out, and handed it to me. “I forgive you.”

I stopped breathing for a moment. That’s all I ever wanted to hear him say. My eyes became watery. I covered my face with the covers.

He tugged at the sheet and eased it away. “Don’t cry. Please. I never want to make you cry again.” He wiped my tears away. “About last night. . . no, period. I’ve been wrong. I should have never let. . . ”

He stopped once I began to talk through my tears, “You don’t have to. . . ”

He put his finger up to my lips. “I know where everything went wrong - my family. I let them destroy something that God put together,” he said and then withdrew his finger away from my lips. “It made you cling to him and doubt my love for you.”

“It was both of our families,” I admitted and wrapped my arms around his neck. “There’s no excuse for what I’ve put you through.”

He pulled me closer. “None of that matters to me anymore. Last night, I checked into a hotel. The walls were bare and the bed was cold. I was running away from you, but then all I thought about was you - you and Jamere. I don't want to be without you or him."

I ran my hand all over his smooth dark chocolate bald head. "We need you. I need you," I muttered with tears streaming down my face. "After you left, I prayed."

"And, that's what I did," he said with tears rolling down his cheeks.

My heart was racing.

We snuggled inside a warm embrace. When we came up for air, he took a hold of my hands. "What if, after church, we took a long ride down Pacific Coast Highway?"

"Okay," I breathed.

He released my hands and stood up. "And, what if. . . " he said and walked over to the closet, slid it open, and reached inside, "I asked you to wear this dress today?" He held the white zippered bag that held my wedding dress inside, in front of me.

I covered my mouth with both hands, as he laid the white bag on top of the bed and made his way back over to me.

He kneeled down in front of me on one knee.

My hands trembled.

He reached inside of his pocket and pulled out the small black box. "Sweetness, our world is not perfect but it's complete and I love you so much. I always have and I want to know if you, Carmella Denise Dixon, will marry me today in Vegas?" He lifted the top of the box. "I realized that he had your body, but he never had your heart. So, what do you say? It's only a four hour drive," he said and smiled. . . wide.

I lowered my head and glazed into his eyes. "Romell Jamere Jefferson, I would be so happy to take that ride down Pacific Coast Highway with you and anywhere else you want me to go."

He loved me and that's all that mattered, it's all I ever needed.

He stood up and reached for my hand.

I held it out, he slipped the ring on my finger, and then I walked into his arms.

"I love you. There's no other man for me but you."

And, there wasn't. He was everything that I ever dreamed of in a man, but I didn't realize that until I'd almost lost him. His grass was much greener than I'd thought.

He kissed my forehead and we rocked a slow rock back and forth with Jamere finding a way to sandwich himself in between us. We hadn't even heard him come into the room.

Romell scooted back a little bit to make more room for Jamere.

"Come on in here, little man. There's a spot for you." He helped Jamere secure a place in between us. "Daddy's boy," he said and rubbed the top of Jamere's head, and then he said to me, "We'll handle this together."

And, a tear escaped and trickled down as I looked at the both of them.

And, all was well.

I had my Sunday tulips, my Sunday dress, my Sunday man, and our Sunday love.

***Cherritta L. Smith** resides in Las Vegas, Nevada and is an aspiring writer who loves learning the craft of writing.*

Mixing Business with Pleasure

By Richelle Denise

"You've got to be kidding me."

I threw my hands up. Cars continued to whiz by me as I sat in my own, stranded on the shoulder of Interstate 45. Of all the things that could happen, I had to have a flat tire on a morning that had the potential to change my bank statements forever. The biggest meeting of my career was about to take place, and I was stuck in my car watching other people make it to their jobs on time.

My opportunity for job advancement relied on my ability to impress Travis Whitaker, our new CEO who was in town from the corporate office in Atlanta. I felt confident in the presentation I'd prepared. I had done extensive research on his leadership style and I read interviews that gave insight to his preferred approach to landing accounts.

"Breathe, Kennedi, breathe." Talking to myself was the only way I could keep calm. I checked the time. "Come on, Kenny," I begged. It had been twenty minutes since I hung up with my brother. The traffic was flowing, and according to my calculations, he should have made it to me in twelve minutes flat. I glanced at my watch again. Eight twenty-three. There were thirty-seven minutes remaining before I was due in the conference room.

The sight of my brother's large pickup truck made me feel a little less anxious. The office was only about twenty minutes from where I was, and there was no traffic. I slipped my heels off and crawled across the front seat to exit nearest the guardrail. I was careful as I climbed over, not wanting to rip the split in my pencil skirt.

"Mama said you have a big meeting today," he said as he approached the trunk of my car to get the spare.

"I do. Do you think you can you hurry? I don't have much time to get there and set up."

"You wanna take my truck? The air isn't working, but once you start driving the wind will keep you cool."

When I weighed my options, I didn't have another choice, if I wanted to arrive on time. I reached up and pecked him on the cheek. "You're the best. Hand me the keys." My brother had been the pillar of strength my mother and I depended on since the day my father walked out.

"All right, knucklehead, get to work. I need to get started, this Houston humidity ain't playin' with a brotha." Sweat dripped from his face at an increasing rate.

I grabbed the items I needed for work out of my car. "Thanks again, Kenny."

"Slide in over here. Those cars are going by so fast, I wouldn't want anyone to sideswipe you." He wiped his forehead with his arm and opened the passenger door for me.

Twenty-five minutes later, I walked into the automatic doors of the twenty-story building which housed the advertising agency I'd been employed at for the last four years. The echo of my high heel shoes resounded through the lobby as I trotted to the elevator. I ran into my office and picked up the additional items I needed for my presentation. I had two minutes to get back on the elevator, run to the conference room, set up, and prepare to walk through a new door of opportunity for my career.

"Ms. Tyler, is everything all right?" my secretary, Mary, who was more like a second mother to me asked as she took her hand and tried to tame my windblown hair. "You didn't forget that Mr. Whitaker was in the office, did you?" She was one of the most organized, helpful people I knew. I didn't want to be annoyed with her but how could anyone, especially her, think I forgot about the meeting I'd spent the last five weeks preparing for?

I brushed past her so fast I could have knocked her down. "No, Mary, I didn't forget. I had a flat tire. Talk to you later," I yelled as I rounded the corner. I pressed the elevator button four times as if that was going to make the doors open faster.

Three minutes after nine, I entered the conference room. The frigid air slapped me in the face along with the aroma of freshly brewed coffee. The members of my team, and my supervisor, Mr. Spencer, sat along the sides of the oblong conference table with agendas in front of them. Sitting at the far end, was the gorgeous man I'd been gawking over every time his pictures popped up when I Googled his name. The images online did no justice to the sight of him in person.

Walking in, I felt like a defendant on a murder case approaching the witness stand. "Good morning, everyone." In an attempt to avoid sounding like I'd just finished running a relay, I took a deep breath. "It's a pleasure to meet you, Mr. Whitaker." I set my things down on the table and extended my right hand.

"Likewise, Ms. Tyler." His handshake was firm and his smile was absent.

"Ms. Tyler, you're late," Mr. Spencer said. It wasn't a surprise, since he had zero tolerance for tardiness or excuses.

It took all of the good sense my mama gave me not to say: *Oh really? I hadn't noticed.* But enjoying the simple things in life such as a car, a roof over my head, and eating daily also helped me respond with a polite, "Yes, sir. I apologize. It will only take me a second to set up."

No one said a word as I fumbled to get my equipment together.

Two hours later, the meeting was over. Everyone began mingling and introducing themselves to Mr. Whitaker. That is. . . everyone, but me. As soon as I saw an opportunity, I darted out of the conference room.

I went to the ladies' room down the hall and peeped under each stall before I walked to the mirror and stared at my reflection. "What just happened to you in there, girl? You blew it." I put my face into my hands and cried. All of the hard work I'd put into the presentation, all of the lost sleep, and all of the time I put in was wasted all because a stupid nail found its way into my tire.

When I had cried enough to feel a bit of relief, I grabbed a few paper towels and patted my face dry. I picked my belongings up and walked into the hall.

"Nice job on your presentation, Ms. Tyler. Very impressive."

Before I turned around to reply, I closed my eyes and inhaled. "Mr. Whitaker, I. . . um, well thank you," I stammered. If there were a way to disappear, I would have done it then. I stood in front of him thinking there was no way he could have thought I was competent.

Then he did it. He flashed a Colgate smile that brightened the hall. Well, that's a slight exaggeration, but his teeth were white. "You're welcome." He looked around; probably to make sure no one could hear our conversation. "Why don't I treat you to lunch? It's time to celebrate."

I felt my brows squish together. "Celebrate?"

He nodded his head and shrugged. "Yes, celebrate. Well, when I get promoted, I like to celebrate. But, maybe that's just me..."

"I got the promotion?"

He nodded and watched me ingest the news.

"Thank you, oh I don't know what to say. I am just at a loss for words."

"I would say you're welcome, but I can't take any credit for the presentation you gave. I've heard many wonderful things about you and the team you supervise. I believe you're going to go far in this company."

"Wow, that means a lot coming from you." I couldn't keep the grin from sneaking up on my face.

"So, do I have to celebrate your promotion alone or are you going to join me?"

If he weren't my boss, I would have accepted his invitation without any reservations. My mind told me to tell him thanks and let him know I had other plans. But my fast beating heart and girlish instincts that had me crushing on him, caused me to cast out all thoughts of logic. I knew going to lunch with my boss, whom I was attracted to, would be against company policy, but I still blurted, "Let me drop these things off in my office." When I realized the casual tone I had taken with my boss, I said, "I apologize for. . . "

He raised his hand. "No need to apologize. We can meet in the parking lot, then you can follow me to the restaurant." Then, him and his broad shoulders proceeded down the hallway.

"Great. I'll see you in a few minutes." No sooner than I had gotten the words out of my mouth, I remembered I had my brother's truck. I was about to have lunch with the CEO of Project Management, Inc. and I had to drive a truck that had no air conditioning on what had to be one of the hottest days of the summer.

I had to get my car from my brother. I knew I wasn't at the top of the corporate ladder and my 2012 Honda Accord was no luxury vehicle, but it sure beat looking like the African American version of Ellie Mae from *The Beverly Hillbillies.* I turned and caught up to him. "On second thought, I have one errand to run. Would it be all right if I meet you at the restaurant?"

"Sure, I'll go ahead and get us a table. Are you familiar with Ruggles Green on West Alabama?"

"Yes, I know where it is. I'll see you there." After breathing a sigh of relief, I made my way to my office, dropped off my things, and scurried out. If I couldn't get a hold of my brother, I needed to get there before Mr. Whitaker. The next order of business was to call Kenny. Lucky for me he was five minutes away because he was out paying bills.

I was conflicted in the way I felt about Mr. Whitaker's lunch invitation. I couldn't figure out if it was all business or if his motivation was personal. If I said I was hoping it was all about business, I'd be lying. Regardless of his motives for inviting me to eat, I knew I shouldn't have felt such an attraction to my boss. But, Mr. Whitaker was my type from his skin tone all the way down to the shiny shoes he had on his feet. My mama always told me that a man's shoes told a lot about him. If that had any truth to it, this man was worth more than impressing in a business meeting. But, since I didn't know his motive, I had to follow his lead. I couldn't afford to lose my job because I flirted with my boss.

***

"I filled it up for you," my brother said as he was getting out of my car.

"Aw, thanks. And thanks for agreeing to meet me at my job I know it was last minute. I have an important lunch meeting and riding with no a/c this time of day would have been no good for me. You need to get it fixed. This Texas heat in the summer is nothing to play with. Do you need me to help you?" I reached into my purse.

"You know I wouldn't feel comfortable taking money from you. I'll get around to it. You go ahead and get to your lunch."

"Speaking of my lunch, I'm going celebrate, because I got the promotion."

"See, you got all the brains and I got the beauty."

I punched him in the arm and hopped in my car. "I gotta go."

It took ten minutes for me to arrive at the restaurant. I didn't need to be escorted to my seat. As soon as I walked in, I spotted Mr. Whitaker sitting at a table in the back corner.

He stood as I approached. "I took the liberty of getting us a table that would allow us a little privacy." Once I sat down in the chair he'd pulled out for me, he returned to his seat across from me.

His charm, poise, and swag combined and made me feel as though no public place would be private enough to do the things I wanted to do with him. "Oh, this is fine. Thanks for offering to bring me to lunch to. . . celebrate."

He chuckled and leaned forward on his elbows. "Why did you hesitate before you said celebrate? Don't you feel the festive mood in here?"

Sensing his humor, I replied, “Of course, I do. This is the best promotion party I’ve ever had.”

He stared at me for a moment then he said, “You are stunning, Kennedi. May I call you Kennedi?”

When I realized it wasn’t a business lunch, I felt my shoulders relax. “Thanks for the compliment. And, of course, you can, *Mr. Whitaker*.” I wasn’t sure if I should follow suit and call him by his first name.

“Travis is fine. We aren’t at work.”

I gulped. “Right, we aren’t.”

“Can I make a confession?”

“Sure. You can, Travis.” I raised an eyebrow and grinned.

“You did well on your presentation, but I didn’t bring you here to talk about work. I want to know a little more about you. Not Kennedi the advertising campaign manager, but Kennedi the woman.” His stare was intense, but his smirk made me feel like a young girl with her first crush.

“Well, there’s not much to know, I love to laugh, I enjoy reading, cooking, and shopping. No kids. No dog. And, I love my job. I think that sums me up. And who are you underneath this designer suit?”

He licked his lips, like L.L. Cool J. I did a good job of keeping my composure when he did that, if I do say so myself. “I am quite simple. There isn’t a whole lot I’m not willing to try. I have a lot to offer.” Then he leaned in across the table like he was about to tell me a secret. “When I see something nice, I want it, and I always get what I want." He lifted his face and stroked his chin.

"Oh, do you now," I teased.

We sat at the restaurant and enjoyed the rest of our lunch laughing and discussing the greatest life lessons we'd ever been taught. I left lunch grateful that the morning that started off wrong, flat tire and all, ended with me feeling like no one could deflate the happiness that welled up inside of me. Not only did I have lunch with a handsome, powerful man. I had gotten a huge raise at work.

Spending time with Travis every other weekend began to take first priority in my life. He was always traveling, so we agreed that he would fix his schedule so he could come to visit me every other Friday. I found myself turning down offers to hang with friends and family in turn for cozy movie nights and take out meals in his Houston high rise or my apartment. Since he was my boss, he suggested that we keep our relationship low key until we decided, in his words, "it was best to come out with it."

The best part of being with Travis was that he wanted me for who I was on the inside, not for my full lips, or my pear shaped body that most men were attracted to. I knew these things because in all the time we had spent together, not once had he tried to make any sexual advances. Kisses came in abundance and though I enjoyed them, I found myself desiring to take our relationship to the next level.

Two months into our relationship, I decided to step it up. . . physically. I was happy our anniversary fell on a Friday he would be in town. I had big plans for us and it would take a few days to recuperate if things went as planned. The last fifteen minutes of work, I sat tapping my pen on my desk. One thing's for sure, looking at a clock every few seconds doesn't make time pass faster. "Come on, turn five already," I mumbled. The bouquet of sunflowers Travis sent revealed even more so that a business tycoon could be sentimental and romantic when he wasn't working.

At five sharp I bounced out of my office. "Have a great weekend, Mary"

"You too, Ms. Tyler. I must say, you've always been a pleasure to be around, but lately you have been even more radiant. Whoever this new guy is, has got to know he is blessed to have someone like you in his life."

"Aw, thanks, Mary. But, you know what? I'm blessed too." I could feel the positive energy surging through my body. I felt the corners of my mouth curve upward.

"I look at you like another daughter, so may I offer you a piece of advice as if you were mine?"

"Of course. You've been married to the same man for nearly forty years. I'd gladly take advice from you. As a matter of fact, maybe I should get my notepad." I pretended to walk to my office.

"You're such a mess. Well, I always tell my girls that no matter how a guy is packaged on the outside or how he makes you feel in the beginning, you must ask the Lord for discernment. Look at his heart. Pray and ask God if he is the man that has been sent to you. He'll let you know. Even if it's a still, silent voice within you, He will reveal it. Just ask."

"Okay, Mary I will." I knew better than to talk back to my elders. But the truth was, I didn't know if I was ready to hear what God had to tell me. I was enjoying my time with Travis and the secrecy of our relationship turned me on. There was something satisfying about knowing I dated the boss without anyone else being aware of it. I felt like a teenaged girl sneaking around with a bad boy her mother had forbidden her to associate with. "I'll see you Monday, and thanks for the advice."

An hour later, I bounced around in my bedroom singing my own rendition of Mary J. Blige's song "Just Fine." I never learned the whole chorus, but the parts I knew, I belted out, as I got dressed for the evening. I even went to the mirror and sang with my brush like I used to do when I was younger.

Three quick knocks at the door let me know that Travis had arrived. I turned my music off and ran to the door. When it swung open, he embraced me. "Do you know how long I've been wanting to do this," he said as he hugged me tighter. He shut the door and our lips met causing our tongues to do a dance that sent currents of sensation throughout my body.

When we pulled away, I answered. "Yep, just about as long as I have. I was counting down the minutes until it was time for me to leave work."

"I got you something else to signify our two month anniversary." He pulled out a light blue bag with a bow on it.

"You already made me cry when you sent me flowers. Before this morning, I had no idea you remembered. We didn't celebrate last month. I thought I was the only one that remembered because I got my promotion that day. And, women just seem to remember sentimental things like this." I opened the bag and pulled out a jewelry box that held a pair of heart-shaped diamond earrings. "Oh Travis, I love them."

"I just wanted to give you something that would bring you to the heights of happiness you have brought into my life since the moment you walked into that conference room." He took the earrings out of my hand and placed them in my ears.

"I didn't buy anything for you, but I do have something special in store for you." I gave him a seductive look and backed away while moving my index finger to beckon him toward my bedroom. The magnetism between us was undeniable. In no time, we were entangled in each other's arms. I kissed him with so much passion the room felt twenty degrees warmer than it did when he entered. He touched me in all the right places and was gentler than I imagined him. When he laid me on the bed, he stopped and whispered, "Are you sure you're ready?"

He nibbled on my ear, traced my neck with his tongue, and lit a fire within me that only he could extinguish. I couldn't answer with words, so I unbuckled his pants, and in the moments thereafter, I showed him that I was more than ready.

In the days that followed, my mind was consumed with ways to please him. My heart raced faster than a greyhound running on a track when he was near me.

The following Friday, I heard Travis' voice in my office corridor. "Good morning, I don't believe we've met before. I need to speak with Ms. Tyler. Is she available," he asked Mary.

She introduced herself, and then she told him what a pleasure it was to meet him.

I had just spoken to him on my lunch break and he hadn't mentioned coming to Houston. W*hat was he doing in Houston this weekend?* So many thoughts were going through my head. I began stacking papers on my desk and making sure everything was organized. Travis made it very clear that we were to be all about business while we were in the office.

I gulped when I heard Mary reply, "Yes, Mr. Whitaker, she's straight through those doors." I could hear their voices getting closer.

"Thank you." He appeared at my door and put his hands in his pockets. "Oh, and please make sure no one interrupts us." No explanations were made. He closed the door and turned his attention my way. "And you, Ms. Tyler have some explaining to do."

Realizing that authoritative demeanor was exchanged for the laid back man I'd grown to know in private, I played along. "I'm sorry, I messed up, Mr. Whitaker. Please don't punish me too bad."

He grabbed my waist and hoisted up my skirt and it didn't take long before he had to cover my mouth to muffle my outbursts of pleasure.

Once we were both presentable again, he walked out with his briefcase as if nothing took place. His power and all about business attitude were just two of the many things that made me desire him. When we were in meetings, I loved watching him take charge.

Summer turned to fall and just like the seasons changed, so did our relationship. It grew to heights beyond explanation.

"I want to be with you all the time, Travis. I don't like when we're apart," I whined as we cuddled on my couch. I didn't care that I sounded like a baby because moments that we held each other made me long for a more committed relationship. One that we could've gone public with.

"You know I want to be with you too, babe, but we can't just come out with our relationship. There is a strict policy about employers and employees having personal relationships."

"I know, that's why I was thinking I could resign, we can get married and everyone could know about our love. It was fun to sneak around at first, but now I'm tired of hiding who's sending me flowers, buying me elaborate gifts, or whisking me off for lunch." I exhaled. "People might begin to think I'm some lonely, desperate woman who's doing all of these things for attention."

"Come on now, we both know you don't want to quit your job." He kissed me on the forehead and headed for the shower.

The next morning, I woke up and attempted to cuddle, but discovered that I was in bed alone. I sat up and positioned myself so I could see into my restroom, which was also empty. Moments later, I heard footsteps coming into the room.

"Good morning, beautiful." He set a tray with a glass of orange juice, oatmeal, and fresh strawberries on the bed. Then, he kissed me. "Breakfast is served, Madame."

"I don't know what to do with you." I shook my head and placed my hand over my chest. "You sure know how to make me feel good. I know we talked about this last night, but let's consider my plan. Or I could start flying out to Atlanta to see you on the weekends you aren't here."

He sighed. "Speaking of Atlanta, while you were asleep I got a phone call. One of the clients we're trying to land an account with wants to meet for lunch. . . today. I gotta be at the airport in an hour."

"What? But this weekend was supposed to be special. This would have been our first time spending three weekends in a row together. Can't you reschedule?" My arms were folded, my bottom lip was stuck out, and I had tears in my eyes just like I was seven years old. "Why didn't you wake me up?"

"You were sleeping so peacefully. I'll still be back next weekend. We'll be right on schedule. I just had to see you yesterday." He kissed my lips. "Go ahead and eat before your food gets cold. And, to make up for my abrupt departure, I left you a little package on your dresser. Go out and buy yourself something nice." He winked.

I clapped my hands with excitement knowing that the "little package" he left was some cash for me to go shopping.

I ate and he gathered his overnight bag. The time he had to spare before he got to the airport felt like five minutes.

When he left, I crawled back into bed and hugged the pillow that he slept on. I inhaled his scent. *He'll let you know.* Mary's words bounced around in my head. I looked around, knowing I was alone, but the urge to get on my knees and pray summoned me out of bed.

I knelt down. "God, it's me, Kennedi." I looked up and took a deep breath. "I know I haven't prayed in a while, but I need help. I need to know if Travis is the one for me. Can you send me a sign? I don't know if I'll be able to hear a still voice inside of me. So, could you give me a sign that I'll be able to understand? In Jesus' name, Amen."

I sat back on the edge of my bed and decided to do some work before I headed out to shop. When I opened my laptop, I decided to peruse Facebook. I went through my timeline and looked at pictures of my former classmates and their families as they went on trips, had family gatherings, or as they posted pictures of their children to show off awards they'd earned. I longed for a family of my own, and I began to fantasize about the day I'd be able to share my love and my family with the world.

Then, something caught my eye. As I scrolled down, I saw a picture of a man and woman, who happened to be my former college roommate's cousin, Christine. Their picture was sprawled across my computer screen. She was gazing into his eyes and he dipped her toward the ground as if they were doing an exotic ballroom dance. Given the fact that I had been longing for the day I could pose for a picture like that, I should have felt jealous. But jealousy was nowhere to be found beneath the layers of my rage. The post on the picture read: *Baby, I'm so proud of the man you've become. You are my world, I can't wait until we become one in a few hours, T.*

"You sure work quick, don't you God," I muttered as I continued to scroll down her timeline. I clicked my laptop touchpad and read comments from her "friends" as well as her responses. While reading, I discovered that she believed he forfeited his bachelor party the night before to go on a business trip, which required him to be in Houston. He was scheduled to catch an early flight and would be returning to Atlanta right in time to get ready for their nuptials. My absence from social media kept me from noticing his presence on her page. Otherwise, I would have made the connection earlier.

I balled my fist up and hit it on the nightstand next to my bed. My heart raced so fast I thought it was going to jump out of my chest. With trembling hands I dialed his number.

"Hey, babe, you caught me just in time. I was about to board the plane."

"Oh, this won't take long. I just called to congratulate you on your wedding today, and can you pass the message on to your future bride?" I hung up before he had a chance to speak.

I faulted myself for not asking if he was in a relationship. *How could I have been so naïve?* The next time I got close to a man, I'd ask questions I yearn to know even if my emotions can't handle the answers.

***Richelle Denise** has always had a passion for reading. She is currently working on her debut novel. Look for her novella, PayDay (with ReShonda Tate Billingsley) coming soon.*

Searching for Mr. Right

By Patrice Tartt

I'm not sure why, but I always get extremely nervous right before a date. You would think I was fifteen going on my first date with my neighborhood crush. In my mid-thirties, I should have been able to shake this feeling off over a decade ago.

Yet, here I was. Nervously standing in front of my mirror, in the fifth outfit that I'd tried on, running late, as usual.

It was almost five and I had to be all the way across town in forty-five minutes. But luckily, my daughter was spending the weekend with her dad so I didn't have to worry about making any kind of arrangements with the sitter.

As I stood in front of the mirror, my phone was steadily buzzing, but I ignored it. I didn't have to check the screen to know that the calls were from my girls trying to make sure I would be on time tonight.

Well, it was too late for that. Plus, even though I was nervous, I wasn't stressing about my tardiness. I was definitely worth the wait for any date.

Finally, I settled into my car, determined to make this a relaxing drive into D.C., even though rush hour would double the normally thirty minute drive from Silver Spring into the district, especially since this was Friday. But like I said, I wasn't going to stress about time since I was nervous enough.

Instead, I used the drive-time to reflect on my love life. There was a lot at stake for me with this dating thing. Not only for me personally, but because of my daughter as well.

Tiffany was eight years old and I was doing everything to build a legacy for her. From my home health care business to my dating life, Tiffany was affected by my choices and I was always aware of that -- especially with bringing a man into her life.

There were times when I wished it wasn't this way -- but as the saying goes, it is what it is. Tiffany's father and I were no longer together. At least I could say that we were amicable, which was a long way from our crazy-love, on-and-off, up-and-down relationship that started back in high school and continued until about two years ago. I was no longer going to waste my life waiting on a man who would never make a commitment, who would never make me his one-and-only. So, Tiffany's father and I were done, with no chance of resurrecting that dead love affair.

But I wasn't bitter because my beautiful daughter came from that union and now, because of her, I had to look at every date and ask was I dating for fun or the future?

It would always be about the future for me and for Tiffany.

That's why in the last two years of dating, I'd tried it all and seen it all. I'd tried everything -- from blind dates to on-line dating. I should own stock in Match.com and eHarmony, or at the very least be hired as a spokeswoman for both sites.

Though now that I think of it, maybe choosing me to advertise for those websites wasn't that great of an idea since not a single date had worked out. I didn't stay in touch with not even one of the dozens of men I'd met. And why would I? From being boring to braggadocios, those men just didn't interest me.

Well...that's not completely true. There was Nathan Lewis. Yeah, Nathan is the only one whose name I remembered. We'd had dinner down at the Harbor and then strolled along the waterfront, chatting easily, about his job as a teacher and my business.

I was definitely feeling Nathan and a second date was in our future -- until I received a text from his wife!

Yup, his wife. His new wife. Of three weeks. Nathan had forgotten to tell me that he'd recently said, "I do," and had just returned from his honeymoon in Tahiti.

Now, as I pulled up to the valet of Nathan Vans, which is where I was meeting my date-du-jour, I wasn't sure that it was such a good idea for me to spend the last fifty or so minutes reminiscing about my dates from hell.

I dropped my keys into the valet's hand, stuffed my ticket into my purse, then made my way inside. I caught a glimpse of my reflection in the ceiling-to-floor mirror behind the hostess stand. My little black dress was a classic, with a scoop neck, the hem hitting right at my knees. But the knit hugged my size ten curves, accentuating my figure, making me look sexy and classy.

The four-inch gold heels that I wore, raised my already tall frame to almost six-feet; so I hoped that my date was at least six-three, which is what he told me, but most men lied on these sites.

When I walked inside the bar area, I did my usual scan, though I pretended that I wasn't really looking for anyone. There was nothing worse than standing there with the "I am searching for someone" look, only to have no one even walk up to you. (I had that happen -- twice. My dates didn't bother to show up; nothing more humiliating than being stood up in public.)

But it didn't seem like I was going to have that problem this time because there he was, Mr. Potential -- at least that's what I'd named him. I gave all of these men a name, hoping that one day, one of them would be Mr. Right.

Mr. Potential was sitting at the bar and looking as fine and sexy as Al Pacino in Scarface. I recognized him right away because he'd been right on the money with his description. He'd said, "I'm tall, I've been told I have an olive tint to my skin and I have light brown eyes."

He'd left off his lips, his full juicy lips that I could see all the way from the other side of the room. I had a thing for lips and already, I began to have a few dirty thoughts.

But, I kept my composure and as I glided over to him; his 'I just won the lotto' smile said that he was one-hundred percent satisfied with me as well.

"Hi, Charles?"

He stood to greet me. "That's me," he replied.

"Nice to met you, I'm…"

As I extended my hand, he finished for me. "Mariah, yes…yes very nice to meet you, Ms. Mariah."

"Likewise," I said, keeping my smile and trying not to snatch my hand away from his, even though he was squeezing the life out of me. I was sure that by the time I got my hand back, my fingers would be numb.

"Let's go to our table," he said, finally releasing his death grip and pointing toward the main dining area. "They're ready for us."

"After you, sir."

He raised a single eyebrow, but then nodded and walked in front of me. In these situations, I always let the guys lead the way. That gave me time to check him out thoroughly. . . from behind.

And my view gave Mr. Potential an A Plus!

"Would you mind if I ordered appetizers for us to share?" he asked when we were seated.

"Go ahead."

He ordered mini crab cakes, and then, while I asked for a seafood salad, he had the steak and lobster.

"So I think this is a great match already," Charles/Mr. Potential said as the waiter walked away with our order.

"Why do you say that?"

"Because I'm an orthopedic surgeon and you're in health care."

"That is interesting," I said. "I have a couple of short-term clients who are recovering from knee and hip replacements and who need assistance just for a few weeks."

"See what I mean?" he said. "So when I talk about how replacing joints is my passion..."

"I'll understand," I finished.

We laughed and then it went that way all the way through the appetizers, dinner, and even the chocolate lava cake we shared. I actually hated to see the night come to an end.

Charles walked me to my car. With his hands caressing my shoulders, and my hair flowing in the light evening breeze, he gave me a kiss on the cheek. With those lips. His lips were so soft, sort of like a king sized down pillow inside of a 1000 thread-count pillowcase.

It's time to say good night, Mariah.

I wanted to tell my inner voice to shut up so I could just grab Charles and kiss him ferociously. But I let my inner voice take charge and bid him good night.

Charles called me the next morning, before I was even out of bed, and said he wanted us to get together again.

I was giddy, especially when he said, "What about tonight?"

Yes! "I would love to."

"You can have dinner at my house."

Yes!

"We'll cook dinner for you."

Yes! Wait! What? We?

My thoughts actually made a screeching sound in my mind. Was this dude married and he was setting me up for some freaky-kind of threesome?

"We?" I said.

"Oh, I forgot to tell you, I live with my mother."

"Why?" The question came out of me before I had a chance to stop it.

"What do you mean, why?"

"Well, you're a surgeon, right? I mean, it's not like you can't provide for yourself. Is something wrong with her? I mean, is she okay; do you have to take care of her?"

“No, there's nothing wrong with my mother," he snapped as if my questions had insulted him. "I just like living with my mother. You got a problem with that? Chicks always asking why, why, why....”

My mouth was wide open as Mr. Potential ranted about how women always wanted to know why he was living with his mother and right then, Mr. Potential turned into...Next!

I hung up the phone and went straight over to my laptop. Yeah, there were probably lots of good guys who lived with their mother, but I wasn't going to hang around to find out if Charles was one of them. It just wasn't natural for a grown man to want to live that way. Talk about being a Mama's boy!

On the website as I clicked from one photo to the next, I actually wished that I could take time off from all of this. It was hard -- dating and finding Mr. Right felt like a full-time job. It just seemed much easier to sit back and wait.

But how would I find Mr. Right that way? Did I really think that he was going to walk up to my front door and ring the bell?

No, I had to put effort into this. Plus, I couldn't stop. I was a thirty-five-year-old woman with needs...lots of needs. And one of those needs was to be a wife. I longed for the day when I'd be dressed in all-white (though that would be a stretch) and be holding onto the arm of my father as he walked me down a long, rose-petal sprinkled aisle.

So, I just kept on clicking, from one photo to the next, until I came to...Stanley Jones: an ex college-basketball star, now a middle-school teacher -- I loved men who had a heart for kids.

So, I messaged him. And he responded.

After a few messages, back and forth, he messaged: *You wanna get together tonight?*

That made me frown and I paused. I guess I must have taken too long to respond because he came back with: *NOT a booty-call. Just feelin' you. Let's go to the movies. Meet me over in Arlington on Jefferson-Davis Hwy?*

I wanted to tell him that this wasn't the way I did things. Usually, after messaging for a few days, I liked to talk on the phone and get a feel for the guy.

But maybe I needed to do something different. Tiffany was going to be with her dad all weekend, so why not be adventurous? I agreed. We exchanged numbers and planned to meet up at seven.

Since I was changing everything, I was determined to get there on time. And I achieved my goal when I jumped in my car and made the trek to the Virginia side. As I turned into the parking lot, I heard someone bumping an old Tupac song so loud, it made my car vibrate. I found the culprit, a dude in a car that only a "D boy" would drive.

I rolled my eyes and shook my head, wondering why guys liked to do that? Why did they feel it was okay to invade everyone's space with their loud music?

As I walked toward the theatre, I saw that I wasn't the only one who felt that way. Everybody was glancing over, frowning, and shaking their heads.

Inside, I stood next to the ticket line, glancing at every guy who walked through the door, though just about all of them were with a woman. After just a few minutes, my phone vibrated with an incoming text.

I'm here, where are you?

Before I had a chance to text back, I heard, "There you are, Sweet Thang."

I looked up and screamed! Well, I screamed inside. It was Mr. Loud Music himself pimp-strutting toward me.

I just knew that a camera was about to pop out and someone would say, 'Surprise! You're on Hell Date!'

"What's up?" Mr. Loud Music asked.

For just a millisecond I thought about saying, *No hablo Ingles,* and then, get the heck out of there.

But it was Saturday night, and I was already here. So, I decided to make the best of it. Well, the best that I could after I saw his sagging pants. I hardly noticed that he was 6'3, the epitome of tall, dark and handsome with hazel eyes. And lips. Lips that I could kiss, though I would never want to be that close to him. It was hard to see any of that since my focus (and everyone else's) was on his underwear that he had on display -- boxers with pink elephants!

Just think about the free movie, and free popcorn, Mariah.

But after he bought the tickets and we walked past the attendant, he kept on moving toward the theatre, not even asking me if I wanted anything to eat.

Who does that? Who comes to a movie and just walks inside?

At least he paid for the ticket.

Then it got worse. I could hardly watch the movie, because he wanted to carry on a conversation.

"So what's up? What you like to do?"

"Uh...."

"I mean, how you make your money?"

"Ssshhh!" came from behind us.

But I seemed to be the only one who heard that because Mr. Loud Talk (I switched from Music because I really couldn't remember his first name now) just kept talking as if the most natural thing in the world to do was to get to know one another in a movie theatre.

I kept slipping down further and further in the seat until I was almost on the floor. Talk about embarrassing.

At the end of the movie, I wanted to stand up and tell everyone, 'Hey guys, I don't even know him for real.'

But at the end, all I did was stand up, look down and say, "Thanks," and then I ran out of there like I was an Olympic sprinter.

When I got into my car, I didn't even turn on the ignition. My first business -- to block all calls and texts coming from Mr. Embarrassing/Loud Music/Louder Talk.

But I didn't stop there; as soon as I got home, I went to my laptop and canceled all of my memberships with those dating sites and then, I deleted the apps from my phone. I was so done.

Yes, I really wanted to be married, more than anything. But then, the words of my grandmother came to me. Right before I went off to college she told me, "Baby, you're going to learn a lot of things out there with all of those people who have all those fancy degrees. But I don't need a degree to tell you one of the most important things you should learn -- always let love find you; never search for it."

I always wondered why she'd given me that advice right then. But I listened to her because even with her sixth grade education, my grandmother was the wisest woman I knew.

But, I guess I'd forgotten because I'd been on one helluva search the last two years.

Looking up to the heavens, I said, "I hear you, Grandma! I really do."

So that was it; that was the end of my on-line dating catastrophes and for the next few weeks, all I did was focus on my business and my daughter. And every day, I told my grandmother, that if this was going to be all there was for me, then it was going to be enough.

The weeks turned into months, and though I couldn't say that I was *really* okay with not dating, I was at least okay with it. Not that it wasn't frustrating; it seemed that every day, no matter where I went -- the grocery store, the cleaners, at Tiffany's school...someone was telling me about her Mr. Right. Not to mention the number of announcements at church. It was like someone out there in the universe was taunting me.

But I kept my grandmother's words close to my heart. And then the next Sunday, it was like God wanted me to remember Him, too.

"You may think that God's forgotten you," the pastor said. "But just remember what the Lord says. He that findeth a wife, findeth a good thing."

Of course I'd heard that scripture before, but now I let it settle into my heart. It was hard, but that's what I was going to do. My Mr. Right was going to find me.

And so, the months became a year, and I couldn't believe that I'd done it. Though I had lonely times, I wasn't lonely. Actually, I looked forward to some days alone. Like the Saturday afternoon when Tiffany was spending the day with her best friend. I was just lounging around, catching up on the magazines that had piled up, when the doorbell rang.

None of my girls had said anything about coming over, but I swung the door open. Then, I froze, blinded by all the fineness in front of me.

"Hello," the man said in a baritone so deep, I expected him to break out in song at any moment.

"Uh...."

"Are you all right?" he asked, that beautiful tone now filled with concern.

"Uh...."

"I'm sorry if I'm disturbing you," he said. "I just wanted to introduce myself to my neighbors."

"Uh...neighbors?" I said, finally managing one intelligible word.

"Yes." He nodded and those light brown eyes of his seemed to glow. "My son and I just moved in next door; and because I have a small son, I wanted to get to know as many of the people around me as I could."

"Oh, your son lives with you?" I asked, finally finding my voice. "And not his mother?"

I didn't know what I said, but the ends of his luscious lips turned down just a bit. "I'm a widower," he said. But then, just as quickly, his cheer returned. "But it's been a few years and this is a new start for me and my son." Then, he shook his head and held out his hand. "Where are my manners? I forgot to introduce myself. My name is Joseph...Joseph Wright."

Joseph Wright? Joseph Wright! Mr. Wright had rung my doorbell!

"I'm Mariah," I said. Tilting my head, I asked, "Would you like to come in for a few minutes?"

He gave me a gleaming grin, with perfect teeth, of course. "Sure!"

As he stepped inside, I checked him out from behind. An A Plus Plus!

And then, right before I closed the door, I looked up to the heavens. “I hear you, Grandma.” I moved to close the door, but then did another glance to the sky. “And thank you, God.”

***Patrice Tartt** is an Amazon #1 best selling author, speaker, coach, and networking expert. She is the CEO and Founder of Mommy Divas on the Move, LLC and Girls Write Too, which is a writing program for young girls. Patrice's debut novel, "Wounds of Deception" and "Mommy Divas on the Move: 16 Successful Secrets for Mompreneurs", are both available on Amazon. Be sure to check out her articles on the Huffington Post and connect on social media. Visit Patrice's websites at patricetartt.com and girlswritetoo.com.*

Open

By Victoria Kennedy

Deanna spoke softly into the phone. The diffused, ambient lighting of her bedroom helped create an atmosphere conducive to seduction, and since she couldn't be with Karim in person, she chose to captivate him with her words and sounds. She resorted to "ah's," and "umm's," to fill pauses between sentences and to caress him with her voice.

Karim was a reserved man and she knew he would never voice some of the thoughts he entertained about her, not over the phone anyway. He was a hands-on type and no amount of sighs from her would motivate him to speak improperly. He was in the United Arab Emirates for a conference on the changing face of Islam around the world and she wouldn't see him for another week. After reading his last postcard, she wished he could see the look of arousal on her face brought on by the suggestive words he'd written. She wondered if he'd let his guard all the way down.

He'd finally expressed physical longing. The most recent postcard set a scene that appealed to her senses of taste, sight and touch in a way to answer her question of whether they wanted the same things from whatever it was they were doing.

For the past year, he'd been polite to a fault. Pecking the backs of her hands with pursed lips when he greeted her and touching her cheek tenderly in parting. She accepted these most recent written endearments as a small victory, some movement in the right direction. Maybe, when they next met, he would take action the way his words had on paper . . . the way he had in her fantasies. She hoped.

Deanna toyed with the postcard, turning it to the picture on the front then re-reading his words on the back.

Greetings from Cairo!, it read, in his chicken-scratch handwriting that looked like it should be scrawled on a prescription pad. She didn't know when she'd learned to decipher it so effortlessly.

The rasp of his voice hummed in her ear, as he continued to talk about the heat in Dubai and the awesome hospitality being extended to him. He said he hadn't eaten in a restaurant, since his arrival, so many homes had hosted him and the only reason he slept in a hotel, instead of a private residence, was because he valued his privacy. It certainly wasn't for lack of offers for everything from sleeping quarters to a few daughters' hands in marriage. That boastful announcement made Deanna feel a little uneasy about his travels and the time spent away from her. She shifted onto her stomach, propping up onto her elbows and balancing the phone between her head and shoulder.

It hadn't dawned on her before that other women would want her Karim but she could certainly understand why they would. She smirked at the notion of referring to him as "hers" but she was in too deep with this unlikely suitor to back off now. She had invested her hopes and emotions in this man who prided himself on being the best at everything he did. He was something of an enigma – obsessing over test scores, chess scores, and IQ's. He talked about maintaining his temple and ran daily, no matter where he was in the world. He often stressed the importance of strength and endurance, which made Deanna slyly consider his bedroom skills.

Karim was a noted historian, a popular professor of Cultural African Studies at Loyola University in Baltimore and as such, represented his institution around the world, courting scholars and professionals in his field of expertise. He was a striking man, tall and lean with graying hair at his temples and dark penetrating eyes that made Deanna feel like the only woman in the world when he peered into hers. He mostly wore a kufi and suspenders with a bow tie. He was formal and seemed most impressed with everything about Deanna that was not – like her unpretentious ways, her talkative nature and how she didn't hesitate to express her feelings, even snorting in her laughter. She made his stiff attempts at humor funny just by responding with her laugh. She was open to learning about him and he was eager to teach her everything.

"Well, since they are offering you virgin brides, it sounds like a golden opportunity to find a nice Muslim wife, Karim," she teased.

He paused a little longer than she expected, in the wake of her deliberate jab. She often asked why he wasted time with a "good, ol' Southern Baptist girl" when there were plenty of women of his faith looking for a great catch like him.

"I've told you before, Deanna. I could have had that a long time ago, if that's what I wanted."

"Well, if you know that's not what you want, stop taunting me with stories of people throwing their daughters at your feet."

The position he'd chosen for his dating life – eschewing Muslim women – puzzled her, but the fact that he wasn't looking for someone like that intrigued her more than the confusion she now pushed to the back of her mind. She could hear the smile in his voice, when he replied, "Duly-noted, my Dear. And while we are addressing taunts, could you please stop torturing me with your breathy sighs?"

Deanna broke into the hearty laughter he loved and his barely constrained chuckle joined hers across the time and distance between them. She was enjoying this new, more relaxed side of Karim. She enjoyed it more, for not having to coax it out of him. He acted as if a layer of stiff formality had been peeled away. She wondered how many more layers it would take to get to the heart of him.

"I think this is the longest period we have spent apart, my Dear. Knowing I have the melody of your sweet voice to look forward to each night before I fall asleep warms my heart."

The intimate nature of Karim's words was pleasantly unexpected and out of character but it had become a part of the turning tide. Each passing day was making him bolder in his declarations. A month earlier, he was in Egypt and that trip had marked a change in their relationship, which until then, had not been defined. The postcard he sent after that had expressed desires, beyond the regular niceties:

Dearest Dee,

Today was a very tiring day. I was in conference then toured the city with, Dr. Hassan, my colleague from the American University. We visited the Khan al-Kahlili Bazaar and the sights made me think of you. I imagined introducing you to the exotic spices and envisioned you in the beautiful silk robes of red and gold. I miss you. And I wish you were here.

Progress, Deanna mused. His old-fashioned attempt at flirtation was extremely endearing.

He wasn't like anyone she'd known, certainly not like Bayard, her last boyfriend, who spoke mostly with his body. She'd let him make body language their primary communication because he spoke it very well but, after a while, the conversations had become predictable and lacked the intellectual stimulation and challenge she sought.

She and Karim had first met when she was a bank teller and he was her customer. Their conversations about the latest headlines or the weather had given way to an exchange of phone numbers, and progressed to nightly phone calls that gave accounts of each other's days. She had looked forward to those talks, but not like she now looked forward to the postcards. They were proof that a thing between them even existed.

Usually, the phone calls included polite pleasantries while the postcards revealed real thoughts and intentions with a formality Deanna found amusing. This special correspondence of theirs, alternating between phone and post, convinced her that the physical relationship she'd had with Bayard would never be enough to sustain her ever again. She realized she needed a man to also make love to her mind. Karim was doing that in spades.

She rolled onto her back with the phone still pressed to her ear. This was month eleven and, she was holding postcard ten.

"Ah," she sighed into the phone, this time unconsciously. He seemed to discern the nature of her sounds while still riding the noticeable shift their earlier exchange had introduced to the conversation. She revisited his desire to cook for her and dress her, while he continued to talk without the need of her response. She wondered if he also wanted to undress her, as she entertained the desire to be filled by him.

His voice lulled her with the inflections of Sierra Leone, even though he hadn't lived there for the past twenty years. Karim recited his daily agenda with as much attention to detail as his daily prayers and filled her in on his itinerary for the remainder of his trip. Ordinarily, this would have been sufficient. She had learned to tolerate the rather dull accounts of his conferences, the panels and discussions he'd participated in. She'd settled for occasional hand-holding on rare lunchtime outings and chaste kisses, but something as simple as his acknowledgement of her sexy sighs had thrown her off balance. She held on tighter, as she felt them make the U-turn she'd been waiting for.

She pulled the other nine postcards from a tin-lidded box in the drawer of her nightstand. She sat up in the bed, spread them out on her quilt and gloried in his global destinations. He had been everywhere, from Sydney to Johannesburg, Reykjavik to Marrakesh, Moscow, Hong Kong and so many other places. She re-read them, as he drawled in her ear about his activities. She could hear him struggling to keep his voice devoid of yearning. Every time he strayed away from his work schedule and restating the topics of discussion he'd planned , his tone softened into a personable rich timber. He'd try to snatch it back into his business voice but he'd already put himself out there. Postcard nine was dated May 12th and showed steep inclining streets in the foreground while the Golden Gate Bridge rose in the distance.

Hello from San Francisco! was printed across the top. She smiled at his first uses of the nickname he'd given her, just a shortened version of Deanna but for Karim, it had been a bold move:

Dear Dee,

San Francisco is a bustling city. I have met interesting people including some eager young men from my country who are anxious for reform, after the Civil War in Sierra Leone. I only want to broaden horizons for Loyola and if that means challenging some traditions, it will require deeper thought on my part. I hope all is well with you and that work isn't too hard. I am working a lot but not too hard to think of you. I should return by the end of the week. You know, I wish you were here.

His mention of the war had shown more openness about the struggles he experienced right before they met. He'd only spoken briefly about the hard times that had divided his family, during the last armed conflict in his homeland.

Postcard eight had a 1950s Parisian scene with people strolling the Champs-Élysées.

Bonjour from Paris!, it read. It was dated April 4th.

Hi Dee,

This has been an exciting week. Major developments are taking place in the Muslim world. I have arranged a most excellent exchange with some Senegalese brethren from The Grand Masjid of Paris. My assistance is needed on their research for a book. They will visit Loyola sometime this year. I'm sorry we haven't had a chance to talk but I'm thinking of you. I wish you were here.

Deanna put the postcards in chronological order. She'd come to appreciate the structure their order brought to her life and even that was tentative. Something was amiss with the dates and places but she was no stranger to confusion. She'd left a chaotic existence, a history of disorder in the Sandtown section of West Baltimore – an abusive father, a passive mother and two underachieving sisters who confounded her with their lack of ambition. She knew Bolton Hill, where Karim lived, wasn't very far but it was a world away from her past and closer to the new beginning she sought.

In this new order, everything had its place and she was trying her best to fit Karim into a space they could both inhabit. It was ironic that he lived mere miles away from her childhood and her dysfunctional family. He represented a possible bridge between her past and her future.

Deanna sighed again, in a whooshing sound more abrasive than seductive.

"Why are you so restless, Sweetheart?"

Sweetheart?

"I don't know. I just really need to see you. I think we need to talk." Her growing impatience was palpable.

"Deanna, I need to see you as well and I'm afraid we've talked too much. I want to hold you. Do you understand?"

"Yes, Karim. I'm waiting for you to come home."

"Good. That's my girl."

All the postcards were postmarked from the same place – Washington, D.C. Deanna noticed nine months ago that the first card wasn't postmarked for Marrakesh, the city he claimed to visit. She assumed he'd been so excited about presenting his scholarly paper at a conference on the history of Morocco and that was why he'd forgotten to mail it before boarding the plane.

She remembered asking him about the discrepancy, after the postcard from Sydney Australia – his fourth trip away. It was during summer break and he participated in a tour where he and a group of scholars traveled the world discussing the friendly nature of Islam and keeping a respectable distance from violent extremists. Deanna had been mesmerized by his appearance on Face the Nation and swelled with pride, when he called her right after his segment aired.

"Karim, why are your postcards always postmarked for Washington, D.C.?" she finally asked.

"That's because I mail them, when I land at Dulles Airport. I write them on the plane. It gives me something to do, during the long flights."

"The postmarks are what give the postcards value. The stamps validate the destinations."

"My words give the postcards value, Deanna, because they are from my heart. No stamp can validate that," he'd said.

Deanna's judgment had been poor, in the past – with her family and with Bayard. They'd all been willing to take what she had to give: hopes, dreams, money, and trust. They took everything for granted and offered nothing in return. With Bay, as she'd affectionately called him, he equated brute strength and a short fuse with epitomizing the qualities of being a man who didn't walk away from conflict. However, walking away for her had been hard but necessary, if she wanted to salvage the remnants of trust left hanging on by a thread. The last straw had been when Bayard wanted to resort to her father's method of resolving disagreements. He'd pummeled a family friend into a bloody pulp because he'd lingered too long in an embrace with Deanna. Now, after dating Karim for nearly a year, she knew he possessed more stability than Bayard was capable of.

She was the first to admit, Karim's latest efforts to make his intentions more physical aroused her, but it was hard to trust the change. It was more urgent than a natural progression. She wondered what had motivated him this way. Was he the man she made him out to be or was he just playing games at a higher level than she was accustomed to?

In the absence of sighs and realizing her quietness, Karim asked, "Are you sleepy, my Dear?"

"I am just a little tired, Karim."

"Not of me, I hope."

"Of course not."

She never thought the postcards wouldn't be enough. She'd been traveling vicariously through him for a year, seeing the journey through his eyes, the destinations as the lens. The usually outspoken Deanna didn't want anything to mar her fantasy of him so she kept her doubts quiet. He was flawed, she knew, but he was still her hero, saving her from a mundane existence. He was closer to perfection than any man she'd known. She told herself she didn't care if he filled out those damned postcards in the bathroom at work, as long as he sent them to her and finally professed his real feelings.

"Goodnight, Deanna, Dear Heart." His breath caressed her name. "I will be home soon."

"Goodnight, Karim. I'll be waiting."

By Wednesday morning, Deanna sat in the lunchroom thinking of her last talk with Karim and how quickly the days had passed, since their night on the phone. Before he'd left, he had come to see her at the bank where she'd been promoted to Assistant Manager. He'd kissed her chastely on the lips in front of her co-workers, both surprising and embarrassing her. The teller line buzzed with chatter, at the public display of affection. Dr. Longo was a regular customer and she knew many were surprised to see him interact intimately with her.

As they entered her office, he grasped and kissed her hands then sat down and filled her in on his itinerary for his time away. After a quick embrace and a tender swipe across her cheek with the back of his hand, he strode out into the branch with a wave good-bye.

* * *

The remainder of the week puttered by at a pace so slowly, it was infuriating. Deanna hadn't spoken to Karim in days yet refused to call his cell so far from home, no matter how badly she wanted to talk to him.

"Deanna, you have a call on line two," the receptionist paged her. Her pulse quickened at the startling announcement and with the prospect of it being Karim. It had been one week since she'd spoken to him. She moved purposefully from the lunchroom at the rear of the building to her office up front. Along the way, familiar customers smiled and admired her polished appearance – the café au lait complexion, the black hair pulled tightly into a low ponytail dangling between her shoulder blades and the navy pencil skirt hugging her shapely hips and nipping in her small, tight waist. The outfit complemented her petite frame; most people standing in the long line noticed the attractive picture she presented. However, she didn't notice anything other than the fact that she had a call waiting for her undivided attention.

"This is Miss Turner," she answered, affecting the husky professional tone she used for Karim.

"Well, hello, Miss Turner."

Her stomach clenched, at the sound of the familiar voice, not the one she'd hoped for.

"Why are you calling me here at work?" Her voice was low and stretched tight.

"As if you would take my calls at home."

"Bayard, there's nothing for us to talk about – at home or work."

"Listen to you – all formal and stuff. I've always been Bay to you, baby. That fancy professor putting thoughts in your head, huh?"

She didn't like the sound of anything relating to Karim coming out of his mouth.

"No," she said. "I have thoughts of my own. Thank you."

"You been thinking of me?"

"No. I haven't."

"I bet your body has."

"Look, Bay – Bayard. Don't call me again. Just let me go."

Her plea went completely ignored. "And by the way, congrats on the promo-"

Deanna hung up before he could finish his compliment. Her hands shook slightly, after she placed the phone on its base. Her body reacted too intensely to Bayard's voice and his words. She sat still until her pulse slowed down and her nipples obeyed the silent command to forget the memories playing on an endless loop of warm lips and tongues devouring secret places.

Karim doesn't know this side of me, she thought.

"Ahem." The baritone voice broke into the thick silence.

She looked up quickly, self-consciously flushing at the intrusion into her private thoughts.

"An irate customer?"

Karim's long frame filled the open doorway. There were no suspenders, no kufi or bow tie in sight, only a dazzling smile and an assessing look in his eye. He was the picture of virility in a crisp white shirt, the sleeves rolled back upon deep brown forearms and the collar relaxed and unbuttoned. Something had changed, starting with the broad smile on his handsome face. He was open.

She felt like she was really seeing him for the first time. She couldn't hold back the happiness bubbling up from her insides. She stood and moved in his direction, stopping at the edge of her desk and sitting, too self-conscious under scrutiny of the customers to throw her arms around him.

She brought the huskiness back in her voice.

"So glad to see you are back from your trip."

"Glad enough to accompany me to dinner this evening?"

"Yes, I believe I am."

"That's perfect," he responded, "because I am ravenous."

His voice dipped to the lower register of his vocal range and aroused her with its implication.

"I'm quite hungry myself. You know you could've called to ask me out, Dr. Longo." She smirked.

"Then I would have missed this beautiful vision before me."

He waved his hand around to emphasize her presence. His compliment hit its mark, as Deanna blushed to the roots of her raven tresses.

After he left the bank, the day passed with more urgency. She narrowly avoided a stupid mistake that could have cost her job. She'd literally had to run a half a block to catch a customer she'd given the wrong loan check. It was because her mind was flooded with all the scenarios she wished for the evening and they had her beside herself. Karim would pick her up at her apartment, after Friday services at the masjid and attending to business on campus.

She found herself smiling often at the memory of his parting kiss – lingering on her lips, not smooching her hands.

She rushed home, at the end of the day, to find something sexy, yet understated to wear. She'd been more than patient with Karim and waited for him to make all the manly moves. It's not like she was aggressive, but his visit this afternoon hinted they may finally be on the same page. She hoped he planned to make good on the promises of postcard ten, of cooking for her, clothing her, coming home to her, longing for her…

Her mailbox was full and she was glad to see her Essence and InStyle magazines. She pulled the sales papers and coupons from the pile of mail, and a postcard dropped out. It was number eleven and had the postmark of the U.A.E.:

Greetings from Dubai! It had a picture of the tallest skyscraper in the world – the Burj Khalifa:

My Darling Deanna,

I sensed a distance in you tonight as we talked on the phone. This is the first time I've felt disconnected from you and I don't like this feeling. I hope you are not pulling away from me. My schedule has been very demanding lately and it is putting a strain on our relationship. You've been too kind to mention it but I am already aware. I want to make amends. Let there be no misunderstanding, you are the woman I want. Please let me prove it to you, my Love. I miss you. I wish you were here with me.

Deanna stared at the postcard, tears welling up that she refused to let fall. A sense of guilt crept up on her. She was so close to having this man, this honorable man who was as different from her as she could ever find. But what she'd wished for was too good to be true. Realistically, she couldn't have the sophisticated professor who traveled the world and commanded the respect of his peers, not without coming clean herself. She didn't have a right to anticipate the pleasure of being with him until she told him the real story of her life. The double standard of requiring transparency while living a lie was not lost on her.

Insecurities from her past taunted her with memories of submission and abuse. She was another person, in another time filled with shame. This new Deanna had made a choice to be cherished and desired by a good man and no longer claimed as the property of a possessive, unstable one. Surely, Karim could relate to the need to start her life over in a new place with better opportunities. That's what he had done, she resolved with a glimmer of optimism.

She showered quickly and chose a simple black sheath that molded perfectly to her curvaceous figure. She was determined to be ready for whatever the evening would bring, as she applied fresh makeup and admired the reflection staring back at her. Her mother's beauty was the one thing she didn't mind inheriting.

The doorbell rang. He was early. Anxiety crackled within her, creating uncertainty, even as she acknowledged her strong will to be with him. Her heart was racing, in spite of her resolve. As soon as she opened the door, the world stopped.

Bayard was standing in her hallway. His facial hair was trimmed neatly, the way she always liked. His hazel eyes locked into hers with pleading. It was impossible to ignore the most notable change in his appearance. He'd traded his usual tee shirt and jeans for a pressed dress shirt tucked into khakis. Her eyes roamed appreciatively over the muscular planes of his torso encased in the crisp cotton. And he was holding a beautiful bouquet.

He spoke before she could find her voice.

"Is this what you want, Dee-Dee?" She assumed he was talking about his new image.

"What?" She didn't recognize her own voice, in its weakened state it was more like a whisper.

The delay caused by her shocked reaction must have been interpreted as a welcome because Bayard reached out to hand her the flowers.

He had never been in her apartment. She refused to move aside to grant him entry and noted the twitch in his left jaw, recognizing it as the switch for his short fuse.

"How could you tell me to let you go?"

"It's time, Bay."

"Never."

The buzzer caused her to jump and Bayard's eyes to darken with contempt. Karim's timing was poetic. The enormity of what could occur planted her heavily in her truth. She couldn't run this time – not down the hall or across town. She faced Bayard with defiance in her dark-rimmed exotic eyes.

"You have to leave. My date is here."

He straightened his shoulders and stood his ground. Just when Deanna was prepared for a face-off with her former controller, he said, "Deanna, Please don't continue with this. I'll give you everything you want."

"I just want you to leave, Bay."

"I can't."

He took hold of her shoulders and tried to pull her into his broad chest. She had a flashback of all the times she'd pleaded with him to stop everything that caused her pain. Anger reared its fire in her. Deanna pushed back. Hard.

"Stop it. I don't want you anymore, Bay!"

Her forceful yell brought him to a startled halt.

"Please… leave me alone."

The normally quiet hallway was filled with the sound of her severing ties that could no longer bind. Her neighbor's door swung open suddenly, causing Bayard to step further away. The old lady looked back and forth between them before resting her eyes on Deanna.

"Are you okay out here?"

"Yes, Ma'am. Sorry about the noise."

Deanna maintained eye contact with her until she was convinced enough to go inside her apartment. The neighbor looked back at Bayard and said, “Don’t make me call the police.”

With that, Bayard gave Deanna one last lingering look then turned to leave.

She finally pressed the button to grant Karim access to the building and breathed deeply to calm her nerves. She couldn’t believe Bayard had left with no further trouble. The mention of the police had been an effective threat. She almost felt sorry for him. Almost.

She smoothed her dress over her hips and checked her reflection once more.

This time, she opened the door before Karim could knock. He was smiling and handing her roses. She noticed it was still there – that look in his eyes she’d seen earlier. It projected realness. More layers had been peeled away. She knew she could trust this man.

Before she could turn away to place the flowers on her table, she was swept into his arms. Deanna’s senses reveled in his smell, his touch and the taste of his lips, as she returned his passionate kiss. She told herself she could have these moments of pleasure with nothing to hide or fear. Her closed heart couldn’t give or receive love but an open heart was free to accept its every desire.

She could feel the hardness of Karim’s body as she ran her hands along his shirt. His gaze met hers with a glint of yearning. He bent toward her and rubbed his nose against hers, closing his eyes.

"I told you, I was coming home to you."

Deanna felt her heart crack wide-open.

"And I said I'd be waiting. There's so much I want to share with you. It's time for us to really talk, Karim; it's time for us to both be open."

Victoria Kennedy *is a writer and singer, currently pursuing an MFA in Creative Writing and the Publishing Arts, finding inspiration in everyday things. She performs regularly and is working on her first novel. To find out more about Victoria, go to www.victoriaadamskennedy.com. You can also find her on Facebook.*

A Good Woman

By Tania Renee Zayid

"It's complicated."

The moment those words cascaded from Jeff's full, sexy lips, Kayla felt a warning jolt in the pit of her stomach. She glanced briefly at him across the dinner table before lowering her eyes and sighing, Kayla unconsciously smirked and thought: "Here comes the drama." She realized that her tone of voice might reveal her thoughts, so she modulated her voice to sound as neutral and as non-judgmental as she possibly could.

"What is complicated? How your last relationship ended? Or are you referring to yourself?" Kayla smiled and asked the question almost jokingly to deflect the sarcasm she felt.

"Kayla, I don't consider myself to be complex. I am a pretty straightforward guy, even a simple man in some ways. I am the dude that actually keeps a spare key under a flower pot near my front door. My last relationship ended on a very bad note and we were both at fault. There is no cut and dry answer to why things ended the way they did. Suffice it to say that we both screwed it up."

Kayla had been in this game for so long that she was an expert at hearing what wasn't said and seeing what wasn't visible. In short, she had become a genuine communication strategist when dealing with a new man. She knew that Jeff had told her, for now, all that he was going to about his most recent relationship. So she changed tactics and quietly replied, "I understand."

Actually, Kayla really didn't care why Jeff's last relationship ended. She knew enough to know that each person in the defunct relationship would have their own truth and their own lies. So it really didn't matter why a connection was terminated; the most critical question was HOW it ended. Was there violence, or unresolved and ongoing desire? Were the two people still emotionally and sexually entangled although they were "broken up?" Those were the answers that Kayla searched for when she first met someone new.

"Thanks, Kayla, for not pushing the issue. That relationship is over and done. I don't believe in lingering in the past; especially when I could be staring right at my future." Jeff smiled sheepishly after he realized how cliché he sounded.

"Damn, that was an old line, wasn't it? I got to step my game up!" Jeff chuckled as he waited for Kayla's response.

"Your game is pretty tight, sir. Trust me."

Kayla smiled as she looked Jeff in his eyes. In fact, Kayla was very attracted to Jeffrey X. Taylor. He was her ideal man, the one she had been patiently waiting for. Jeff was 6'3, muscular, and he had one of the most handsome faces Kayla had seen in a long time. His skin was smooth and dark and he had slick, black facial hair. His beard was neat and his mustache was on point.

But it was Jeff's eyes that had captured Kayla. He had long, curly eyelashes that almost touched his cheeks when he blinked. His eyes were clear and healthy and he had the darkest pupils that Kayla had ever seen. It was like looking into a pool of shimmery, black, priceless oil.

Jeff's melodic voice gently coaxed her out of her thoughts of his sexiness.

"So Ms. Kayla Danyell, tell me. Why are you still single? You are a beautiful, intelligent, successful woman. So why hasn't some dude claimed you for life?"

Kayla had anticipated this question and had her answer ready. It never failed that a man who expressed interest in her also wanted to know why she wasn't already taken. Kayla, through trial and error, learned that most guys really didn't care for her honest answer to that question. The truth was that Kayla had been more interested in becoming successful in her career than in becoming someone's wife. Sure, in her early twenties, Kayla had the same desperate desire that most women do: to find and secure a husband. But when that fantasy man never appeared, Kayla moved on to other things, like her career. She pursued her MBA and completed several programming certifications after she graduated with her undergrad computer engineering degree. She was twenty-two when she received her first degree. Now, at thirty-six, Kayla was single, childless and the Chief Operating Officer at an employment agency that placed computer experts in careers at various Fortune 500 companies. The very accomplishments that defined Kayla were also unspoken deal breakers in the dating game.

"I decided a long time ago that I never want to be divorced. So I took the time to make sure that I am prepared for that type of commitment."

That answer was actually a version of one of Kayla's truths. All of her girlfriends were married by their late twenties or early thirties. Kayla had felt like the social outcast for many years. Even when she had a couple of long term relationships, she felt, deep down, that her friends always questioned the validity of her relationships if the end result wasn't a walk down the aisle.

Now, a decade later, half of her friends were either divorced or separated. And ALL of her friends were saddled with the responsibilities of children. Kayla was a source of secret envy in her circle of friends. She was still relatively young, beautiful and free. She had all of her time and resources to herself and she could construct her life using her own blueprints. Kayla was well aware of her freedom and she enjoyed every minute of it. While Kayla still had a longing for a life partner, she wasn't desperate to be legally bound to another person. She was in a good place, and she knew it.

"So, Ms. Kayla, are you prepared? Are you ready to go to the next level?"

Kayla knew that she must REALLY be feeling Jeff because any other man referring to her as "Ms. Kayla" would have worked her last nerve. But when Jeff called her "Ms. Kayla" it sounded sweet, endearing and sexy.

"Yes, Mr. Jeff, I am ready for marriage if I find a man who is ready as well." Kayla winked and gave Jeff a sexy and knowing half-smile.

"Damn, you are one beautiful woman. And I am not just saying that, I mean it. I think I may have hit the online dating jackpot, baby girl."

Kayla was grateful that Jeff made a concerted effort to comment on her beauty and not her sex appeal. She knew that she was a sexy woman and she worked hard to stay that way. But she also knew that she was naturally beautiful in a dark, mysterious sort of way. Kayla was 5'7, 140 pounds soaking wet, and she was the color of hot, cream-filled coffee. She had dark thick eyebrows that had never seen a piece of thread, wax or a razor. Her expressive brown eyes were protected by long lashes that never needed a stroke of mascara.

She had a small, upturned nose, full perfectly sculpted lips, and deep dimples in both cheeks. Kayla had thick, naturally waved hair that used to be the bane of her existence. "Indian Hair" is how Kayla's mother described the unruly, dark, deeply waved mop of shoulder-length hair on Kayla's head. When all of her friends were going to the beauty shop every two weeks to get their hair permed and cut into the latest style, Kayla's hair laid on her shoulders like a heavy burden. Now, it was ironic that so many women were actually paying to get "Indian Hair" weaved into their own.

Kayla had developed a health and beauty regimen in her younger years that served her very well now. She ate well, but limited sugar, salt and fat intake. She exercised a minimum of six hours a week, and she had managed to maintain a svelte figure although she carried a few extra pounds. She got facials, manicures and pedicures faithfully, every two weeks, every season of the year. She was actually surprised that she never caught pneumonia in the winter when she wore sandals out of the nail shop in freezing weather just so she wouldn't ruin her fresh pedicure.

Kayla was beautiful and she knew it, but she was grateful for her looks. She wasn't vain and she knew that her looks didn't define her. Kayla's serene self-confidence gave her a gracefulness that both men and women immediately noticed.

"Jeff, I appreciate the compliment, but man, you ain't so bad yourself! Maybe we BOTH have hit the lottery."

"Is this your first time doing online dating?"

"No, this isn't the first time that I have dated a man that I 'met' online. However, it IS the first time that I actually met someone in real life that seems like an all-around good match."

"I understand that. I have met a few women online and we never got past a phone convo. And I have met a couple of young ladies online who in real life looked, how shall I put this, totally different than their profile pictures."

"Totally different how? Were they different ages, different sizes, what?"

"All of the above and then some. One chick told me she was 5'9, and "model-size", and her one profile picture supported that, but she was actually about 5'4 and plus size. Now don't get me wrong, I'm not hung up on size or looks, but like any man I like a good looking woman. What got me was the deceit. If you can lie about something as obvious as height and weight, what else would you lie about?"

"I never understood that either. Why lie about something like that? I mean at some point the two of you are going to meet and the jig is up, right?"

"Right! It made me wonder if maybe the young ladies weren't a bit off balance for even trying to pull that off. What about you? Did you meet some jokers too?"

"Man, I met several jokers. Married guys parading as single, unemployed guys parading as "business men", and even one dude who was incognegro."

"Girl, what is incognegro??" Jeff's eyes danced with amusement.

"Incognegro is a white dude who posts pictures of a black dude online, who poses as a black dude online, but who has blond hair and blue eyes in real life."

"Kayla, you ARE joking right?" Jeff was incredulous about this online dating revelation.

"Nope, I kid you not." Kayla laughed out loud when she thought back to meeting "Ray," whose real name was Chad.

"Well damn, that's a first; a white dude wanting to be black. But I can certainly understand. I would have pretended too if I saw pictures of that fine Kayla."

"Well I am glad I joined this site because I get to sit across from this FINE Jeff!"

Kayla had actually just joined the exclusive online dating site that was geared toward professional African- American singles who were serious about finding committed relationships. The monthly fee was expensive, but necessary because it stopped those who were ardent game players from joining. People who spent the monthly equivalent of rent just to find companionship were pretty serious.

Jeffrey X. Taylor was Kayla's first match on the site. His bio stated that he was 37, never married, no children and that he owned his own business. His profile picture was gorgeous. Kayla's interest was immediately piqued so she initiated the online conversation. Jeff responded the same day and their dating relationship started.

First there were the pleasant e-mails. Then there was the exchange of phone numbers. Jeff and Kayla sent what seemed like thousands of text messages and talked on the phone for hours for the first two weeks. They finally had their first date in a small, eclectic jazz restaurant during the third week of communicating. Now, tonight, they were on their second date in less than a week. Things were progressing quite well.

Kayla decided that one of the things she like best about Jeff was his honesty and his consistency. He told her that he was a CPA who owned his own financial planning business. Kayla was pleasantly surprised when she looked him up online and found that he was telling the truth. His website was very impressive indeed. Kayla was also very glad that Jeff had an unusual name. "Jeffrey X. Taylor" sort of cleared the path for her Internet searches. She found out early in their conversations that the "X" actually stood for "Xavier." His credentials pulled up immediately under their state board of accountancy.

Kayla had learned that you can find anything you wanted to know about a person if you just listened. In this day and time of social media and advanced Internet searches, all one needed was a valid name and birth date. Men and women were both guilty these days of sharing way too much information. Jeff had described the general location of his home and specific details about the unique architecture. In less than fifteen minutes, Kayla had his address at her disposal. When she drove through his subdivision just to see the houses, she found his immediately, even without the address. He had told her that he lived in the only "Tudor-style" house on his street. Jeff had not been lying about the architecture either. His property was absolutely amazing.

Kayla realized that after a few days of talking to Jeff, she never EVER thought about William, her ex anymore. That revelation was truly shocking. William had been her man, or so she thought, for two years. She truly loved him. She found out, unexpectedly, that William had another woman who also truly loved him. The woman had shown up in a restaurant where Kayla and William were dining for their two-year anniversary. Kayla had fully expected to get a ring at the end of the night. Instead, she got the wrath of the other woman.

Kayla had excused herself and left when the woman began to shout obscenities at William in the middle of the exclusive restaurant. The one thing that Kayla refused to tolerate was drama. ESPECIALLY ghetto, side-chick, cheating man drama. From that day forward, Kayla refused to accept William's calls, text messages or e-mails. She was confused, hurt, angry and mystified. The greatest feeling that Kayla had was embarrassment. She was so embarrassed that she had absolutely no clue that the man she loved was a cheater.

Kayla was particularly embarrassed that she was a computer expert who never even thought to do her research on the man she loved. In the end, she found out that SHE was the side chick and that William and Evelyn had been "on and off" for three years. William had married Evelyn a year ago and Kayla's heart had been shattered for a second time. After William got married, something inside of Kayla changed forever. She had lost her faith in herself and she felt so stupid for being so trusting.

Kayla became obsessed with William and his "wife." She used every tool at her disposal to find out everything about Evelyn. She had to know what Evelyn had (besides William) that she didn't. Not a day went by for almost a year that she didn't check all the social media sites to see what Evelyn and William were doing. She studied every picture, every post on both of their social media pages. She was giving up her life to watch Evelyn and William live theirs.

One day, Kayla still didn't understand why, she had a major lapse in judgment and sent William a connection request on his social media account. She didn't realize that Evelyn was the administrator of their account but she sure found out when Evelyn sent her a scathing message telling

Kayla to "never contact my husband again." Kayla was so pissed that she actually drove down William's street that same day. In the most bizarre twist of fate EVER, Evelyn was outside in their yard and she saw Kayla driving slowly past.

The next day, Kayla received an e-mail from William from an account that Evelyn obviously had no access to. True to form, William's communication was brief and to the point. "Kayla. Please don't contact me anymore and for God's sake don't drive down our street anymore. I am sorry that things ended the way they did with us, but you don't know my wife. If she sees you driving past our home again or you try to contact me on my page, Evelyn will file a restraining order and tell the police that you are a stalker. Please. For your sake, let it go. William".

Kayla believed that it was the word "stalker" that made her cease and desist contact. She had worked too long and too hard to get tangled in a legal dispute with William and Evelyn. So she stopped spying, stopped snooping and vowed never to ride on William's street again.

But she had never stopped thinking about William. Not even for a day. It wasn't even love anymore that kept her mind preoccupied with the man who betrayed her. It was the rejection. She could not understand the rejection of a man she had been intimate with for two years.

When Kayla met Jeff, William became a distant memory; a ghost. Jeff was helping her to give up that ghost. The one thing that Kayla took from that dreadful experience was that no matter who she met, she would do her due diligence. Never again would she be fooled by an imposter. Kayla would forever do her research.

After their pleasant second dinner date, Kayla and Jeff mutually agreed that they would try exclusive dating. So far, everything was working out nicely. They had had a few very enjoyable dates and they basked in each other's company. Kayla and Jeff were truly a perfect match. They held the same core values and both decided not to pursue a sexual relationship until they got to really know each other. After all, they were both almost forty and there was a lot at stake here.

But then, Kayla began noticing small changes in Jeff's behavior after about six weeks. Normally Jeff and Kayla would speak on the phone every night, but for the last two nights, Jeff had sent "good night" text messages. Yes, they did speak during the day, but good night TEXT messages....really? Kayla felt a small knot of fear tying itself over and over in her belly. What the hell? On the second text message night, Kayla called Jeff but his phone went straight to voicemail. She decided not to leave a message.

Kayla and Jeff had scheduled a date night for the upcoming Friday. On Tuesday afternoon, Kayla's cell phone rang.

"Hello."

"Hey, baby girl. How is your day going so far?"

"So far so good, JT. How about you, baby? How is your day?" Kayla's smile lit up her office as she talked to her man. He had been so sweet lately that the warning bells that had been ringing loudly when his behavior briefly shifted were intermittent chimes now.

"I have been busy, baby. Real busy. On that note, I am afraid that I have a bit of bad news. I need to reschedule our Friday night date. I have some projects that I have to finish and they will keep me tied up well past midnight."

"I understand, baby. Duty calls. No problem. Would you like to come over to my house for a bit on Saturday? Or maybe I could finally get to see your house."

The silence on the phone was so loud that Kayla wasn't sure if she should say anything else. That had been a small bone of contention for Kayla; the fact that Jeff hadn't invited her over to his home yet. Jeff had promised that they would eventually "get around" to home visits, but something just didn't sit right with Kayla. He had been to her home albeit briefly a couple of times to pick her up for a date. It occurred to Kayla a couple of weeks ago that they had never REALLY spent any time alone.

Kayla had subtly asked Jeff about spending "alone" time and he told her that he didn't want to put them in a situation that would encroach on their agreement to delay intimacy. Kayla felt mixed emotions that truly surprised her. She always desired a man who wanted to get to know her intimately and not just sexually. Now the man had appeared and she felt like something was missing because he wasn't rushing to bed her. She at first found herself questioning her attractiveness and her sex appeal, but now she was starting to silently question Jeff. Was he hiding something? Was there someone else? Jeff gave every indication that he was truthful, and her woman's intuition told her that he was very attracted to her and wanted her. Plus, her research of him had panned out. Everything that he told her had been true so far. So why was the warning bell messing up her peace?

"Kayla, I promise you that we will get there. Unfortunately, it just won't be this week. I had some unexpected audits to come up so I really will be tied up. It is my plan to see you on Sunday. How about an early Sunday dinner?"

"Sure Jeff. That will be just fine. Don't work too hard, baby. I will talk to you tonight."

"Okay, my pretty Kayla. I will talk to you later."

After hanging up the phone, Kayla had a sudden pang of regret that she played it too cool and didn't drown Jeff with well placed questions about his last relationship. She didn't even know his ex's name. Had he and his ex gotten back in contact recently? Kayla knew that for many women the most attractive man was one who was taken. Had his ex somehow found out that he had a woman and was now trying to slither her way into Jeff's life again?

That night, Kayla sent but did not receive a good night text. The next morning, Jeff called before Kayla headed off to her office.

"Good morning, baby girl. I'm sorry I missed your text last night. I was so tired, baby that I just crashed." Jeff indeed sounded tired.

"You know, you need a break. You can't work yourself to the point of exhaustion, baby."

"Seeing your face on Sunday will be just the break that I need, Ms. Kayla. I miss you. I promise you that this is not the norm. We will be back on track soon."

"I know, Jeff. I look forward to Sunday, too."

Everything seemed all right, but Kayla couldn't shake the feeling that everything was starting to be all wrong. She had finally admitted to herself that she loved Jeff and that she wanted him more than she had ever wanted anyone.

On Friday, Jeff and Kayla were back to their "normal." Although Jeff was going to work late that night, he made a point to talk to Kayla several times during the day. On Friday night, Kayla decided to go to bed early and do some reading. She called Jeff at his office to tell him goodnight.

"Hey, Jeff. Just want to say good night early. I know that you're working and I'm going to bed early."

"Good night, Kayla. You sure you are okay? It's not even nine yet. You not becoming an old lady on me already, are you?" Jeff giggled like a school boy telling a dirty joke.

Kayla loved his laugh. “Man, you are older than I am. I'm getting my rest so I can stay young and fine.” Kayla laughed like a flirty teenager.

“Well baby, sleep on. Because that sleep thang is working righteously for you. You are most definitely young and fine.”

“Night, Jeff."

“Good night, Kayla. Sweet dreams, baby girl.”

Kayla woke up on Sunday morning with a smile on her face. Fifteen minutes later she was near tears when she heard Jeff’s voicemail. She hadn’t even heard her phone ring. She must have been in the shower when the call came in. But she'd called her voicemail service and heard Jeff’s smooth sexy voice: “Hey, baby girl. There has been a change of plans for tonight. Don’t want to go into detail on this machine, so call me later. I will be at church so call me after one. Talk to you later, baby.”

Kayla’s eyes filled with unbidden tears and a million thoughts went through her mind. Was his ex going to be at church? Was Jeff blowing her off to spend time rekindling the flames with his ex? What was REALLY going on?

Kayla spent the next few hours running the gamut of emotions. She paced the floor. She cried a little. She became furious that Jeff was trying to play her. What happened to all that honesty? She ran through that cycle several times. At 12:48 pm, Kayla talked herself down from the ledge. At

1:00 pm, she called Jeff. No answer. His phone went straight to damn voicemail.

At 2 pm, Kayla's phone vibrated.

"Hmmm. A text message from Jeffrey Xavier Taylor. Wonder what it says?" It never occurred to Kayla that she was talking out loud. To herself.

K. Can we do a late dinner? Something has come up. I was thinking around 8? Hit me back.

Why did he text instead of calling?

Kayla never knew what triggered her next actions. All she knew was that she was NOT going to be played ever again by any man, including Jeff. After she read his text message, Kayla decided that she had had enough. She was going to get herself together, go to his house, and resolve this once and for all.

When Kayla arrived at Jeff's house, she noticed that his car was not in the driveway. Where was he? She knew he wasn't home because his unique "Tudor-style" home was the only one on the street that didn't have a garage. Kayla didn't know what she was thinking, if she was thinking at all. She was full of fear and confusion and deep sadness.

She parked her car across the street from Jeff's house and walked up the cobblestone pathway to his front door.

Suddenly, she came to herself. "What are you doing Kayla?" Again, she didn't realize that she was talking to herself.

Almost magically, something Jeff said came to her mind: he was a "simple" man who kept a spare key under the plant by his front door. He forgot to mention that the "plant" was actually a small tree in a massive pot. She put her purse down and started pushing the pot with all her might. Good thing she wore jeans and tennis shoes. Good thing indeed. All those years of weight training had finally yielded a return on her investment. The huge pot moved and there, on the concrete patio, was the extra key.

Kayla held her breath as she turned the key in the lock. She went inside and for some reason went straight to the dining room. There was all the proof she needed. His table was perfectly set for two with beautiful champagne glasses, fresh white roses, chocolates and an ornate ice bucket with a bottle of the best champagne chilling inside. So, he had gotten back with his ex.

Before Kayla could gather her thoughts, she heard the front door open. In an instant, Jeff was inside and staring at her in disbelief.

"Kayla! What the hell are you doing in my house? How did you know where I lived? How did you get in here?" The words exploded out of Jeff in an avalanche of sheer confusion, anger and bewilderment.

Before Kayla could utter a word, she saw Jeff's hand reach behind his back. In a split second she was staring down the barrel of a 9 millimeter.

"Don't you move one inch, Kayla. Not one inch. I go to the trouble of creating a romantic night for you in my home and this is what you do? You break into my house?"

The last lucid thought that Kayla had that Sunday was, "Damn. He was telling the truth."

As Kayla sat mute and handcuffed in the back of the patrol car, her mind was blank. She couldn't believe what she had done. *Oh GOD! What had she done?*

The tears rolled down her face as she looked at Jeff talking to the police officer. She could hear the conversation because her window was down. He was going to press charges. The officers got into the front seat and started the patrol car.

Jeff's handsome face was twisted in rage and anger and he refused to even look in Kayla's direction. At the last second, before the car pulled away from the curb, Jeff finally looked at Kayla with sadness and spoke so softly that she had to strain to hear him.

"I actually thought you were the one, Kayla. I thought you were a good woman."

***Tania Renee Zayid** is a Registered Nurse from Memphis, Tennessee who is finally following her first passion: writing. Tania has been writing poetry since she was twelve and has had her poetry published in a local Memphis newspaper. This is her first attempt at writing fiction. Tania is currently working on her first book.*

The What If? Game

By Gina Torres

One look and a half of a smile was all it took to make the hackles on my oblivious, never-jealous boyfriend rise. For a split second I heard that sexy opening guitar riff and Bill Withers singing "Who is he and what is he to you?"

Until this moment, I had never crossed paths with any men associated with my past. But when Jason and I walked into the club, the first person I saw was Marcus - all six feet two inches of milk chocolate, square jawed, chiseled featured feast for the eyes.

He saw me, too and I semi-smirked. I am not sure how Jason, who was ahead of me, saw any of this. Frankly I didn't see the big deal.

True, I had once been interested in Marcus. We used to work together. We had even shared a poorly executed kiss, blech, blech, blech. Why do we assume attractive people are skilled in intimate endeavors? He was the second most gorgeous dude I encountered that was a horrible kisser. DEAL BREAKER!

After the very brief look that passed between me and Marcus, Jason turned around and began interrogating me.

"Who was that? Why are you smiling?"

I started laughing at that one. Then the man that I loved, and with whom I wanted nothing more than to spend time with, utterly and completely lost it. Without waiting for an answer, he snatched my wrist and dragged me out of the club with a vice-like grip. He'd become a bonafide Neanderthal with "you my woman" behavior.

I was stunned into absolute silence as I passively allowed him to drag me outside. Shock morphed into perverse delight at the fact that something so innocent would get this reaction. I was high on the control, but I feigned anger and disgust once we were outside.

"Let go of me," I growled. I twisted my arm trying to break free.

He came to his senses releasing his grip and dropping his arm. "Go back in then," he said, walking toward the car.

Until that moment I believed he was truly aloof. This incident allowed me a glimpse into his insecurities. I was hit on often, many times by his friends. He never really reacted in front of me, which got on my nerves. He usually addressed it privately. I assumed it was because he knew he had nothing to worry about. But something about this exchange caused him worry.

He didn't need to worry. But I loved every ratchet second! I didn't do much to make him feel better. I didn't want him to feel better. I wanted to bask in his concern, fear, and territorialism. I wanted revenge for when he didn't rescue me from unwanted attention. That was my agenda, but he switched modes on me. He met my faux anger with faux indifference. I wanted to fight with indignant "How dare yous" and "What do you mean, I smiled? So what, I smile at folks I know!"

He wanted to distance himself from the dramatic outburst. I didn't want him to believe that I would go back in. What would I look like chasing behind a non-kissing drunk when I had the assurance of a talented kisser and an equally skilled lover?

He didn't know any of that, though. So we had to get through this part. His long legs devoured the space as he walked rapidly through the large full parking lot. I trailed behind at a leisurely pace. I didn't keep up on purpose and refused to move faster to avoid appearing anxious or agreeable. We got into the car and drove back to my place.

He stared straight ahead. I stared out of the window. Nobody said anything. When the car stopped I got out and slammed the door. I went into my apartment alone. My roommate was in her room but she was not alone.

***

Jason and I remained incommunicado for three days. I decided enough was enough and called him. We made up after a screaming match. Yes, he was still in control. I couldn't help myself; he owned me. Nobody else pleased my eye as much or titillated my senses the way Jason did. I was Narcissus mesmerized by his perfection of male beauty. I could barely tear myself away to complete simple tasks.

The first time he kissed me, Jason held my face in both of his hands and gently placed his lips on mine. As if I was delicate and lovely. It was so tender and delicious.

My greatest desire was for our limbs to be entangled, breath synchronized as we shared the most intimate embraces, soft sighs, and softer kisses. I could and did kiss him for hours. I wanted to become a part of him, I wanted to possess him. I wanted to be intertwined as if we were a DNA chain.

For all of my strong black woman bravado I was weak to his caramel colored skin, washboard abs, and shoulder length light brown dreads. In short, I simply couldn't get enough of him.

When I saw him, it lifted my spirits. When he smiled, I couldn't help but smile. When our bodies joined it was more than on a merely physical level; it was spiritual.

I felt like this most of the time. But the rest of the time I wanted to kill him. He could take me from speaking in unknown tongues of lust and passion to wanting for him to go away forever. As if I never met him.

His dirt, disorder, and general lack of awareness about how civilized people conduct themselves drove me to absolute and total insanity.

Jason was also not open to moving. He loved our Ohio town and the sports teams. I wanted to travel and explore other places. I wanted to be a resident of the world.

In one sense he owned me. In another, I had to force myself from fleeing. I wanted to reclaim my heart and soul. I questioned over and over at what cost is this? Would I lose myself, my sanity, or my very little focus? The roller coaster of aloofness and tender passionate loving was too much. I felt like I was drowning.

***

Months later, I found out I was pregnant, I panicked. When I told Jason, he was silent and then went MIA for a week, to process. It felt immature to me. This was the time to be supportive of each other. Instead he went away to sulk. I knew on some level this couldn't continue, forcing it was unwise. But when he finally resurfaced, we tried. We played house and pretended we could build a life together. We couldn't. I wanted to do things the way enlightened people did them. I wanted him to attend the doctor visits and birthing classes. When he did, he acted anti-social and sullen like a spoiled unhappy child. He caused me no end of embarrassment.

We often do things for men we are either indifferent toward or uncomfortable with out of some undefined idea of submission. Which isn't what it is commonly believed to be and it darn sure doesn't apply to boyfriends. Or it is out of some misplaced idea that being "enough" will keep him with you: Sexy enough, sexing him enough, serving enough, catering to him enough. When that doesn't work we cannibalize other women.

***

My roommate, Christina was a true redbone. She was uber pale, freckled, and had the most shocking shade of red hair I had seen on anyone of any nationality. Men couldn't resist her. Because she was built like a King Magazine model and all of her assets were real, she couldn't resist men. Her first impulse was to sleep with them, then determine where they fit in her life. For her sleeping with a man was like a handshake or a dog smelling another dog's butt. Jason called her Raggedy Ann and didn't particularly care for her. She was baffled by his indifference.

"What is wrong with your dude? He doesn't even look at me."

"I'm not sure how to respond to that, Christina. Would you prefer that he come in your room and mount you after I fall asleep?"

"I can't say that has never happened to me. But naaah. Something ain't right with him. And by the way, you don't know how stupid you look always following him around like a love sick puppy," she said. "Dudes are good for two things: their money and their dangly bits. And you never ever let them know how much you are into them."

"Okay, my man isn't trying to screw you behind my back so something is wrong with him? I should break up with him, adopt your lifestyle, and sleep around with whomever? Got it. But wait, I don't think I could have a threesome, or a foursome, or a fivesome, or an infinitysome. That seems like too many private parts and unique odors in a confined space."

"Don't knock it till you try it, Boo-Boo," she said and then threw a pillow at me. "It's your turn to spot the pizza. So what movie are we watching tonight? I rented four."

I just shook my head. I knew Christina was a free love Hippy. She made us herbal tea. I ordered the pizza and settled in for roommate bonding time, absently stroking my tight little belly.

***

A couple of weeks later I woke up to mild cramping. I thought it odd but not terribly bothersome. I figured I would call the doctor's office from work. By the time I had driven a few blocks, the waves of pain were unbearable. When I realized my seat was wet I drove another block and pulled into the emergency room parking lot.

My body had rejected our baby. The perfect little curly haired mini us (or that is what I dreamed of) was no more. I couldn't reach Jason. No answer to my texts and his phone went straight to voicemail. When I finally got home from the hospital, I walked into our living room and Christina had her arms around Jason's neck. Her robe was a blue pool at her feet. All I saw was her large red freckled white butt crack and side boob. When they heard me, they jumped apart like they had just touched fire.

I couldn't speak. I was so disgusted. He called my name and ran after me. I ignored him and my lingering discomfort as I dashed down the stairs. I made it to my car before he did and I pulled away. I drove to my sister's house an hour away.

He called and left message after message. I deleted them without listening. He texted. I caught a few words of those as I deleted them. Disjointed words: *Talk! Not what you think! Her Fault!*

Whatever. I cried for days. I felt like my soul had been severed from my body. My sister took care of my wounded heart and traumatized body. She shored me up with "Forget that trifling fool! I will cut him if you need me to!" She made me laugh. But she would literally cut him.

I went back when I knew the whore wasn't there to collect my belongings several days later. I couldn't live with that freckled faced slut bag anymore. I couldn't look at her. Jason must have been watching my place because he caught me in the hallway on one of my trips down.

'Why haven't you called me back? I was worried!"

I whipped my neck around. Clearly this fool was retarded.

"Really? Why do YOU think I didn't call you back? If you were worried, why were you up against my naked roommate?"

"You know she isn't my type. She let me in and said you would be there shortly. Next thing I know, she dropped her robe and had her arms around me. You saw me trying to push her away."

"Oh, so you're a strong man. But you can't get a girl to stop touching you? Mmm kay."

"Look, I don't hit or hurt women. She let me in. I thought you were home. She was straight out of the shower. She just dropped that robe and was trying to kiss me. I pushed her away."

"I called you all day," I said. "It went to voicemail and you didn't answer your texts."

"My phone was dead. I didn't charge the night before and I had to work a double shift. I came over when I got off. Where were you?"

"I was at the hospital."

"Hospital? Hospital why? Are you are all right?" He paused and swallowed. "Is the baby all right?"

"There is no baby. I lost the baby," I whispered. The emotion of everything made my knees buckle and I began to slide down the wall. He caught me and I cried. He brushed my tears away. He cupped my face with both hands resting lightly on each side of my face. He stepped closer, leaving no retreat, filling my senses with him. I could smell his clean skin and the light mist of cologne. I could see his glistening eyes. I was keenly aware of his body leaning into mine. He brushed his lips against mine and kissed me.

Briefly I relaxed into the familiarity and the need. As if I was strung out and only a hit from him would be my fix. Our emotions were on 1000. Our attraction, fear, and sadness radiated off of our bodies, clashing in midair into a terrible jumble of confusion. We wanted to touch, fight, and make love on the spot.

Our need was immediate. I couldn't. I wouldn't. I would hate myself for that display of reckless weakness. I wasn't about to hate myself. Besides I wasn't healed from the miscarriage or the D&C. I could still feel the scraping.

"No. No. I don't want to do this." I pushed him away. Far enough for me to catch my breath and think. I had to gather all of my inner reserves to walk away from this cocoon of emotions. That, coupled with days of crying, had left me physically and emotionally spent. But I had to go. I wouldn't allow myself to look into his eyes again or note how his lashes grew or how moist his lips were, or how his neatly trimmed mustache framed the lips that drove me mad when I felt them against my own. I didn't even want to look at him. When I saw his face I thought of a big white freckled behind.

"What do you mean? I told you what happened. This is actually like a blessing in disguise. We can always have another baby, later."

And there it was. Relief. And confirmation for me.

"Maybe we can. But it won't be together. I don't know if your accounting of events was accurate or not. At this point, I don't care. This," I pointed between me and him, "is done."

"You cannot be serious. Just last week we were planning the rest of our lives."

"Yeah, I still am. Just not with you."

"You love me and I love you."

"But is that enough? I told you our baby died. Our. Baby. DIED. You act happy. I mean was this the perfect time? No. This was not some random arrangement of cells. This was a human with a body, fingers and toes." I wiped the tears from my face. "Look, I don't want to start hating you or resenting you. We are not on the same path. At this point, I want to be the only person responsible for my failures. I don't want to blame you for diminishing me."

"Well then, we can have another baby now. If that is what you want."

I gave him the blankest stare for a moment. "You don't get it. That isn't what I want. It isn't even what I wanted. I was willing to work with it. Your baby and mine. Now the baby is gone. Maybe this is the clue that we have gone as far as we should?" I hefted the last box and I walked away. Jason stood there like I'd slapped him.

***

He continued to call and text me. I changed my number. He sent flowers to my job. I found another job. I couldn't afford to falter. I had to define how I wanted to live my life. It was painful but I did it.

I became a buyer for an upscale boutique chain. I now lived far from Ohio. Several times a year I traveled to exotic locals to choose pretty fabrics and baubles to sell stateside. I was content.

After five years of a less than stunning dating life, I met my husband, Ian. He was completely cool and laid back. A photographer by trade, he was an outdoorsy thrill seeker type: always hiking, kayaking, and biking in the outer reaches of somewhere. He pushed me physically. He had to. I certainly wouldn't have initiated it.

Ours was a nice and peaceful existence. There was mutual respect and appreciation. Our passion was reasonable. It wasn't an all-consuming passion that could easily take a turn into dramatic loud arguments. We cooked together and had wine on our rooftop terrace in the big city. We behaved like adults.

So why did I suddenly feel like I was missing something a few years into marriage?

"Ian, do you regret not having kids?" I was scooping paella onto plates as he filled our glasses with a lovely white wine.

"Yes and no. We both travel a lot. And we have plenty of nieces and nephews."

"That we do," I giggled. "Sometimes I would like to know what we are missing. We have a nice life, I would love to share it."

"Aren't we too old?"

"Do you think 33 is too old? I would love to meet a mini you or a mini me or a mini us. You are beautiful, you know." I looked into his blue eyes. He was ruggedly athletically handsome. I took a sip of wine and smiled as the setting sun framed the city outline. I had an overwhelming sense of joy and peace. I loved him for wanting to take this journey with me. It was time.

***

Several months later I went to surprise my sister with the news. She was finally going to be an aunt. I felt bad keeping the first trimester a secret. But I feared another miscarriage. Ian and I decided not to share this news until we were ready. So I wanted to tell her in person.

I'd stopped at the mall to pick up a few things. I stopped at the food court because I had graduated from daily nausea to ravenous hunger. I saw a sort of frumpy but pretty lady with three beautiful children. Inexplicably, they seemed familiar. They were all laughing and talking to her as they decided where to eat. She beamed at them.

A few steps behind them I saw HIM. He was watching the lady and the children. Then he looked at me. He was still gorgeous. His neatly trimmed goatee framed his lovely mouth. Clearly he still loved clothes and working out because he was wearing the heck out of those jeans and designer loafers.

For a few seconds it seemed like nobody was there but us. Time stopped, people slowed down. A look of sadness crossed his face. I knew my emotions were plainly etched in my own visage. I had not seen him since the day I left him in my apartment hallway over a decade ago. I couldn't process my feelings. I didn't know I still needed to. Nor could I process that realization that the happy people belonged to him. The kids looked like him.

In that eternity, my memories came back in such a flood I feared I would be overcome. Those deep sensuous kisses, showering together, loving, arguing, lost baby and a big white freckled butt. There it was. The butt.

I gave an almost imperceptible nod of acknowledgement. He responded in kind. Then HER spider senses must have tingled because she looked at me, then looked at him. There was that sexy guitar riff again. A look of intense displeasure contorted her pleasant beige features. I arranged my eternity scarf, hefted my massive Louis Vuitton purse, and walked away without looking back. I wondered about the life we could have had together and what our children would have looked like. I wondered what if? I waited until I got to my rental car to give into the hyperventilating and soul wracking sobs. Then I felt my baby kick. I realized everything was as it should be. I wiped my face and started the car.

Gina Torres *is NOT an actress. She is a Facebook addicted, arm-chair psychologist, political commentator, often militant, pop culture junkie. She loves the written word and the subtle, or not so subtle, turn of a phrase. She has been a freelance writer for many years, writing copy, articles, and web content. She has a B.A. in Communications from Trinity International University. Follow her on Twitter @geeshouse and www.geeshouse.blogspot.com.*

We Ain't The Huxtables

By LaChelle Weaver

Never in my wildest dreams would I have imagined my day ending like this. But, this wasn't a dream. It was my life, and it was about to change in a major way. Things don't always go as planned, but in life, what does? I'd planned on landing my dream job, getting married to my high-school sweetie, Jared, and having kids all by the age of thirty. In our young minds, we were going to be like the Huxtables, our favorite TV family. Jared dreamed of becoming a doctor, and I an attorney. That was circa 1993, the year we graduated high school. However, as with many adolescent relationships, Jared and I drifted apart after heading to different colleges that fall. We made occasional reappearances in each other's lives the first few years, but eventually that waned and we lost all contact--until a few months ago. Ironically, we reconnected through someone else I had also lost contact with.

Home in Charlotte for a weekend visit, I was at the grocery store shopping with my mother when I heard a female voice call me from behind.

"Martika?"

I turned in the direction of the voice, and after a moment, a wide smile spread across my face. It was my childhood friend, Shayla.

"Oh my goodness! Shayla, how are you?" I greeted my long lost friend with a big, warm hug. We hadn't seen each other in over twenty years. We embraced for what seemed like forever. Shayla was one of the few people that I always thought about over the years. We were both on the track and softball teams in high school. Back then, we were best friends, but just like with Jared, we lost contact after we went to different colleges.

"Not as good as you are, Miss Thing. I hear you're a big shot attorney now," Shayla said when we finally separated. I chuckled at her comment because that's something that I heard all the time when I came home and ran into people I hadn't seen in years. My mother stood back, wearing a proud smile because she enjoyed hearing people refer to her daughter as a big shot lawyer. She prided herself on having raised a successful child despite the fact she was a single parent. My father died when I was really young, so my mom did it all, without complaint. She sacrificed so much to send me to college at Howard University and then law school at Georgetown. I always told her I was just as proud of her as she was proud of me.

"I don't know about all of that 'big shot' stuff. But yes, I am an attorney," I said.

"I'm not surprised at all. That's all you ever talked about when we were younger, so you were destined to become one. I'm so proud of you, Martika!"

I smiled and thanked her. I introduced her to my mother since they'd never officially met face to face. After their brief introduction, my mother said she was headed to the meat department and she'd meet up with me later.

"It really is so good to see you, Shayla," I said once my mother walked away. "I've thought about you over the years and wondered how you were doing. You look great."

Shayla was always beautiful, with her high-fashion good looks and thin, statuesque frame. She'd filled out some, and her long, bone-straight hair was now a mane of natural, golden curls. Other than that, she looked to be the same Shayla, gorgeous as ever.

"So do you. I know people always say this when they see someone they haven't seen in years and, for the most part, they're lying when they say it. But you haven't changed one bit," she said.

I chuckled again. "What have you been doing with yourself?"

"Girl, what haven't I been doing? Hopefully, we can get together and catch up. It's been way too long."

"I'd love that. I'm in town just for the weekend, but maybe we can do brunch on Sunday before I head back to D.C."

"Sounds great to me. I'm always ready to indulge in a good Mimosa. You pick the place and I'm there," Shayla said. We both pulled out our cell phones and saved each other's numbers.

"You know, it's so funny that I would see you today," Shayla continued, as she tucked her phone back into her purse, then looked back at me.

"How so?"

"Well," Shayla began, dragging out the word. "I saw somebody else from our past the other day that you might be interested in hearing about," she said coyly, wearing a big grin.

"Really now? And who might that be?"

"Walk with me while I grab a few things and I'll give you the four-one-one." We both laughed because *What's the 411?* by Mary J. Blige was one of our favorite songs in high school, and we always said that to each other when we had something juicy to talk about.

"So, who is this mystery person?" I inquired as we strolled along the produce section.

"Let's just say, he still probably has that hideous sweater you bought him back in the day."

We burst out laughing, garnering a few looks from some of the afternoon shoppers.

"I'll never forget how you wanted to beat me up over that sweater," Shayla said, jokingly reminiscing.

"How could I forget? I spent all of my Pizza Hut paycheck on that sweater for his birthday, and when I showed it to you, you fell out laughing in my face and made fun of it. I could've killed you I was so mad," I said, playfully rolling my eyes at her. "You know I thought he was going to look like a younger version of Cliff Huxtable in that sweater."

"I apologized for hurting your feelings. It didn't matter what I thought anyway because he loved it. You still wouldn't speak to me for about a week. That is, until I bought you that new TLC CD! After that, we were best friends again."

"Ah yes! I loved that CD. We'd listen to it for hours when I spent the night over your house. *What About Your Friends* is still one of my favorite songs 'til this day," I said. As we reminisced about the fun times we had together as youngsters, my mind kept going back to Jared.

"How is he? When did you see him?" Shayla had successfully piqued my interest. I hadn't seen Jared in over twenty years. The last thing I'd heard was that he'd moved to

New Orleans after graduating college, but I didn't know much more than that.

"I ran into him just yesterday, in fact--at the gym. I hadn't seen him in a while. He looked good. Really good," Shayla said, dragging out the last two words. I laughed at her trying to overemphasize his good looks.

"You're a mess," I said.

"Just calling it like I see it. I'm not beyond flirting, honey. My husband was with me, so I had to check him out on the low. But trust me when I tell you, he's like wine and cheese. He's gotten better with age," Shayla said as we laughed out loud again. She quickly examined some red apples and placed the ones to her satisfaction in a plastic bag.

"He was living in New Orleans, but he's been back in Charlotte the past year. Sadly, his mother is very ill, and he moved back home to look after her," Shayla said.

"Oh, wow. I'm very sorry to hear that Mrs. Wallace is sick. I was really close with her back then. She was like a second mother to me," I said. Even though I hadn't seen Jared's mother in years, my sadness was genuine.

"Well, I know she's in good hands with her son being a doctor and all," Shayla said, grinning at me again. I couldn't help but grin also at this little revelation. I was happy to know that he'd followed his dreams of becoming a doctor.

"You're smiling real hard, girl!"

"I'm just glad to hear that he's doing well. I know how much he wanted to become a doctor," I said.

"Mmm...hmm. Those old flames aren't reigniting, are they?" Shayla asked.

I couldn't help but blush. I felt a bit silly, but something was stirring inside me. I wasn't quite sure what it was.

"I'm just curious. That's all. Nothing more," I said, trying to convince her otherwise.

She wasn't buying it, though. Shayla gave me major side eye and grinned continuously. "If you say so, Miss Thing. I'm curious about something as well," she said as we made our way out of the produce section.

"What's that?" I asked her. We stopped in front of the bakery and checked out the freshly baked desserts. We noticed a red velvet cake before Shayla got back to her question.

"Well, it's probably none of my business, but I'll ask anyway. I don't see a ring on your finger," she said, pointing to my left hand. "And not that that means anything, but did you ever find your Cliff Huxtable or anybody close to him?"

I usually didn't like discussing my love life, or lack thereof, but it wasn't like it went unnoticed by people close to me. I got this often. They always wondered why somebody like me, a successful, and what many considered beautiful lawyer, didn't have a man in my life. That was a question I couldn't answer because I didn't quite know myself. It wasn't like I wasn't trying.

I had relationships with men who I thought would be the one, but ultimately, we weren't a good fit. At almost forty years old, I was too old for the foolishness. As a professional, black woman living and dating in a big city, I'd seen and experienced more than enough of it.

My last date sealed the casket on my dating life. As a skilled attorney, I still couldn't believe how I could be so wrong about a person. I met Eli on one of my morning jogs around the Martin Luther King Memorial. He had the warmest set of brown eyes behind a pair of stylish eye glasses. He looked like the intellectual type, which always attracted me. I loved a man who could stimulate my mind first, then my body. He was walking his dog and I was doing my cool-down stretches when we made eye contact and struck up a conversation. He made me laugh and I felt comfortable enough to give him my number when he asked. I even petted his black Lab when we parted ways, even though I wasn't a dog person. We talked later that evening and decided that we would meet the following Saturday for dinner.

I didn’t know what I was getting myself into. My first indicator should've been the weather. It was cold and rainy most of the day. At Eli's suggestion, we decided to meet at an Ethiopian restaurant on U Street. I'd never been to an Ethiopian restaurant before, but I was open to trying something different, even though I didn't want to travel all the way to U Street.

Traffic was horrible, especially with the rain and tourists that flooded that area. I’d usually hop on the Metro on a day like this. Since I was dressed for a nice evening out, wearing an expensive pair of high-heeled boots, I decided to drive.

Eli was already waiting inside the restaurant when I arrived a few minutes late for our seven o'clock reservation. He stood to greet me with a hug, but it was lukewarm. I didn't know much about him but as I settled across from him at the small table for two, I definitely noticed there was something off in his mood. He seemed annoyed about something, but I didn't address it right at that moment.

"This is a quaint, little place. You come here often?" I asked him, my eyes scanning the eclectic decor of the dining room. But instead of responding to my question, he stared at me like I had something hanging out of my nose.

"Is something wrong? Do I have something stuck in my teeth?" I asked him, trying to lighten the mood.

He lightly tapped the face of his watch with his forefinger, and then looked at me pointedly. "You're late. Not a good impression for a first date, miss," he finally said. His eyes chastised me. If I wasn't mistaken in my hearing, which I hardly ever was, there was an attitude in his tone. It caught me off guard.

"I apologize for being a few minutes late, but as you must know being a D.C. resident yourself, traffic is pretty bad this time of the day in this area, especially with all this rain," I responded, trying to keep my budding annoyance at bay. Surely, he wasn't trying to chastise me like I was a kid.

"Cool beans. It's just that tardiness is a pet peeve of mine. My mother always told me that if a person doesn't respect your time, they don't respect you. I don't like it, and I just wanted to make you aware of it from the giddy-up. I'm about establishing boundaries from the very beginning."

I was speechless. Was this man really serious right now? I pursed my lips to prevent myself from saying something I wouldn't be able to take back, and then, inhaled. I needed a woosah moment.

The waitress came at just the right time, and I was thankful for the reprieve. She introduced herself and then went through her rundown of the specials of the day. Since, I'd never been to an Ethiopian restaurant, I let Eli order for the both of us. I figured maybe letting him feel like he was in control of something would loosen him up a bit. We managed to fill the time before we received our food with small talk and a bottle of Ethiopian wine, which was actually pretty good. I learned that Eli was divorced with no children, which didn't surprise me any. I had only been in a room with him for about thirty minutes and I wanted to run for the hills. Yes, he was handsome and smart, but he lacked a lot of substance. I knew this wouldn't be a love connection. I just wanted to get through the rest of the date.

When our food arrived, things really headed south. The array of colorful dishes looked and smelled good, and I was ready to dig in because I had skipped lunch in anticipation of the date. Since I'd never eaten at an Ethiopian restaurant before, I kindly asked the waitress for silverware because there wasn't any on the table. Big mistake! She gave me a weird look, and Eli laughed.

I frowned at him. "What's so funny?" I asked, annoyed by his behavior.

"We eat with our hands. There's no silverware here, so you'll have to get those perfectly manicured fingers of yours dirty," he replied with an amused expression.

I didn't see anything funny. I was embarrassed enough, but he didn't have to try to humiliate me in the process. I apologized to the waitress and she went on her way.

"Why would you do that?" I hissed at him. "You should have told me that we have to eat with our hands. Then, you try to embarrass me? I don't appreciate that," I lit into him. My blood was boiling.

He threw his hands up in a defensive stance, still laughing. "I thought you were a cultured woman despite the glitzy exterior. Guess I was wrong," he retorted, shaking his head.

"I told you I've never been to an Ethiopian restaurant before," I spat back at him. "Thanks for the heads up."

"You're an attorney, right?" he asked me.

"What's your point?" I glared at him.

"My point is, just like you do your research for cases, you should've done the same for this date. A quick internet search and a few customer reviews would've saved you the embarrassment."

This man was a complete fool, and as my mother taught me, you never argue with fools. I was done. I pushed my seat back with my feet and stood to leave.

"You're a piece of work, and hopefully, our paths will never cross again. What an idiot!" I said, before grabbing my purse and umbrella, and storming away.

I heard him yell out, laughing, "So, we're not gonna go Dutch?" After this disaster, I changed my jogging route and made the decision to take a dating sabbatical. It wasn't worth the headache anymore. At this point, I accepted the reality that I may never have the man or the family I wanted. I was okay with that--at least that's what I told myself.

"No. No Cliff Huxtable, yet. Just my career for now." I sighed, snapping back to reality.

Shayla looked at me with seriousness. "Martika, you do know that he doesn't exist, don't you?" she asked me.

I laughed. "Of course I do. But can't a girl have her fantasy? All women have one."

"I'm not talking about that. I'm talking about that image you've made up in your head about the 'perfect man'," Shayla said, making air quotes with her fingers. "He doesn't exist. There's no such person. Once you let go of that, the man you're destined to be with will come. Trust me, I had to learn this myself. It took a nasty divorce for me to learn it."

I pondered her words as we made our way down another aisle. Then she dug into her purse, pulled out a small, white card and handed it to me.

"That's Jared's business card. You should give him a call before you head back to D.C.," she said, winking at me. "You never know. Us running into each other could be the catalyst for your destiny."

We shared a laugh before giving each other one last hug, and promised to get together for Sunday brunch before parting ways. As I stood there with Jared's business card in my hand, I couldn't help but wonder if there was something to rekindle with him. I wouldn't have to wonder much longer.

Now here I was sitting at a bistro, sipping a glass of red wine, awaiting Jared's arrival. I'd got up the nerve to call him this afternoon after going back and forth about it.

Our initial conversation was short, but pleasant, even though when I dialed his number and waited for an answer, I could hear my heart thudding against my chest. I didn't realize that I'd been holding my breath until I heard a male voice on the other end.

"Hello."

His voice was unfamiliar now after over two decades, but the sweet baritone eased my anxiety.

"Hi, Jared. This is Martika. Martika Jordan," I answered, adding my last name just in case he needed a reminder of who I was, even though he shouldn't have. I was his first true love.

There was a brief pause before he replied.

"Martika? Wow! What a pleasant surprise. How are you?"

My heart smiled and so did I. Then, I silently chastised myself for having these schoolgirl feelings. I had no idea if this man was already attached to someone, but hearing the excitement in his voice warmed me from the inside out.

"I'm doing well. I hope I didn't catch you at a bad time? Are you free to talk?"

He chuckled before responding.

"You have no idea how free I am. Where are you? I'd love to see you and catch up, that is if you're free?" he said.

My heart was smiling again and I couldn't agree fast enough to meet him. When we ended our conversation, my anxiety returned. I didn't know what to expect, but I would soon find out.

A few minutes later, as I sat glancing out the window, I heard the deep baritone of his voice. It was like listening to my favorite love song. Pleasing to my ears.

"Just as beautiful as you were since I laid eyes on you last."

I looked up to see my high-school sweetie and first true love smiling at me with the whitest of teeth against a smooth, dark chocolate-brown complexion. The only sign that Jared had aged at all was in his voice.

My smile was wide until I noticed his formal attire. I frowned, confused. He was wearing a black tuxedo. He looked handsome and svelte. Some of the patrons glanced at him, too. It just seemed a bit odd, but maybe he was coming from a wedding or some black tie event. I stood to greet him and he swept me up in a big, strong hug. I could've melted right there as I took in the fragrant scent of his woodsy cologne.

"It's so good to see you after all of these years, Martika," he said. He held me at arm's length, doing a once over with his eyes. "You look great."

I blushed, thanking him. I felt all kinds of emotions that I probably shouldn't have felt, and I had no control over them. *Lord, give me strength*, I prayed silently. We took our seats across from each other at the table, and stared at each other a few more seconds, both of us wearing big smiles. It was a sweet moment until I asked him about the tuxedo he was wearing.

"Oh yeah, about that," Jared said, as if he'd forgotten that he was even wearing it. "I was supposed to get married today."

My eyes bulged in surprise. Once again, a man had rendered me speechless, and not in a good way.

"What do you mean you were supposed to get married today?" I was perplexed by his casual announcement. He seemed a bit cavalier for having left someone at the altar.

"I was supposed to get married at noon today, but I couldn't go through with it. I knew that I would be making the biggest mistake of my life." He said this with a hint of sadness in his eyes. It was four o'clock in the afternoon, so I couldn't help wondering what he'd been doing the last four hours. My mind raced with questions.

"Did you just leave her at the altar?" I was curious to know. I'd heard of things like this happening, and I always wondered what would cause someone to make such a split decision. Why wouldn't he have decided this earlier—preferably, before their actual wedding day? I couldn't wrap my mind around it. What could've been so bad to crush someone's heart like that? As a woman, I couldn't imagine being in such a predicament. I didn't know his fiancée, but I was sure that she wasn't a happy camper right about now. I know I wouldn't be.

"Well, not literally. Figuratively, maybe. I love Rita, don't get me wrong, but I'm not in love with her. I never was," Jared said, waving the waiter over and asking for a beer.

"And you just figured this out on your wedding day? Obviously, you'd been having doubts before then. Why get to the day of, get dressed and then decide not to go through with it?" I quizzed him.

He put his hands up. "Whoa, Counselor. Can I explain myself here?" Jared joked, but I didn't think it was funny. I really felt bad for this poor woman, and I was having serious doubts about Jared's character. What kind of man would do such a thing? Why would he tell me to meet him just hours after breaking some woman's heart?

“It just seems a bit cold and cruel,” I responded. “I can't imagine what she's feeling.”

Jared got serious after my response. “You may not believe this, but she's actually okay with it. Well, she's made peace with it.”

The waiter brought Jared the beer he'd ordered, placed it in front of him and walked off. I furrowed my brow at his words as he took a swig of his beer.

“Really now?” I asked, my tone full of doubt.

“Yeah. We met up at a neutral place and talked things out. It wasn't nice at first. She slapped me and I let her have that. I deserved it, but we couldn't keep up with appearances.”

“Meaning what exactly?”

Jared was talking in circles and I wanted him to get to the bones of what he was trying to say.

“We were only getting married for my mother's sake. I don't know if you know this, but she's terminally ill. She's had a long battle with breast cancer, and she's losing. She won't be here much longer. Probably a few more weeks, if that,” Jared said sadly.

I reached across the table and took his hand in mine. “I'm sorry to hear about your mother, Jared. Shayla told me she was sick, but I didn't realize the extent.”

He smiled at me. “I appreciate that. I've come to terms with it. She's watched me accomplish so much and she's been my biggest cheerleader. The one thing she wanted more than anything was for me to get married and have a family of my own. She said she didn't want me to be alone."

I nodded in understanding because my mother wanted the same for me.

"So, I was trying to make part of her wish a reality, but when I woke up this morning and started going through the motions of getting dressed, I realized that I didn't want my mother to leave this earth with me having lied to her. As I stated, I do love Rita, and she's been a great friend and confidante. But I can't continue to live a lie, no matter how much I care about her."

"Have you told your mother yet?" I asked, my heart full for him. I couldn't imagine my life without my mother. He nodded his head. "Yeah. That's where I've been the past few hours. With her."

"How did she take the news?"

"Surprisingly, well. She was disappointed because she loves Rita like a daughter, but she said that she understood that I had to live my life for me, not for her or anyone else. When she gets to heaven, she promised to send me an angel here on earth."

A tear fell from my eye and I quickly wiped it away. It was hard watching Jared choke up talking about his mother. The love he had for her was palpable.

"If anybody can work their magic in the afterlife, it would be Wilma Wallace. I told her to just make sure whomever she chooses to send, that she can cook."

We both laughed, lightening the mood. We sat and talked until the bistro closed.

***

Robin Thicke's soulful voice serenaded us as we swayed together on the dance floor to his beautiful ballad, *Angels*, wrapped tightly in each other's arms.

We were surrounded by relatives and close friends who'd come to New Orleans, our new place of residence, to celebrate and rejoice in our recent union as Dr. and Mrs. Jared Earving Wallace.

Essence Magazine was on hand to capture the special moments throughout the day for their online wedding feature, that I enjoyed reading over the years. I couldn't be happier. Shayla was right by my side as my matron-of-honor, but sadly, Mrs. Wallace was missing from our joyous occasion. It was definitely bittersweet. She'd succumbed to her illness just weeks after Jared and I reconnected, but I was thankful that I had the chance to visit with her before she passed.

Our courtship was fast, four months to be exact. We couldn't put off what we felt for each other any longer. Life was too short, and we'd already been apart more than twenty years.

Jared isn't the perfect man by far. He doesn't fit into that Cliff Huxtable image I'd dreamed of all of these years. We ain't the Huxtables -- far from it, but we have a genuine love that has been in the making for over twenty years. Our future as the Wallaces was bright, and I looked forward to it. After all, I married my first and true love.

***LaChelle Weaver** is a native North Carolinian and avid reader whose love for writing and storytelling spans back to childhood. An English graduate of North Carolina State University, she's always had a passion for weaving words together to create an entertaining and engaging reading experience. She aspires to write in the genre of contemporary fiction, focusing on issues that affect women to spark great discussions, and hopefully to inspire. She's currently writing her debut novel, Sunday Dinner. For more about LaChelle and to stay informed about her future projects, you can visit her at lachelleweaverwrites.com.*

The $8 Deal

By Trenekia Danielle

No one could tell my 22-year-old self that I wasn't a grown woman the summer after graduating from college. I was living in a one-bedroom townhouse in one of the most coveted neighborhoods for college students. I was accepted into a dynamic graduate school. I was paying for it all on my own with a cute car to drive up and down the Californian Coast. Okay, my parents were paying for the car but I felt free and powerful that year. I lived in San Diego, a city ready to champion the single me. There was downtown, the Gaslamp District – with its outdoor mall – restaurants, clubs, and Petco Park where the San Diego Padres Baseball team played. Old Town provided the history of Mexican civilization with rows of shops and authentic Mexican food. If Old Town was not authentic enough, you could be in Mexico in thirty minutes, eating, shopping, and dancing in the clubs. Of course, there were the beach cities, with the rolling waves of the Pacific Ocean blanketing sandy beaches. The beach cities had their liberal vibes with runners, bikers, and skaters gliding down the beach path. There were old and modern hippies selling organic homemade attire and food. In other words, this tourist town had many things to do and all kinds of people to meet. It was a miracle that anyone graduated from any college there with so many distractions.

But I was bored. I had been living there for four years and assumed that I had done it all. Downtown, Old Town, Mexico, whatever, was not exciting to me. And when you think you have done it all, boredom slides right in and starts unpacking. Boredom is the worst companion for a single woman. Instead of taking advantage of my city with three major colleges surrounding it, I decided to answer this phone call.

"What's up, Girrrrrlllll?" Casey yelled. "Whatcha doin?"

"Nothing. Watching TV," I said.

Casey replied with her sometimes deep raspy voice, "Come to the V.F.W with me tonight."

See, right there, I should have hung up the phone but boredom will keep you listening to nonsense. Now, don't get me wrong. I loved Casey. She was my girl. I'd known her since middle school and we ended up at the same college. Casey was a genius. We shouldn't have ended up at the same college. She should have been at an Ivy League school that would have challenged her. Instead she was a six year college student partying all over San Diego. Plus, I always knew these nights would lead to partially bad decisions and colorful stories to tell my grandchildren.

San Diego is also a military city with several Naval and Marine bases. There was double the number of V.F.Ws (Veterans of Foreign Wars) Halls in the city as military bases. Many veterans stayed in San Diego after they left the military. It was better than harsh winters, humid summers, and little to no opportunities from where they came from. Although they were a great support to its veterans, they were not known as the popular clubbing spots. Everyone knew that no one under 50 years old went to the V.F.W. to go clubbing in San Diego. The young military men and veterans went to the city clubs. Civilians knew that a 22-year-old going to the V.F.W. on a Wednesday night only meant comedy, frustration, one-night stands, or potential sugar daddies. Boredom talked me into going for comedy. It's funny how boredom never talked me into going to Wednesday bible class at the church, which my mom and the church ladies always encouraged me to do when I went to church on Sundays.

The smoked filled fellowship hall/juke joint was filled with drunken senior citizens who hadn't realized that sober nor intoxicated, their bodies could not perform the latest dances. Then there were the pick-up lines…

"Hey young thang! Wanna ride my bicycle?" said the long haired man in a wheelchair.

"I may be old but I'm ready," said a balding round man in full military fatigues trying to sing like Keith Sweat.

Another gray haired man with a gold cane next to him shouted to us as we walked by, "If I was 20 years younger. . . Oooo weee!"

It wasn't all bad. There were a couple of tables in the back where men and women argued while playing dominoes and spades. Others sat at the bar nodding their heads and sipping drinks as the DJ blasted Motown, Soul, and Hip Hop jams through the small hall. Then there were those who found these two young girls a form of entertainment while we passed by.

"Who let these babies in here? Who the hell left the gate open?"

"Babies, are you lost? I can see Similac dripping behind you ears."

"Your young self. I'll break ya!"

We endured these comments all night in between fits of laughter.

I stopped Casey at the bar and said, "What are we doing here?"

Casey replied, "Girl, to party. Plus, it was free to get in. The drinks are cheap and not watered down like the other clubs."

"But I don't drink," I said.

She calmly snapped back, "And you didn't have nothing to do either."

Casey danced off with some fifty-something year old man murmuring about her dark skin and voluptuous chest. I sat down at a rickety round table thinking I should've stayed home or at least gone to Wednesday night bible class. Boredom is a dumb friend.

"Excuse me. Would you like to dance?"

I looked up and saw a young, handsome, well-dressed man. He was kinda short, though.

"Sure," I said.

We danced for a little while and then I had to ask.

"What are you doing here? You look young. Wait! How old are you?"

He chuckled. "Shouldn't I be asking you the same thing?"

"Right." I laughed.

"Hi, I'm Donald Wesley. I'm 27. I'm hangin' out here with some of my buddies."

I replied, "Which branch are you in?"

"None. I work on the Naval Base as a civilian."

I had never heard this before so I said, "Doin' What?"

He laughed and shook his head at me. "There are many of us who work on the bases but are not enlisted. Somebody still has to man the base if the soldiers go off to war."

We danced and talked the rest of the night. Casey stumbled over to us.

She said, "I'm ready to go. Did you drink?"

"No," I replied.

She continued. "Good. I wanna go to Tijuana tonight."

I said to her, "Casey. I'm not going to TJ tonight. I'm taking you home."

"Boooo!" she loudly replied to me. "Hey Anthony, can you take me to TJ?"

I was flustered with my friend and situation as the designated driver. I turned to Donald and said, "I gotta go."

"I see, to save your friend, right?" he said.

"Apparently." As I began to turn around, he stepped in front of me and said, "Can I get your number before you go?"

"Yeah," I said, as I wrote it down on a cocktail napkin. He smiled and gave me a hug.

He whispered in my ear, "It was really nice meeting you."

His smile was so beautiful. He was like a mini Morris Chestnut with pearly white straight teeth. I turned quickly before I embarrassed myself from blushing.

After that night, we spent days talking about our families, careers, goals, and hobbies. Okay, mainly my career, goals and hobbies. His hobbies were work, getting paid, and clubbing.

"Hello," I said after I picked up the phone.

"Hey pretty girl," Donald tried to say in his sexiest voice.

"Hi Donald. How was your day?"

"It was cool. Got some new parts in for the ships and then I got paid."

"That's cool. I was watching the news about the president cutting welfare checks. What's your take on it?"

He said, "Shoot. I don't care cuz I just got paid! When you gon' let me take you out?"

"When you seriously answer my question."

He laughed at my comment and continued, "College girl, save that for them nerd boys on your campus. I'm about workin', getting paid, and taking you to the club."

"Donald, I met you at a club. That better not be our first date."

"Naw, babe, I'm just kiddin'. Wherever you wanna go tomorrow. My treat."

"Donald, I still have some questions before we get there."

"Damn!" he replied.

I was not going to let him think I was desperate for a date. Besides, I was following my dating safety rules. Finally, I agreed to go out with him on a date but it would be during the day, in public, and I would meet him there. My mama and girlfriends taught me right.

We decided to go to a matinee movie in a high traffic shopping center. I was wearing a white flower print dress. It flowed in the breeze and accentuated my curvy silhouette. When he saw me, he caught up with me and said hello. He gave me his arm and escorted me to the theater. He placed his arm around my shoulder as we watched the movie. Later, we continued our conversations outside in the courtyard. We shared more of our lives and how we felt about living in San Diego. It was funny. As much as that beautiful city had to offer, all the locals hated it and were screaming to get out of there. All in all, he was a complete gentleman during the whole date. I would later tell this to Casey over the phone a few days later.

"That dude is settin' you up."

"He is not," I said.

"He's one of those slick ones," she said. "I didn't trust him when I saw him that night."

I replied, "You were drunk the whole time. How would you know?"

Casey shot back at me, "Shut-up, girl. I can still see when I'm drunk. And you know I can hold my liquor."

"Whatever, Casey," I said.

Casey responded, "Look I've dated military dudes a long time. They will do all that but they want just one thing. SEX!"

I said, "I've dated military too."

There was a pause and then she said, "One military dude. He was stupid."

She did have a point. So, I responded, "Yeah, you're right. But, Donald's not in the military. He's a civilian that works on the base."

"Yea, yea, girl. Don't call me back cryin," said Casey.

Before I could respond back to Casey, the phone beeped to alert me that I had another call.

"Casey, I'll call you back. It's Donald."

She quickly said, "Remember what I said."

"Bye, Casey." I clicked over.

His cool wannabe sexy voice chimed in. "Hey beautiful. How's it going?

"Fine," I said.

He replied, "What you doin'?"

This is where I let boredom take the wheel. I had not done anything all day but sleep and paint my toes. That didn't sound interesting, so I decided to invent something to sound sexy and flirtatious.

I responded, "I'm taking a bubble bath surrounded by candles. Just relaxing."

He coughed. "Damn. . . I mean wow! Can I come over and rub your back?"

"No, silly. I said I'm relaxing."

"You know I got something to relax you more," he said.

"Yea, sure you do but I'm good," I said.

"When you think you gon' let me get in that bath tub with you?"

I started giggling. "Not for a long time. We just met two weeks ago."

His voice sounded a little irritated. "We've been talking a WHOLE lot. How much more of me do you need to know?"

He was right. He may have been handsome but his brain was all hot air. If it wasn't about work or clubbing, there was just dead space on the phone. Despite the huge warning signs, boredom kept egging me on to toy with this man for comedy, like asking him Jeopardy questions I knew he could not answer.

I said, "Okay, Donald, Are you watching Jeopardy right now?"

"I can't believe you got me doing this."

"Did you hear the question?"

He mumbled something under his breath and then said, "Uh, yeah."

"You are not watching," I said.

He groaned. "What's the question?"

"The answer is name a process in which sodium bicarbonate or disodium phosphate is added to water to make Coca Cola."

He responded, "Okay. But what was the question?"

"In Jeopardy, the answer is the question but you answer with a question," I said.

"What?"

I continued, "For example, this number twice makes four. The answer would be 'What is the number two'."

He repeated, "What?"

"Donald, just start your answer with 'what is'."

He replied, "But you still haven't given me the question."

"I did. I'll repeat it. The answer is name a process in which sodium bicarbonate or disodium phosphate is added to water to make Coca Cola."

He shot back, "You keep saying the answer but what is the question?"

Usually, by then, my face is buried in a pillow while I am screaming laughing and holding my stomach from the pain. Donald is usually cursing now in frustration and asking if I am still on the phone.

One thing I knew for sure was that our conversations may have been pointless but they were never boring. I was beginning to like Donald. He made me laugh.

However, this current situation was becoming less and less of a laughing matter.

What I could not see is that boredom never brings you to the happily ever after. Boredom will drive you down the slippery slope of dumb decisions, embarrassment, and bad consequences that you will try to etch from your mind when you're older.

It was at this point that I did not notice that boredom just took a left turn to the wrong side of town and I had no chance to get back home.

I giggled. “You are funny.”

He snapped back at me, “Baby, this ain’t no joke. I’m a man. You know what men want and need.”

I started laughing. “After two weeks? Wow. You could have a disease or something. Are you current on your HIV status?”

He replied, “Okay. You playin’. You actin' like a little girl. You like to flirt and toy with a man but you ain’t ‘bout it.”

“Dude, for real? Calm down,” I said.

He continued, “Look here. I’ve been a gentleman this entire time. I took you out and spent money on you. So, I should get something in return for that.”

“You spent eight dollars,” I said.

“What?”

I continued, “You heard me. You spent eight dollars on me. I’m supposed to have sex with you because you spent eight dollars on me!” I burst out in laughter with tears running down my face.

“You one of them bougie girls. My boys told me not to mess with you. You like them officer chicks. Listen clearly. Donald always gets what he wants. This whole dating game is all about men getting in the panties. Are you down or not?”

“Not,” I quickly said.

“What?”

"No. I'm not down. Because your cheap, Happy Meal, matinee, broke, two marbles left in the tank thinks you are entitled to my magnificently designed and awe-inspiring self. I am more than mere flesh to satisfy you. I am intelligent, dynamic, gifted, and complete class. And I will not waste all this on your two minutes!"

But I did not say any of that because he would have got stuck after magnificently. Okay seriously, I didn't because I was stunned. I just said, "No, I'm not down."

He growled back at me. "Shhhh. . . You think I'm a spend another dime on you. This conversation is over."

The phone clicked and all I heard was the dial tone. What just happened there? Did he just proposition me for sex for $8.00? Casey was right. I wanted to cry. Dang it! I should've gone to Wednesday night bible class!

I felt cheapened. I felt like a drugged up prostitute pushed out of a slow moving, stinky, rusty, 57 Chevy onto a pee infested alleyway with a few dollars thrown at me.

After a few minutes, I picked up my disheveled emotions off this pee-infested dramedy. I put myself here due to boredom. I realized the joke was on me the whole time and boredom was laughing herself to the bank. It was time to not waste my life doing trivial things for kicks.

In that moment, I recognized that I wasn't nearly as grown as I thought.

An adult woman has purpose in all things in her life, including dating. My first intentional act would be to kick boredom out the door. I started thinking about the things that needed to be done before I began graduate school, positive and more engaging activities I could participate in the city, volunteer work, mentoring and going to Wednesday night bible class.

This experience made me realize that I was not so free and powerful. I still had some learning to do. It was time to give dating a rest.

My thoughts were interrupted by my new neighbor's bass-laden music vibrating through our connecting wall. He was a Navy man living off base.

The smell of charcoal and sweet grilled meat breezed through my window. I could hear male voices with southern drawls growing louder over the music. It sounded like they were playing a game of dominoes.

Just as I was getting ready to bang on the wall to signal for him to turn the music down, I heard a Georgia accented deep voice pierce through my screen door.

"'Scuse me."

A six foot–two inches deep-chocolate skinned muscular African god was standing in front of my door holding a case of Coors.

"Is this Eric's house?"

"No. Next door to the right."

"Thank ya, Miss."

My eyes continued to stare at the door after he left. I thought to myself, *I wonder if Casey would like to come over today.*

Trenekia Danielle *is an emerging writer whose love for human interactions led her to express them oratorically and now through the written word. Her first screenplay, I.E.P, was aired nationally in 2012 on the African American Shorts Film program. She is the content creator of the web series, Ladies Small Group. Her future goals include screenwriting feature films and publishing a children's book series.*

Only a Dog Wants a Bone!

By Natalie Woods Leffall

My Daddy always told me, "Baby girl, only a dog wants a bone!" I guess he didn't know that if you're not skin and bones, all you attract are dogs! Chihuahua dogs, little pieces of men barely five feet tall, weighing about 125 pounds soaking wet, who want to prove their manhood by mounting a big girl. Pit Bulls, who seek to control a big girl because they think you should be happy just to share the air they breathe. Pah-leeze! These are just two of the canines Daddy never knew I would encounter on my journey to love and happiness.

Daddy says when I was born the doctors marveled at how beautiful I was. He says I get my smooth caramel skin and firecracker personality from my Great Aunt Annie Mae. I call her Nana. She is living proof that a woman of size can capture a man's eyes! My Nana is a 68-year-old BBW, a Big, Beautiful Woman. She stands almost six feet tall and although I can't tell you exactly how much she weighs, my guess would be at least 350 pounds. Big girls never tell how much they weigh. It's a part of the fat girl code! Nana taught me to be proud of my curves, show off my big legs, push-up my cantaloupe sized breasts, gird-up my gut, and walk with a strut!

I'm the ultimate Daddy's girl. My Daddy named me Angel, because he said the moment he held me in his arms, he knew I had ascended from heaven! Daddy was the first man to ever love me! He loved me more than he loved my mama, which is probably why they were divorced by the time I was seven. So, when daddy died nine years ago, a piece of me died with him. I was 23 years old and a senior in college when I got the life shattering news. Daddy suffered a massive heart attack at age 45 and died on the floor of my grandmother's living room before the paramedics arrived. I was devastated. Who would be my cheerleader? My number one fan? Who would help me separate the men from the dogs? Daddy was gone!

My name is Angel Nicole Williams. I am 32 years old, single, successful, and FAT! I'm obese, overweight, and unapologetic (on most days). Proudly standing at five feet, 3 inches inch tall, I am 248 pounds of beauty and brains.

According to my doctor, I'm relatively healthy, even though she is always encouraging me to lose weight. Lord knows I have numerous testimonies of diet successes and failures. I have tried the Hollywood Diet, Apple Cider Vinegar Diet, Cabbage Diet, Atkins Diet, Daniel Fast, Slim Fast, Sugar Busters, Weight Watcher's, Quick Weight Loss, Jenny Craig, and even my neighbor Craig donated his personal training services. In the end, he was really looking to be served personally so that didn't last long! I have Walked Away the Pounds, Sweated to the Oldies, suffered Insanity, Hip-Hopped my Abs and zoomed into Zumba! I've ingested enough protein shakes, appetite suppressants, and fat burners to fund a fat camp.

So, I've just resolved that I'm a fat girl who works as the Program Director for a local talk radio station, drives a 500 series BMW, and who lives alone in a gorgeous two-story townhome in Houston, Texas.

Dating can be daunting for an overweight girl! The average man is looking for 36-24-36! When your measurements come in slightly shy at 48–38-46, men don't always flock at your feet, but they do come sniffing around your door.

My first real dating experience was as a freshman in college with a Chihuahua named James Bradley Johnson III! JB was a lil' piece of man with the stature of Kevin Hart, but carried himself as if he were Shaquille O'Neal. Baby, you couldn't tell him he wasn't seven feet tall, even though

JB was barely five and a half feet! It was hilarious and sexy all at the same time. What was even sexier was JB's appreciation of my size 18 frame. He was a southern gentleman from Natchez, Mississippi with an appreciation for a good three piece, and I'm not talking about chicken. He used to say, "Gurl, only a real man can 'preciate legs, thighs and breasts like yours!"

I would giggle like a schoolgirl and let him explore my parts, until one day, I found out I wasn't the only three piece JB found finger licking good! I discovered he had a concubine of overweight lovers on campus. Since Daddy didn't raise no fool, I told that Chihuahua adios!

Fat Girl Code # 97: Just because you're a little chunky, you don't have to accept being treated funky! If we don't like to share our food, sharing a man is definitely not on the menu!

A few years after I graduated from college, I encountered my first Pit Bull. If only I knew then what I know now! I was on top of the world because I landed my first job as a radio producer for KJWK, Houston's premiere talk radio station. When you're not a size six, you work harder to convince the world that you're not fat and lazy!

One day, I was shopping for furniture for my new apartment. I noticed one of the salesmen watching me as I browsed the store for furniture to compliment the red walls in my new place. Every good sister of Delta Sigma Theta Sorority, Incorporated has at least one red wall in her home.

I was so caught up in a set of red leather club chairs that I didn't even notice the salesman was standing behind me. "Hello! Welcome to Elite Furniture." I turned around. I swear my lips locked. My tongue was frozen. I could not utter a sound! I'm many things, but speechless is seldom on the list. But this man was FINE! I'm talking Idris Elba, Morris Chestnut, sprinkled with a little Sheriff Troy from Tyler Perry's Why Did I Get Married? fine!

"Are you okay angel?"

Startled, I replied, "How do you know my name?"

"I don't know your name, but if I did, you can be sure I would call it all the time." Was this gorgeous man flirting with me? I was still trying to catch my breath when he said, "Let's start over. My name is Darren and might I say you look like an angel?"

Finally able to speak, I said. "I am."

"You are what?"

"An angel," I replied. "I mean, my name is Angel!"

"Get outta here!" he yelled, exposing the most beautiful set of perfect white teeth I had ever seen. "Why don't I help you find some furniture since my father owns the place, and then tonight, you can help me by joining me for dinner?"

Trying to play hard to get, I replied, "I don't even know you! For all I know, you could be a mass murderer!"

Darren grabbed my hand. "Look at this face. With me, is the safest place you'll ever be."

I totally forgot we were in the middle of a furniture store.

In that moment, I would've followed Darren to a house fire with gasoline panties on!

Darren quickly became a fixture in my life. One dinner turned into a series of breakfasts, lunches, snacks, and an apartment full of designer furniture. When we were out together, I could hear the stares of anorexic Annies inquiring, "How did that fat girl get that fine man?" Darren was a showstopper and he knew it!

The first few weeks with Darren were magical, but the magic soon turned into Voodoo! Under all that fineness was a stone cold fool! Some days I felt like a perpetual contestant in a horrible game of twenty questions.

"Angel, why didn't you call me on your way to work? Why didn't you text me once you made it to work? I came by your house last night. Where were you? Where are you right now?" Darren was like Inspector Gadget on crack!

"Look, I don't appreciate you policing my every move," I calmly explained. "I can't update you on my whereabouts every minute of the day!"

This Pit Bull said, "So can I ask you a question?"

I hesitantly responded, "Yes" because I could feel the drama coming.

"Did you pee today?"

Confused, I replied, "Did I do what?"

He repeated, "Did you go pee today? Have you gone to the bathroom?"

Getting seriously agitated, I said, "Darren, what do my

bodily functions have to do with you wanting to control my point A to point B?"

As if he was schooling me in the art of checking-in, Darren explained, "If you had time to sit on the toilet and pee, then you had time to call me!"

I almost died! This man was literally connecting my urination with our communication! There's nothing scarier than a Pit Bull. You never knew when they would go from being the protector to the attacker! My Daddy would roll over in his grave if I allowed some pretty boy to man handle me. I didn't care if Darren looked like a GQ model, I am the prize. Obviously, Darren missed the awards ceremony!

Fat Girl Code #104: Just because you're overweight, doesn't mean you have to put up with an overbearing man who thinks he can control you!

With age comes wisdom and unfortunately a few more pounds!

By the time I was 30, I was a solid size 22. I could spot a Chihuahua and Pit Bull a mile away so it was easy to avoid these canines! Most of my twenties were spent focusing on my career. I was climbing the corporate ladder and had been promoted to Station Program Director. I was the youngest and only black woman to ever hold the title. Professionally I was on top of the world, but personally I was longing to be loved.

"When are you going to get married? You ain't gettin' no younger Angel!"

I loved visiting my Nana. She would say anything. This lady had no filter.

"You don't want to be fat and lonely! You're too pretty for that."

Looking back, I knew she meant well. Remember, Nana was a big girl herself. But still, she would always say that to me.

It always baffled me how people craft compliments of attractive overweight women. They said things like, "You have such a pretty face!"

So did that mean the rest of me is ugly? What they really wanted to say was, "You're pretty... for a fat girl!" How rude!

"Nana, as soon as I get a man I will let you know. As a matter of fact, I have a date tonight."

"Oh really," she replied.

I could tell I had stirred the pot!

Nana sat straight up in her favorite chair, turned down the volume on the Oprah Winfrey show that she watched religiously, "Do tell."

"Well, it's not much to tell. His name is Marvin. I met him at church."

"Marvin, like Marvin Sapp? That man knows he can sang!" Nana waved her hand and belted out, "Never would've made it!"

I fell out laughing!

"No, not like Marvin Sapp. His name is Marvin Conner."

"Can he sing? There's nothing like a man that can sing chile!"

"I don't know, but he seems very nice."

"Well, keep me posted, baby! It's great that you met him at church, but you know just cuz they in church, don't mean the church is in them!"

Shaking my head, I said, "Yes ma'am. I know." Nana was always dropping wisdom.

***

My doorbell rang. I let out a loud, "Ugggh!" He would be on time! Marvin had arrived and I wasn't ready.

I screamed, "Coming!" as I adjusted my Spanx. Every good big girl knows how to gird up her gut! As I opened the door, I was met with a confused surprise. Marvin was standing there with flowers in hand, dressed in blue jeans and an Alpha Phi Alpha t-shirt. He looked great, but instead of being dressed for an elegant dinner at Eddie V's, he looked more like we were headed to Mickey D's!

"Wow," he said with delight. "You look amazing!"

I did a little twirl, showing off my legs that looked amazing in a short, red one-shoulder dress I picked up at Torrid in the Galleria. "Thank you," I replied. "I'm actually not quite ready. Come on in. I need about five more minutes."

As I walked into the kitchen to place the fragrant flowers in a vase, Marvin followed me. "You know, I was thinking maybe we could just order some Chinese and stay here and watch a movie."

Hesitantly, I replied, "OOOO-kay. I'm a little overdressed for the couch, but I guess I can run upstairs and change. Is everything all right?"

"I just had an extra long day," Marvin explained as he slowly approached me. "I would rather relax here with you." He pulled me close to him and wrapped his arms around my waist. "Wouldn't you rather be here, alone with me, instead of some stuffy restaurant crowded with strangers?"

I was mesmerized by the scent of Marvin's cologne. I heard myself say, "Sure." Afraid of the intensity of the moment, I escaped his grasp and ran upstairs to change.

I learned a lot about Marvin that night over shrimp fried rice. He was a native Houstonian who graduated from Jack Yates High School. He attended Morehouse on an academic scholarship and was raised by a single mother. He was 35 years old and worked as a engineer for NASA. Needless to say, I was impressed!

"So when you saw me at church, what made you ask for my number?" I asked while fumbling with my chopsticks.

Marvin threw up his hands as if praising the Lord. "I guess the Spirit moved me!"

I reached over and slapped his hand, "Stop! That's not funny. You don't play with the Lord!"

"No, seriously," he said. "I was watching you all through service."

"Aren't you supposed to be focused on God?"

"Yeah, but if you want any man to be in Christ, don't ever wear that green dress you had on last week." Pointing directly at me he said, "You led me into temptation!" Marvin was hilarious. "Girl, I'm serious. I couldn't wait until the benediction to get your attention!"

"Well I'm glad you did!" I smiled and suddenly I could feel the atmosphere in the room change. There was an awkward silence.

Marvin leaned in and passionately kissed me. I was startled at first, but it didn't take long for me to give in. Oh yeah, this man was something.

After an amazing weekend with Marvin, I arrived at work on Monday morning feeling like I'd just hit five of the six Powerball numbers.

"Angel, you have a package at the front desk," the radio station receptionist Sheila informed me over the phone.

"Thanks. I'll be there as soon as I finish my morning production meeting."

"Okay, but you may not want to take too long!" Sheila replied.

I hung up the phone and walked to the reception area to find the most beautiful red roses I'd ever seen in my life. This had the makings of Marvin all over it. We had been dating for a couple of months and had become quite the couple. Marvin was a hopeless romantic. He loved holding hands, sending poetic text messages and even an occasional sexy pic to let me know he was a REAL man. For the first time in a long time, I thought I was in love.

"Read the card!" Sheila demanded.

She was more excited than I was. I opened the card and read it to myself: *Who knew I would encounter an Angel on earth! Enjoy 61 roses to celebrate 61 days with the most amazing woman in the world! Join me for dinner tonight at my place at 8:00 p.m. With anticipation, MC*

I closed the card, took a deep breath. This man was too much!

On the way home, I was so excited! I decided to call Nana. It was days like this when I wished Daddy was alive so I could share with him, but Nana was the next best thing.

"Hey Nana! It's Angel," I said when she answered the phone.

"Girl, I know who this is. I'm old, but I ain't senile!"

"You sounding mighty chipper. What's going on, baby?" Nana asked.

Eager to share my news, I replied, "Marvin sent me 61 roses today, one for every day we've been dating."

"Hey! Hey! That's nice. So, you and Marvin Sapp are doing well?"

"Yes, Nana. Marvin Conner and I just may have a love connection."

"Love?" Nana said, sounding like she was shocked. "I don't hear you use that word often! So what nice places has he taken you to?"

I stopped to think. "Well ... we usually have dinner at my

place ... Ummm, we've gone to the park a few times .... tonight he's cooking dinner for me at his house in Clear Lake!"

In sure Nana fashion, she responded, "That man makes all that money working at NASA and he hasn't even taken you to Pappadeaux's? Chile it's a dead cat on that line."

Quickly jumping to Marvin's defense, I said, "Nana, he works long hours. He's always really tired. I truly enjoy our intimate time."

"Have you met any of his family or friends?"

I honestly had to think before I responded. "No, but I haven't introduced him to any of my family or friends either. It's just been 61 days!"

"Baby, God created heaven and earth in 6 days and rested on the 7th! In 61 days, you haven't been out on the town once or met any of his houseboys?"

I loved when Nana tried to talk like she was young! "You mean homeboys, Nana?

"Hell, you know what I mean! I'm happy for you, Angel. But you listen to me; you're too phenomenal to be some man's private possession and their public secret! You hear me?"

Like a little girl, I responded, "Yes ma'am. I hear you." Once again, Nana's wisdom had been imparted.

As I walked through the doors of Marvin's bachelor pad a few hours later, it smelled amazing! I made myself at home in his gourmet kitchen. Marvin was hard at work, looking extra yummy in a black apron. I bumped him with my right hip. "Move over Emeril Lagasse and G. Garvin, cuz Chef Marvin is in the house!" I watched as he skillfully prepared steak and lobster.

"This looks awesome! "What's for dessert?"

With a mischievous look in his eyes, Marvin replied, "Angel Food Cake!" He walked over and gave me the sweetest kiss. I felt my knees buckle. I wanted to give Marvin all of me, but I was plagued by Nana's words. Why hadn't we spent any time in public? Was Marvin trying to hide me? I was trying not to let my big girl insecurities get the best of me.

Dinner was fabulous! I had to give it to Marvin, he was a beast in the kitchen. "You're the talk of the town at my job. Thanks for the roses and dinner! I want to do something nice for you," I explained.

The look on Marvin's face was priceless. "You don't owe me anything. I truly enjoy making you smile."

"I just want to show you how much I appreciate you!" I got up from the table and sat in his lap. "Saturday is Marvin's Day. We will begin with breakfast at the breakfast klub and the rest will be a surprise."

"The breakfast klub?" Marvin didn't seem thrilled. "That place is always flooded with tons of people."

"Never fear, darling! My sorority sister and her husband are the owners. I will see if I can pull some strings to get us past the line." I wrapped my arms around his neck. "Don't you worry about the details. I will be here to pick you up this Saturday at 9:00 a.m. sharp." All I could hear was him groaning.

"Was that a yes?"

He grunted, "Ugh Yes! But my leg is going to sleep!"

I'd totally forgotten that I was sitting on his lap! Poor baby! These are the war wounds associated with dating a plus sized diva! I hopped up with a grin.

"Well, it's official Marvin's Day is this Saturday!"

I was ready to take the show on the road. I wasn't sure Nana was right this time. Marvin was a keeper!

***

Marvin's Day was here! I woke up listening to "Cater to You" by Destiny's Child. I was so busy getting my Beyonce' on in the mirror, I almost didn't hear my cell phone ringing around 7:30 a.m. When I answered, it was Marvin sounding like he had been hit by a Tsunami.

"Hey, babe. I'm sorry, but I'm going to have to reschedule today. I think I have strep throat. I'm running a 102 fever and was up all night," Marvin growled.

"Oh my God, I'm on my way over there!"

"No need for both of us to be sick. My doctor says it's highly contagious. I promise to make this up to you."

"Are you sure you don't want me to come and take care of you? I can be there in thirty minutes!" I pleaded with him.

"Angel, I'll be fine. I've taken a cocktail of drugs that are already putting me to sleep."

I was disappointed. He sounded so awful. There was no way I could be angry. "Okaaay, Marvin. I'll be praying you feel better. Please call me as soon as you wake up."

Sounding miserable, Marvin mumbled, "I promise." I was just about to hang up when I heard Marvin's raspy voice say, "Hey Angel ... I love you."

I stopped breathing! Did he say what I thought he said? Trying to hold back the tears, I said, "I love you, too, Marvin."

When we hung up, I clutched the phone to my heart, paused Destiny's Child, and climbed back into bed. Marvin's Day had officially been cancelled . . . but my life with Marvin was just beginning.

When my phone rang around 11:00 a.m. I just knew it was Marvin. Still in bed, I rolled over with anticipation of hearing his voice. "Hey baby!"

The voice on the other end was instantly recognizable.

"Baby? Who the hell is baby?" It was my best friend, Sunshine.

"Girl, I thought you were Marvin," I replied, wiping the crust from my eyes.

"Well, you thought long and wrong!"

Sunshine had the gift of gab. I never knew I would meet someone who talked more than me! Sunshine and I met in college and had been friends for over 14 years. "It sounds like you were sleeping. I thought today was Marvin's day?"

Sunshine jokingly asked.

Disappointed, I replied, "It was Marvin's Day, but he's sick ... called this morning and said he has strep throat."

"Awww, Angel, I'm so sorry. I know how much you were looking forward to this."

"Yeah, I'm real ..." Before I could even finish expressing my feeling, Sunshine rudely interrupted, "Well, since Marvin's Day is a no go, let's go grab some lunch."

I sat up in my bed. "I am starving."

"Girl, you're always starving! Get dressed and meet me at Grand Lux Cafe by the Galleria at 12:30 p.m. Those fresh baked chocolate chip pecan cookies are calling my name!"

At exactly 12:30, Sunshine and I met at Grand Lux Cafe. It was packed! We had to wait 45 minutes to get a table. As the hostess finally escorted us to our table, I could've sworn I saw Marvin, but I was sure my eyes were playing tricks on me.

Sunshine and I took our seats in a booth and I kept staring in the direction of this man who so greatly resembled Marvin that it was scary!

"What are you looking at?" Sunshine finally asked.

"Uh nothing! I just thought I saw someone I knew," I said as I continued to look in the direction of the Marvin look-a-like and the attractive young lady who was sitting across from him.

"Girl, you know everybody! Remember that time we were in Jamaica and you ran into someone you knew from high school..."

Sunshine was talking, but I wasn't hearing a word she was saying. I had zeroed in on the couple in question like an Eagle focused on her prey.

"Angel! Are you listening to me?"

As Sunshine yelled my name, I watched my man lean over and kiss that skinny heffa on the lips. Even from afar, I knew that kiss.

"That's Marvin," I said in a very sober tone.

"Your Marvin?" Sunshine looked around. "Where?"

Still calm, I explained, "Marvin is sitting in the booth, four rows down with another woman."

"Girl shut the front door," Sunshine replied in disbelief. "I thought he was supposed to be sick!"

"Not as sick as he's going to be!" Hot as fish grease, I felt myself sliding out of the booth. Of course, it took me a minute to maneuver all this fineness to the floor. All I could hear was Sunshine saying, "Oh Lord, it's about to go down!"

With every step I took, the hotter I got! I may have been angry, but I was cute.

As I approached the table where Marvin and the Chipmunk were sitting, I took a moment to smooth out my sexy purple Donna Karan sundress. You never face the enemy looking like you're going to battle! I learned this from Nana.

Marvin was sitting on one side of the booth. His female

companion was on the opposite side. They were so engrossed in conversation that neither of them saw me coming.

"Oh my God! Baby, I'm so happy to see you're feeling better!" I said while smothering Marvin with kisses. I used the force of my hip to push him over just enough to take my rightful place next to him in the booth. You are HEALED!" With eyes of disbelief, I shook my head. "Marvin, you are a modern day miracle."

The chipmunk said, "Marvin, who is this woman?"

As Marvin opened his mouth to respond, I took a huge fork full of caramel chicken off of his plate and stuffed it into his mouth, making it impossible for him to speak.

I looked up at chipmunk, finally acknowledging her presence. "Hello, I'm Angel"

I took a sip out of Marvin's glass of wine as he said, "Debra, I can explain . . . "

So chipmunk had a name. Debra. She looked like a bad contestant on Jeopardy! She did not have a clue!

"Marvin, you have three seconds to tell me who this woman is or I'm leaving!" Debra demanded.

Marvin looked as scared as a whore in church.

"Yeah Marvin, tell Debbie who I am!" If looks could kill, Chipmunk would have ended my life that day.

"Look, ladies. . . " Marvin attempted to speak, but I pinched his thigh so hard under the table that he let out a loud, "Ahhhh!"

I chuckled as if I wasn't responsible for the pain.

Then the chipmunk threw a jab, "I tell you what Marvin, you can have this fat bitch!" If Chipmunk thought calling me fat was going to get a rise out of me, she was highly mistaken. I scooted closer to Marvin, literally pinning his body to the wall at the end of the booth. He was sweating like a jalapeno on Cinco De Mayo!

I placed my big breasts in his face, and looked directly into his frightened eyes. In my seductive, sultry voice, I said, "You didn't have to lie, Marvin." I kissed his left cheek. "You didn't have to send roses. Cook romantic dinners," I kissed his right cheek. "You didn't even have to tell me you love me!" I kissed him gently on the lips. Marvin was close to cardiac arrest! "I'm a big girl, Marvin, in more ways than one! So, why don't you tell Debbie how you much you wanted this fat bitch ... while I leave you here with her skinny ass!"

I took the last sip of Marvin's wine and exited the booth. I was done with Marvin and his chipmunk!

As much as I hated to admit it, Nana was right. . . AGAIN!

Fat Girl Code #384: Never let 'em see you sweat. Big girls don't cry. . . at least not in public!

I was too upset to drive. I left my BMW at Grand Lux. Sunshine drove me home as I finally released hot tears that burned my checks as they rolled down my face.

"Girl, I haven't heard you cuss in ten years! I know

you're hurt, but if it's any consolation, you did that! If Marvin wasn't sick earlier, he is now!"

Turning my face toward the window, I never responded. I needed my Daddy now more than ever!

In the days after the Grand Lux scandal, Marvin flooded my phone with calls, voicemails, and text messages. I just didn't have the energy to respond. I had fallen in love with a breed of dog I hadn't encountered before. Marvin Conner was a Hound Dog. This is the man who hunts skinny heffas by day and is a chubby chaser by night! Marvin preferred meat on his bone, but in the world Marvin lived in, his woman had to be thin. He couldn't take a fat girl to the company Christmas Party or the Alpha Phi Alpha Black and Gold Pageant. Everyone expected him to emerge with a Tyra Banks, Halle Berry look alike. Marvin was a romantic coward.

In his last text message, he wrote:

`I foolishly allowed what others would think to cause me to lose the ONLY woman I have ever truly loved. Please forgive me! Lost without you, MC`

There were days when I wanted to give Marvin a second chance. That's what real love would do!

But Nana put it as plain as pudding, "Angel, you can't teach an old dog new tricks. . . and even if you could, I didn't raise you to be a dog trainer!"

Once again, Nana's wisdom had prevailed, but I will always wonder if I made the right decision.

Natalie Woods Leffall *is a successful Marketing and Event Planning professional from Houston, Texas. Natalie found writing not only to be a meaningful form of expression, but a powerful agent for healing. Through the use of humor and wit, she inspires you to love who you are unconditionally and unapologetically. Natalie has been married for 15 years and has 3 amazing children. She loves motivational speaking and her role as Worship Leader at her church in Crosby, Texas. Learn more about Natalie at www.sincerelynatalie.net and follow her blog at www.nunatalie.blogspot.com.*

A Beautiful Letter

By Cheryl Ashford Daniels

Chapter One

Elle leaned back in her plush executive leather chair and looked out the window of her high-rise corner office. After a few seconds, she folded the letter in her hand, picked up the envelope it came in and turned it over. There wasn't a trace of evidence of who sent the letter or where it came from.

Who would dare set her up on a blind date?

Fanning the envelope, she smirked. Who was she kidding? She knew exactly who had the nerve - her best friend and secretary - Barbara. There was no return address on the envelope which means it came straight from the mail room. Everyone she worked with avoided her like she'd eat their young alive. Barbara was the only employee who didn't care that her title was CEO.

Elle pressed the intercom on her phone. "Barb, could you come in here for a second?"

"Sure, just let me grab my notebook."

"You won't need it."

Barbara giggled. "So this conversation is more for your best friend than your secretary?"

Elle sighed. *She's incorrigible!* "Just get in here."

Barb walked into her office smiling. Every blond strand of hair was in place. Her voluptuous breasts moved in tandem with every step she took. She was beautiful and knew it. Her persona demanded everyone else know it too. Elle had spoken with her numerous times about wearing her skirts too short to no avail. She picked her battles with Barb, and since she was one hell of a secretary and even greater friend, Elle let her win the battle of her hemline.

Barb smiled, and her pale blue eyes twinkled. "What's up? I hope it's hot and juicy office gossip."

Elle scowled. "When have I ever repeated office gossip?"

"Never," she said with a sigh. "The rest of the staff won't tell me anything either. They whisper as soon as I walk into a room. I'm a leper amongst my peers just because I happen to love you dearly."

She sat sideways in the chair across from Elle's desk with downward eyes. Elle knew it was because while sitting, Barb was well aware of how short her skirt was and hoped Ellen Winters the CEO didn't come out.

Elle grinned to put her at ease. "Barb, I'm so sorry you're not allowed inside a group of people who have nothing better to do than speculate about someone else's business." She rubbed her thumb and index finger together mimicking a violin. "Here's a song especially for you and your weighty little plight."

"Oh, now you're a comedian. You don't know how it feels to be shunned."

Elle cocked her eyebrows. "I don't?"

"Maybe you do, but you're supposed to be. You rule this place with an iron fist."

Elle scoffed. "That's not true. I'm only thirty-four and shouldn't even have this job. When the owner made me CEO instead of his son David…." Her spine stiffened, and her adrenaline spiked just thinking about him.

"Elle honey, is everything okay?" Barb's eyes bunched together like they did when she was being motherly.

Elle raked her hand through her long black hair. She held her breath for a second then let out a loud sigh of exasperation. "It's hard to run this place when everyone dislikes you just because you're young, black, a woman and an outsider. The other board members have been here for at least fifteen years. I've only been here for three and have been CEO for two of those. Never mind that I've put this company on Fortune's list of top 100 companies. Everyone's waiting for me to make a mistake. I can't pacify my employees and keep this company in the black too. It's too exhausting."

Barb's mouth was slightly ajar. Frown lines appeared in her forehead, and she sat in what looked like stunned silence.

"Say something, Barb."

With a quick, Barb flashed a smile. "Honey, maybe I'm a little under qualified for this conversation. You need someone with a medical degree."

Elle chuckled. "You're probably right, but right now I need to know something else more central to me on a personal basis." She tossed the letter across her desk. "Did you send this to me?"

Barb picked up the letter, then shook her head.

"How do you know?" Elle leaned back into her chair and clasped her hands behind her head." You didn't even open it."

Barb picked up a different piece of paper off Elle's desk and placed it in front of her. "Our company uses a heavier stock of ivory linen paper." She then held up the folder letter that Elle gave her. "This paper is your standard white copier sheet." She pushed the letter back to Elle. "What is it?"

Using her finger, Elle slid the letter back to her. "Open it."

Barb picked up the letter, opened it and read it out loud. "Ellen, it would give me great pleasure if you would join me on Friday, June 18th at 6:30 P.M. for a romantic evening of dining and dancing." A crooked smile spread across her face. "I didn't do it. I've set you up on six blind dates over the last five months, and I'm contemplating never doing it again. I'm still embarrassed by the one a few weeks ago where you excused yourself to go to the ladies' room and never came back."

Elle huffed. "He was boring. The gossip in the ladies' room stall was more entertaining."

"And the one before him?" Barb pursed her lips and crossed her arms.

"He was a pervert! He touched my legs without provocation or permission. 'I want to see if your legs are as smooth, silky and muscular as they look,'" she said, mimicking the man's tone of voice.

Barb hissed, "That's a compliment. You do have nice legs!"

"Well will you look at that? You gave me the same compliment without molesting me. Was it too much for me to expect him to do the same?"

"Oh whatever, Elle!" Barb waved dismissively. "He came highly recommended."

Elle chuckled. “Yes, by your massage therapist friend. She probably gives happy endings.”

Barb rolled her eyes and tossed the envelope across the desk. “Let’s get back to this letter. Are you going? Rondelle’s is an elegant restaurant. It takes forever to get a reservation.”

“It’s probably a joke.” Elle picked up the letter, placed it back in the envelope and threw it in the trash can. “Well, the joke’s on them. I’m done entertaining this.” She tented her fingers on the desk in front of her. “When you get a second, would you bring me the Colson file?”

“Wait a minute!” Barb shot up from her chair and retrieved the letter. “Let’s call to RSVP and see if the reservation is legit. She picked up Elle’s headset and dialed the phone number. “Hi, I’m calling to confirm a reservation.”

Elle pressed the speaker phone button. For some reason, her heart beat rapidly. She wanted to hear firsthand what was said.

“Reservation code?” The woman on the other end sounded impatient.

Barb put her hand on her hip and frowned. “Honey, you should at least pretend you like your job when a customer calls. The reservation code is 756.”

The woman gasped. “That’s a priority code. Let me transfer you to my manager.” The woman hesitated. “And I’m sorry about before.”

Barb looked at Elle and shrugged. “Not a problem, sweetie.”

The line was quiet all of two seconds, but felt like two hours to Elle. Was it real? She hadn’t been exactly cordial to men. In fact, she made it a point not to look at them even when she felt their eyes on her. The only men she interacted with were colleagues on the board, but it couldn’t be one of them. They all but give her the finger anytime a meeting convened.

“Good afternoon, this is Pierre.” The man on the line had a deep baritone voice with a subtle French accent. “I understand you’re calling to RSVP for priority code 756.”

“Yes I am,” Elle responded before Barb had a chance.

“Wonderful, Miss Winters. The party joining you has already confirmed also.”

Elle twirled her hair around her fingers. “May I ask the name of the party joining me?”

Pierre sounded as if he laughed. “I’m afraid I don’t have that information in front of me. However, I’m sure you’re going to have a great time.”

What’s with the secrecy? Part of the reason she hated dating, aside from feeling like she was cheating on her deceased husband, was that men tended to be reserved. Andrew was an open book from the beginning. Where were those types of men hiding?

“Can I help you with anything else, Miss Winters?”

She sighed heavily. “No, I guess that’s it.”

"Have a great day, ma'am." Pierre hung up the phone.

Barb sat on the edge of Elle's desk. "Whoever he is, he must be very successful to afford a place like that. Let's hope he has a personality similar to Andrew's, and you don't have to bag his face."

Elle looked blankly into space. "There is no one else like Andrew. It's only been two years since he died. Why am I in a hurry?" She picked up the phone. "I should call back and cancel."

Barb took the phone from her. "You will do no such thing. I agree Andrew was phenomenal, but someone else out there is too. You have to give people a chance."

Elle got out of her chair and paced back and forth, staring out the window. "I hate this dating game. You have to kiss a hundred frogs. I don't have time for that. After five minutes into a date, I can tell I've wasted my time. Do you know how depressing that is?"

"Girl, you're preaching to the choir! I'm four years older and have never been married. I haven't even come close." She got off the desk and grabbed both of Elle's arms, turning her around to face her. "But Elle amongst those frogs is another prince for you. That's why I do it. I'd kiss a thousand of those wart bearing bastards to find my prince charming."

Elle shrugged and pulled away, trying to keep her tears at bay. "What if I already have? What if my only prince charming was Andrew?"

"No one is meant to be alone. Honey, there's another perfect man out there for you." Barb pointed to the letter on Elle's desk. "Maybe he's just a week away."

"Not sure why, but I'm going to go on this date. If for no other reason, the food should be delicious, and the intrigue and mystery has my interest piqued."

"And if you don't excuse yourself to go to the restroom, this man may have a small chance of at least finishing a meal with you."

They laughed.

"What can I say? I get bored fast. Now can you bring me the Colson file?"

"Yeah, I'll go get it."

When Barb went out of the office, Elle tapped her fingers on her desk. Who could it be? The letter was signed Anonymous Friend.

Barb returned with a file in her hand. After balling the letter up, Elle threw it in the trash. Enough time on men and dating. She had a business to run. Her focus turned to work. She'd focus on her strange but interesting date when the time came.

Chapter Two

Wrapped in a towel, drops of water still clung to Elle's skin as she looked at herself in the floor length mirror and rubbed lotion on her honey colored skin. She exercised twice a day. Her body was sculpted and lean. People thought she was a health fanatic. She wasn't. She only did it to keep her sanity by having healthy endorphins flow through her body.

One look at the clock told her if she didn't hurry, she'd be late. Sighing, she went to her walk in closet and sifted through her clothes.

"No! Please tell me you're not wearing that."

Elle flinched from the intrusion into her silence. "Damn it, Barb! You nearly gave me a heart attack."

Barbara took her shoes off and lay across the bed. "Keep shifting through your clothes. I'll tell you when to stop."

Elle's hand hovered over the black business pantsuit hanging in her closet. "I can dress myself, thank you. And if you don't start calling first, I'm going to take my key back."

"I only came because I knew you needed me tonight."

Elle stepped away from the closet and lay across from Barb. "What difference does it make? I may as well go in this towel."

"Although he may actually like to see you half naked, you're too much of a prude to pull that off." Barb smiled wickedly then winked. “You’d better leave those types of antics to me.”

"Or better yet,” Elle said with a sigh. “I shouldn’t go at all." Chauncey, her cat, jumped on the bed and snuggle underneath her. "That's right boy. All I need is you."

“Oh no you don’t.” Barb jumped off the bed and sailed to the closet. Going to the back, she pulled out a black sheath dress. “You’re going on this date and wearing this.”

Elle stroked Chauncey’s fur, making him purr. “That dress is too short and too tight.”

“All the right adjectives needed.” She placed the dress on the bed then went back to the closet for some black pumps. “You’re going to look….” She trailed off when she turned to see Elle carefully rubbing her hand across the dress. She went and sat next to her. “Tell me.”

“It’s the last thing Andrew bought me before he died. He made me promise to wear it some place special, but not his funeral.”

Barb lifted her chin. “It’s time you started living again. Drew would want that, and you deserve it.”

Elle rose from the bed. “I agreed to this date, but I’m making no promises.”

“None needed.” Barb smiled. “Let’s get you dressed and out the door.”

Chapter Three

When the valet at the restaurant opened her car door, Elle froze. Her knuckles hurt from tightly holding on to the steering wheel. Finally, she let go of the steering wheel then rubbed her knuckles. After she stepped out of the car, her chest felt heavy. What was wrong with her? Since talking about Andrew with Barb, she'd felt off. For God's sake, she was wearing a dress he bought her! Was it guilt she felt?

"Would you do me a favor?"

The valet nodded. "Yes ma'am."

"Would you keep my car parked close so you'll be able to get to it quickly?" She grinned nervously. "Blind date."

The valet chuckled. "Yes ma'am, but if I may say so, you look beautiful. He's going to like you."

"Thanks."

Elle wasn't worried about being liked. Men paid attention to her whether she wanted them to or not. More often than not their attention annoyed her. But it wasn't like that with Andrew. He'd swept her off her feet almost immediately. They married after dating only two months and cancer took him a year later.

She walked slowly toward the restaurant's entryway. The doorman opened the heavy wooden front door for her. When she stepped inside she gasped softly. The sophisticated atmosphere had dark mahogany wood, arched entryways, high ceilings, fireplaces, candles, fresh flowers and plants and the dim lighting gave the place a soft glow.

"May I help you ma'am," the hostess asked with a smile.

Elle didn't even know the man's name she was meeting. "I'm Ellen Winters."

The hostess' smile grew wider. "Welcome to Rondelle's, Miss Winters. We've been expecting you. Give me one second." She picked up the desk phone and whispered into it. Seconds later, she put the phone down and smiled at Elle again. "Someone will be right with you to escort you to your room."

"Room?"

"Yes ma'am. You must be excited to finally be here. Your reservation was made over two years ago."

Elle frowned. "You must be mistaken. I was just told about this date last week."

The hostess looked at Elle confusedly. No doubt because of the confused expression that had to be on her face. A man walked from behind the hostess dressed in a black suit. "Miss Winters, I'm Pierre. We spoke on the phone last week. If you'll follow me, I'll take you to your room."

Elle willed her feet to move. She wanted to turn around and high tail it back to her car. Instead, she followed Pierre through a maze of elegantly decorated tables. She didn't see one empty table.

After taking an elevator to the twentieth floor then up a flight of stairs, Elle wondered where they were going. A red velvet rope sectioned off the stairs from a long corridor. A sign warned the section was private. Pierre unhooked the rope just long enough for the two of them to pass through then latched the rope back into place. As they walked, lights came on automatically, showcasing art pieces – paintings and sculptures. He stopped in front of a red door then smiled at her.

"Here's where I take my leave." After reaching inside his suit coat, he had a pearly colored envelope in his hand. "This is for you."

Elle gasped. She knew the envelope well. If she went into Andrew's old office, she'd find boxes of them. The shiny silver "W" embossed in the upper left hand corner confirmed that the envelope was his. She swallowed hard then took the envelope from Pierre.

"Thank you."

He nodded and opened the door. "I hope you enjoy your dinner."

After she crossed the threshold, he closed it.

Elle stayed by the door and glanced around the room. Two waiters in the back of the room smiled at her. Perplexed by everything she'd seen thus far, she didn't smile back. The lone round vintage pine table for two had a vase filled with a small bouquet of colorful flowers in the middle. The two chairs around the table were dressed in a satiny white slip covers.

One wall was nothing but windows. Even from where she stood, the outside world from such a height looked beautiful. The curved walls in the room had tall custom gold mirrors on them. Deep rich colors and art deco mixed with elegant modern contemporary completed the romantic atmosphere. Countless fragrant candles were lit, and the chandelier above was dimmed. Wherever she looked, she saw thick long-stemmed vases of fresh red roses. Soft music wafted past her ears.

She turned when she heard a side door open. A man, she presumed to be her date, walked in with a glass of wine in his hand. The room wasn't lit properly, but she knew his walk, his athletic build and thick dark wavy hair. If he looked at her, she knew he'd have beautiful green eyes. It was Ethan, Andrew's best friend.

Ethan smiled widely as he slowly strode over to her, showing both deep dimples. With a quick, he stopped walking and smiling when recognizance set in. Smiling again, he rushed toward her with his arms opened.

"Elle, it's great to see you."

When Elle drew back from him, he looked hurt.

"What are you doing here?" they said simultaneously.

"If you're here for the same reason I am, it's not what you think." Ethan took a gulp of his wine. "I received a letter last week requesting I be here to meet the girl of my dreams."

Elle stumbled back, placing her hand on the door for support. Or was she planning to run away? She'd received the same letter telling her she'd meet the man of her dreams. "Was it signed, Anonymous Friend?"

Ethan nodded. "How did you know?"

"I received the same letter last week. What does this mean? If you didn't send the letter who did?"

He shrugged, and pointed at the envelope in her hand. "I was just given one of those too. It's Drew's. Isn't it?"

Elle nodded. "I believe so."

He pulled his letter from the inside of his suit coat pocket. "Let's open the letters and read them together."

The waiters chose that moment to start their duties. "Would you like some wine, ma'am? Or maybe order some hors d'oeuvres?"

"No! We'd like some privacy." Elle raked her hands through her hair. It was unlike her to be rude. She helped little old ladies across the street and fed stray animals. "I'm sorry I yelled."

"No problem, ma'am. We'll just be in the back of the room until you call for us." Even after the apology, the men hurried back to where they were when she first walked in.

She felt tears threatening to fall from her eyes. "Ethan…"

He took her into his arms. Arms she felt at home inside of. She lived inside those arms from the moment Andrew was diagnosed with stage four prostate cancer to when he closed his eyes and took his last breath.

"We'll figure this out – together."

She shook her head. "I've leaned on you too much – a lifetime's worth already. I promised myself I'd let you have a life and not depend on you. And I did, Ethan. I did – until now."

"What?" He stepped back, releasing her. "Are you saying you purposely didn't return my calls and letters? You purposely kept me out of your life?"

She wiped at one stray tear. "I had to."

"Why?" His eyes were misty.

"You were at my beck and call twenty-four hours a day, seven days a week. I told myself when Andrew was alive that it was your duty as his best friend. But when he died, what would be my reason for needing you in my life? You would've given up your life to give me whatever I needed for however long I needed you."

He raked his hand through his hair and turned his back to her. "Elle, do you know how lost I've been? My life was you and Drew. When he died, I should've still had you to help me through my grief. You stole that from me."

Elle stood in front of him and cupped his face. "I thought I was helping you."

With a derisive laugh, he removed her hand. "You didn't."

She shrank away from him. He'd never been so cold to her.

Ethan gently grabbed her hand, placing it back on his cheek. "That was mean. I'm sorry, Elle."

With her eyes downcast, Elle removed her hand. "No, maybe you're right."

Ethan took her envelope and opened it. After taking the sticker sealed letter out, he gave it back to her then opened his, which was also sealed. They unsealed the letters at the same time.

Tears fell down Elle's face. It was Andrew's handwriting.

Chapter Four

My dearest Elle and Ethan:

I know you must be confused. But please allow me to explain. I hope afterwards you will forgive me for what I've done.

Ethan and I were more like brothers. There was nothing we wouldn't do for each other, including me introducing him to the girl of his dreams because he was shy. He first told me about you Elle before I ever saw you.

He talked about the girl in our office building that he rode with on the elevator daily. The two of you were always early and always shared an elevator. He said he was smitten by your doe brown eyes and beautiful smile. Whenever you were around, he said his heart would pound like it would explode.

When you and I met Elle, it was because I was helping Ethan out on a project. He had the flu. I went to work early that day. You looked up at me and smiled then said good morning. I knew you were Ethan's elevator girl from the moment I saw you. I too was smitten immediately by those same eyes and smile.

I was always the smooth talker. Conversation flowed from my mouth easily. We talked the entire time in the elevator. For a week my best friend was on bed rest, and I had lunch with his dream girl every day. I knew Ethan would soon be back to work, so I invited you to dinner. We kissed for the first time that night, solidifying you were mine. You'd given a two-week notice to your employer prior to meeting me, but you had one more day left in our building. One more day where Ethan had a chance to steal you from me.

When he finally came back to work, I kissed you at the elevator, Elle. You didn't think anyone was there. But I saw Ethan, which is why I kissed you. I needed him to see you belonged to me.

Not long after, the elevator doors opened and we went inside. When I introduced you as my girlfriend neither of you said anything about the other – ever.

But I saw the looks you gave each other. I knew the attraction was still there. But the two of you loved me enough that you didn't act upon the attraction.

As I write this letter, I'm awake in the hospice bed while the two of you are asleep on the sofa. Ethan's arms are around you, Elle. The two of you look beautiful together. Meant to be.

I couldn't give Elle to you, Ethan when I wanted her for myself. You've been a rock for both of us during this time.

Please let this letter serve as my last will and testament.

Ethan, I'm leaving you with the most precious and beloved gift ever given to me - Elle.

I hope the two of you give each other the chance I stole from you. Take care of her and love her like I know you will.

To Elle – sweetheart, my life didn't begin until you walked into it. My heart didn't beat in rhythm until I fell in love with you.

It's okay for the two of you to be in love with each other. You always have been.

Your love is what has gotten me through this. It's a beautiful love that anyone can see and feel when the two of you are together.

Be together.

Let the rest of the world feel that warmth and security I feel being around that powerful electrical emotion that emulates from the two of you just by being in your presence. I believe it's what's sustained me longer than the doctors anticipated.

With all my heart, I love you both.

Andrew Winters

Elle folded the letter then looked up at Ethan. His eyes were red. His cheeks were wet with tears. She'd felt her tears flow continually after reading the first word.

Her hand shivered as she wiped her eyes. "What does he expect for us to do with this?"

Ethan took her into his arms and rocked her.

"I'm famished, and I hear the food here is delectable. Your husband, my best friend, has paid for us to have any and everything we want on the menu. So I say let's just enjoy our date."

Her voice was muffled against his jacket.

"How do you know Andrew paid for this?"

"Pierre told me a friend of mine paid for this entire night and that one meal or all meals were included, as well as any reserved labeled bottles of wine."

"Pierre?"

"Pierre Rondelle. Don't you know that Drew and I were the principal architects for this restaurant?"

She shook her head. "I didn't know that."

Ethan let go of her and pulled out a chair for her to sit. Once she did, he pulled his chair from across from her to her side. He held his hand up for the waiters.

"I think we're ready for at least a glass of wine."

Both waiters rushed to their sides, pouring wine and placing menus on the table.

Elle picked up her glass and smiled. "What should we toast to?"

"Andrew Taylor Winters, and to us – sharing a beautiful love."

"I agree – to both."

After they took a sip of wine, Ethan leaned over and kissed her on the lips. "I've wanted to do that for what seems like forever."

Elle leaned over and imitated Ethan, kissing his lips. "Turnabout is fair play because so have I."

Cheryl Ashford Daniels *is an aspiring writer who has a passionate love for reading and writing. She woke up one morning and decided that instead of reading another book, she wanted to write one. She enrolled in several online writing courses that literally changed her life! She lives in Houston, Texas with her husband Keith, daughter Meaghan and Sasha - her finicky, spoiled rotten diva-ish blue pit bull who has the most beautiful gray eyes! Write to her at: cheryladnls@aol.com or visit her website: cherylashforddaniels.com*

Strangers. Friends. Lovers.

By M.C. Walker

Chapter One

atalie, when was the last time you had sex?" My mother's words almost make me fall out of my seat.

"Mom!" I exclaim.

"What?" She shrugs. "Oh, Chile, please...you old enough to know that thing between your legs does more than just pee."

I glance over my shoulder, making sure no one is eavesdropping on our conversation.

I lean forward and reply, "Mom, I don't want to discuss my sex life with you. Can we just sit here and have a normal conversation like regular people?"

She rolls her eyes, shrugs and avoids eye contact as she pushes a spoonful of pasta into her mouth.

After a few bites she says, "It ain't my fault people in the family are worried about you. They think you. . . you know. . . you might like the ladies a little bit more than you supposed too."

I nearly choke on my shrimp at the sound of words. "Oh. My. God. Mom, please. . . just stop it." I throw up my hands in defeat.

She laughs and sips her wine. I get the waiter's attention with two snaps. Within a matter of seconds, he rushes to our table to rescue me from the invasion upon my sex life from my wanna-be Ace Detective Mother.

With a broad smile, the pencil thin waiter with boyish good looks and olive skin greets us with a smile. "Is everything all right ladies?"

"Yes," I reply. "May we have the check, please?"

"And a refill, please. A lady's glass should never be as empty as her heart." Is my mother really flirting with this young boy?

The waiter flashes his boyish smile and dimpled chin and replies, "Yes, ma'am. I apologize. Right away I will take care of that for you."

He walks away swiftly. I toss my napkin across the table at my mother.

"Shame on you, flirting with that babyface teenager," I scoff. "What would daddy think?"

She laughs. “He'd probably send him a thank you card and pay his cell phone bill.”

I shake my head in disbelief. “What am I going to do with you?”

“If nothing else, Natalie, I hope you learn to live in the moment. Before you know it you're old with arthritis, smell like Bengay, married to a grumpy old man, and you live out your fantasies through dirty books, and your thirty-year-old daughter.”

I want to laugh, but the fact that my mother is talking about herself makes me sad.

The waiter returns with the check and wishes us a goodnight. My mom winks at him. “Until next time, my dear.”

I open my wallet, pull out my credit card and pay the bill. “I don't think you understand me at all, mom.” I shake my head. “I 'm happy with the way things are in my life. Why can't you see that?”

My mom reaches for my hand. She holds my hand in hers, looks me in my eyes and says, “You're not happy. You're content, not happy. There is a difference.” She gives me a reaffirming squeeze and lowers her voice. “Sometimes the greatest pleasures in life are meant to be shared with someone you love. Trust me.”

While still in the moment of her words, my mom finishes off the last of her wine. She grabs her clutch and shawl and begins to strut away from the table. She snaps her fingers and says, "Now lets go find mommy some dessert."

***

Long after the embarrassment of my mother's theatrics have worn off of me. I find myself restless in bed. I can't sleep. I keep tossing and turning between the sheets, trying to find a comfortable position. Too many thoughts are running through my mind. The stillness of the condo, which I usually embrace, is irritating.

I don't know if it's the summer humidity, or the thickness of the air, but I feel like I'm on the verge of suffocating so I welcome the breeze that's sifting in from my bedroom window. I glance at the clock on the nightstand. A quarter past midnight. I should be sleeping like the restof the world. A busy day lies ahead of me. There's too much on my mental plate.

My mothers nagging voice is on repeat, causing my mind to swirl in a thousand different directions. Is it so bad to put my love life on hold while I pursue partnership at the firm? I don't want to be limited by my ovaries. Who says I have to know what I want right now anyway? I can always freeze my eggs, buy a boyfriend, and pretend to have life figured out like everybody else in this world. My mother is old school. Screw love! If love wants to come find me it better be in my corner office overlooking the city.

Okay, stop it!

I can't breathe and I realize it's not the air that's suffocating me, it's my thoughts.

The glass of water I had before bed two hoursago has made its way to my bladder. I kick back the covers and crawl out of bed, rushing toward the bathroom. A slight breeze slides up my legs and down the middle of my back as I run past the window. After handling my business, I head to the kitchen to make a cup of chamomile tea.

Minutes later, I take my tea and head into the living room, thinking maybe TV, along with the tea will lull me to sleep.

As soon as I walk into the living area, my serene night is interrupted by the loud sounds of Jay Z coming from outside. I head toward the patio, stick my head out the door and see my neighbor, shirtless, painting on a canvas. I'd heard a nice-looking man had moved into the apartment vacated by Old Lady Lewis, but I'd yet to bump into him. And now that I had, "nice-looking" was an understatement.

The muscles in his back briefly distract me from my irritation. I don't want to come off as an uptight prude so I slowly count to ten to calm my nerves. I tighten my robe and clear my throat.

"Emm...emmm?"

No response soI try again, a little bit louder.

"Emm…emmmm?"

This time, I catch his attention and he turns around.

His chest is covered in multiple hues from the paint. Holding the paintbrush in his hands, he briefly smiles in my direction.He waves.I nod, trying desperately not to get distracted by his perfectly chiseled chest, six pack abs, and the never ending detour of the heavenly being standing before me.

Focus, Natalie. Focus.

"The music. . . it's too loud!" I yell.

"What?"

"Turn the music down." I point toward my ears.

"Oh!" he replies, dropping his paintbrush. He darts inside his apartment. The music stops and he returns, his chest heaving slowly. He bends to catch his breath and the moonlight and the city lights combine to bring him into clear focus. I can see all of him. From a short distance he looks like Omari Hardwick but much slender and more rugged around the edges. *I like that. I like that A LOT.* The light from his apartment brushes his cinnamon complexion. Beads of sweat slide down his body. Tattoos cover most of his torso. Every fiber of my being wants to throw him inside the shower and wash every part of his angelic body. He's attractive and easy on the eyes. But, he's not for me. He reminds of the guys I used to date during my rebellious years. Heartbreaker is written all over him.

He looks up at me with a brief smile and says, "I'm sorry. Did I wake you?"

"No. I was already awake. I was just making some tea."

"Hmm. I like tea."He flashed a wicked smile.

"Not going to happen. Goodnight." I wag my index finger.

He laughs and I do, too. "A woman of principles...I like that."

"M-hmm." I nod. "Keep the music down," I add, walking away before I took him up on his offer.

"I'm Matthew by the way!"he calls out after me.

"Pleasure. I'm sure," I say over my shoulder as I head back inside my condo.

I lock the patio door behind me. A slight smirk covers my face. He's definitely a ten. But he's just a good lay at best. Definitely not husband material. He'd have me pulling a Jazmine Sullivan and trying to bust some windows out his car.

I take a few sips of tea, then return to my bed. I rest my head on my pillow and close my eyes. Despite my best efforts, I can't seem to get Matthew out of my head.

Chapter Two

I'm partially well-rested as I roll out of bed and jump in the shower. I toss my hair into a quick bun, throw on some make-up, jump into my favorite black pant suit, and head out the door.

Just as I'm locking the door to myapartment, the elevator doors open. I walk quickly as possible to catch the elevator. Matthew is coming down the hall toward the elevator as well. He's dressed in a pair of dark denim jeans, a printed t-shirt with a silly character in bold colors, and a black messenger bag across his torso. A pair of colorful headphones complete his outfit. *Just as I suspected, he's a kid in a grown man's body.*

Matthew's much cuter in the right lighting. He's at least six-foot-three. His full lips and hazel eyes make him unflinchingly gorgeous. He's the kind of guy girls fight over and grown women stalk. He smiles briefly in my direction and I smirk in response. He reaches the elevator in just enough time to catch and hold the door. Just as I'm about to step on, I stumble and nearly drop my purse and laptop. I quickly recover and manage a polite, "Thank you," as I step on the elevator.

"You're welcome," Matthew replies, stepping on behind me.

It's just the two of us inside the elevator. I step back, strategically placing a distance between us. He presses the ground floor button. As soon as the doors close, I immediately regret living on the tenth floor. I begin counting to ten and praying that Matthew doesn't strike up a conversation. *Dear God, please do not lead me into temptation with this man. The devil is a lie. The devil is a lie. In Jesus name, Amen.*

God ignores my prayers as Matthew turns in my direction."Morning. You look beautiful today." When I don't reply, he adds,"Sorry about last night. I'm an artist. So. . . "

The elevator stops and a few more people get on. I welcome the interruption. But, that doesn't deter Matthew from talking. He blabs on and on about being an artist from Queens, New York. We're so close I can smell the mint on his breath and a hint of his light, woodsy smelling cologne. I reply only with a half smile and a head nod. I've already decided that I don't want to get to know him. I'm a decorated attorney. The last thing on my mind is being friends with a man who dresses like a fifteen-year-old kid and probably smokes weed.

More people get on the elevator and we're squished into a small corner.We're standing shoulder to shoulder when he asks, "Can I take you out sometime?"

I look up and realize we're on the first floor. My patience has run thin and I'm dying for my morning cup of coffee from Starbucks. I don't want to hurt his feelings, so, I politely reply,"I don't think so."

"Why not?" he asks without hesitation.

I shrug, deciding to be honest. "You're not my type."

A few heads turn in our direction just as the doors open. I ignore them all and start moving toward the door.

Matthew seems a little shocked, but then he just says, "Have a nice day."

Before I can respond, he places his headphones on his ears and walks off.

Later, I'm sitting at my desk reviewing a case when Jacqueline, my best friend since college bursts into my office. She closes the door behind her and locks it immediately.

"Stop whatever it is you're doing. I need to talk to you."

I stop and casually walk around my desk. I know this is not a life or death situation. Jacqueline has a flair for the dramatic. She's brilliant in the courtroom. Dumb in love. Same as me. Every week she comes into my office to ask for my help with some love conundrum. Either she's broken a nail, broken up with a boyfriend, or is just plain broke.

I cross my arms and legs and rest against my desk. "Breathe, Jacque. Just breathe and tell me what's going on."

"I think Jon is cheating on me. I went through his phone and found some text messages."She's on the verge of tears.

"Here we go again." I roll my eyes and walk back to my chair behind the desk.

"I know what you're going to say. I'm paranoid. But, I promise you, Na, I'm not. I know I have issues bigger than Vogue."

"I can't argue with that."

She ignores my dig. "But I know what I know. Men don't send pics of their stuff unless you're sending them pics of your stuff."

I laugh. She did have a point there.

"Well, I guess that means that it's over?" I knew Jacqueline. Once she thought a guy was cheating, she moved on. With a quickness. "I was just starting to like this one."

"Over like yesterday's news," Jacqueline confirms.

We chat some more, then finally she asks, "How's your mom? Still waiting on Prince Charming to come and scoop you up?"

I nod. "Yep, still counting my ovaries and monitoring my 'situation'."

Jacqueline laughs and says, "I'm surprised she hasn't posted your picture in the single section of the newspaper."

"Give her time, she will."

A mischievous grin crosses Jacqueline's face. "I have a confession. I made us online profiles."

"Us?"

"Yep. You and me."

"Jacqueline, I done told you. . ."

Jacqueline heads toward the door. "All work and no play gives your coochie cobwebs."

"Leave my vagina to me and gynecologist, please."

"Now what kind of friend would I be if I had all the fun for the both of us?"

"The kind that I treat to lunch."

We both laugh.

She stops just before opening my office door. "Come out with me tonight."

"No thanks." I shake my head. "The last time we went out I had to break up a fight between you and a little person. No ma'am."

"That chick shouldn't have been talking all that smack. Just because you small don't mean you can't get a karate chop to the throat." Jacqueline makes a karate move that makes me burst out laughing.

"You are so crazy but the answer is still no."

She shrugs. "Suit yourself. Don't call me when your vibrator dies."

"No, you didn't go there."

She planted her hands on her hips as a wide grin spread across her face. "What's the matter, counselor? Vibrator got you sprung?"

"That's it! You have worked my last nerve," I say, wagging my finger at her. "I can get a man. I just don't have time."

"Make time."

"Why don't you find me one, then?"

"Done!" It was as if that's all she was waiting on. She raced out of my office before I could say another word. I was kidding, but I knew my friend. I'd given her the go-ahead and she wasn't going to rest until she'd found me the perfect date. Or at something close to it in today's market.

Chapter Three

Two weeks and three terrible dates later. I was done with the opposite sex *and* Jacqueline. Each guy was worse than the last that she set me up with.

The first date was a realtor named Brandon. The fact that I could see the ring imprint from his wedding band was a turn off within itself. But then, he compared me to his ex-wife repeatedly throughout the night, which took the date to a whole other level of crazy. Between the sob stories and pathetic look on his face, my vagina checked out long before I did.

Then there was Robert, the university IT consultant. For our date we had dinner at a seafood restaurant in Lithia Springs. He was super sweet. He brought me tulips instead of roses, pulled out my chair, and even offered to split the desert with me over dinner. The date was almost perfect. Almost. If it wasn't for Robert's obsession with big butts and his wandering eyes. He salivated every time a woman with a large behind walked past our table. He had the nerve to ask me if I ever considered butt implants. I nearly slapped him and his momma for that dumb question.

After my date with Robert, I needed a hot bath and a tetanus shot. Jacqueline kept trying to convince me that it would only get better the more I dated.

"You've got to kiss a couple of frogs before they turn into a prince," she said over lunch one day.

"Mm-hmm," I replied and continued eating my salad.A few days later, Jacqueline persuaded me to go out with Andrew, the athletic trainer. He was ooh la la fine from head to toe. He looked like Boris Kodjoe but dipped in dark chocolate. Andrew was well-educated, charming, and quite the comedian. For our date, we went to the Aquarium. Simple, but classy. Occasionally, throughout the date he'd mention going to the gym, his celebrity clientele, and his dream of opening a gym of his own. I admired his enthusiasm and ambition. A man with a plan. I liked that. Homerun, I thought, a little relieved.

After the Aquarium, we went to dinner at a local steakhouse. I was having a decent time until the bill arrived. Andrew grabbed my hand, stared into my eyes, and with a straight face asked if I would write a check on his behalf for $1,000 as an investment for his business.

I wanted to knock the taste out of his mouth. But instead, I snatched my hand away, put my half of the bill back in my pocket, threw my drink in his face and walked out of the restaurant.

With all of those bad dates behind me I just want to relax and live in the here and now. Taking a break from dating, sitting on my patio alone, grilling salmon, sipping red wine, and allowing Marvin Gaye and Nina Simone to take my concerns away.

I allow the sunset and the aroma from the fish to stir all of my senses into a place of tranquility. I kick my feet up, lie back in my recliner, and rest my eyes.

"Looks like a perfect evening for two," Matthew announces from a distance.

Startled, I jump and look in his direction.I hadn't seen him around since that day on the elevator. I actually thought that he'd been avoiding me.

"You scared me," I say. "I didn't see you standing there."

"Sorry. I didn't mean to startle you." He hesitates, then asks, "Mind if I join you?"

"Actually I do." I reply, folding my arms.

"That's a shame. I'm a lot of fun." Matthew professes, leaning on the brick wall of the patio.

I ignore his penetrating stare and tend to my food. I flip the salmon over and pour a little more wine inside my glass. I can see Matthew out the side of my right eye. I glance over and he's setting up his canvas and paint brushes. I watch for a few more seconds and I walk back to my chair. The curious side of me wants to watch what becomes of the blank page in front of him. The other side of me says I should mind my own damn business.

When the salmon is done, I complete the meal with a spinach salad. Marvin and the gang are on repeat. I turn the music down low and sit out on the patio to enjoy my dinner. Matthew hasn't said another word to me.

From a distance I see a painting of a woman's face. An array of light browns and soft blues. The colors are bold but not overwhelming enough to pull away from the art. It's beautiful. Matthew is in his own world. I finish my dinner and walk over to the brick wall.

"It's beautiful."

"You think so?" He doesn't take his eyes away from the canvas.

"Yes. Someone special?" I ask.

He inhales deeply and says, "She used to be."

"Oh!" I reply, confused about what to say next.

I begin to walk away. Suddenly he says, "I loved her once upon a time."

"It shows." I make my way back over to clear the table.

"Didn't think you'd notice," he calls out over his shoulder.

I take a deep breath. "I guess I deserve that," I reply with a smirk." Just a little bit."

"Just a little."

I actually feel ashamed. "About that...I...I'm sorry."

"Don't worry about." He laughs and runs his fingers through his mane. "Been shot down before. Just never inside a crowded elevator."

I chuckle and cover my hand with my mouth.

"You have a beautiful smile, don't hide it."

I blush and reply with a soft, "Thank you."

Before long, my walls come down and we begin to talk. This time around I'm actually listening as Matthew speaks. In my eyes he was only a young punk with headphones and paintbrush. But, there was more to him than his youthful appearance and sly grin. I never would have marked him for a successful mogul of a mobile headphones corporation. Even CEO's wear sneakers and jeans on occasion, he reminds me. He speaks of his passion for painting and how he turned it into a career.

I'm apprehensive about sharing certain aspects of my life with a stranger. He encourages me. I grow to be comfortable with him. We share a laugh and occasionally, our eyes meet. Since I'm on my third glass of wine and I feel myself getting woozy, I finally say, "Well, I'd better call it a night."

So soon?"

"I'm afraid so. Duty calls. Shut eye required."

"Well, I won't hold you up." Matthew stands, and heads toward the patio door.

"Goodnight."

"Goodnight, Natalie."

I pause. *How does he know my name?*

Chapter Four

At work Jacqueline convinces me to allow her set me up on one more date. I wasn't really up for it. But this time around she promised if I didn't have a good time she'd buy me Beyonce tickets for the next concert. Since I love me some Bey, here I am, getting ready for date number four.

I slip my womanly physique inside a sleeveless jersey dress with an asymmetric hem with a wrapover skirt. Simple and chic for any type of event. It's a little after six and the sun is preparing to say goodbye for the evening. To calm my nerves a little bit I turn on the radio and play some Beyonce. I kick off my heels, turn up the music, and shake what my mama and the good Lord gave me. "Single Ladies" is my anthem. I sing every word with all of my might, swing my hair back and forth, and even drop it like it hot a few times. By the time "Drunk in Love" begins, I'm a bit hoarse. Suddenly, I notice I'm being watched by Matthew.

I'm looking at him and he's looking at me. He claps his hands and smiles. I'm shocked and slightly embarrassed. Part of me wants to close the window , throw up the blinds, and run away. It's too late.

Big girl panties. Big girl panties, Natalie. I chant in my head.I stand near the window with my glass in my hand and reply. "Do you watch all of your neighbor embarrass themselves?" I ask.

"Only the beautiful ones."

I smile. "I'm a cop. So, if you try anything funny...I have a right to shoot you."

He laughs and says, " Beautiful with a sense of humor...I'm liking you more every day. But you're not a cop. You're a big shot lawyer downtown."

Okay, that wiped my smile away. "How does a stranger know my business?"

"I live next door and your UPS guy sucks."

I laugh. Matthew was right about that. Despite the fact that I was constantly getting packages, my delivery guy was always leaving my package at the wrong door.

"Going somewhere?" he asks, pointing to dress.

"Blind date," I admit.

"Ouch! Those are the worst."

"Tell me about it."My cell phone chimes and I excuse myself to answer it. It's a text from Jacqueline. I reply to the text and return to the window. Matthew's not there anymore. I gather my things and head for the door. I go to close the window when Matthew reappears.

"Have fun on your date, Natalie."

"I will."

Half of me is not as excited as I initially was to go on the blind date. There's a tingle in my stomach and other places the more I get to know Matthew. A tingle that wishes to be explored.

It takes me about thirty minutes to arrive at the Woodruff Arts Center Museum. Jacqueline is standing at the entry door of the museum. She looks cute in her sparkly silver dress and strappy sandals. She waves at me with a big bright smile. Standing next to Jacqueline is a short stocky man with a thick mustache. I hope to God he's not my date. Jacqueline and I exchange hellos and air kisses.

After admiring my dress she introduces me to the stranger standing next to her.

"Natalie, this is my date Kenneth. He's a budget analyst with a small firm in Buckhead."

Kenneth smiles and wraps his pudgy hands around Jacqueline's waist.

"Nice to meet you, Kenneth,"I say.

"Pleasure," he politely replies.

We're all standing in a triangle for a few minutes when Jacqueline clears her throat, grabs me by the wrist, and points toward my date. A broad shoulder stranger headed in our direction." Natalie, this is Charles... your date." *Easy on the eyes. Check.*

Charles greets all of us with a bright smile. I extend my hand to formally introduce myself and he declines.

"Germaphobe. Sorry," he replies with a partial smile, then walks away as if nothing ever happened.

Throughout the night I try to connect with Charles and give Jacqueline and her date some space. Every effort I make, Charles shoots it down quickly with a negative remark or an educated fact. During the museum exhibit I ask, " What do you do for a living?"

"I teach high school kids in the inner city."

"Oh wow! That must be amazing teaching our young minds."

"I hate my job," he replies with a cringe. "The kids are idiots and their parents are even bigger idiots."

After I while I try again with a more neutral topic like favorite foods. Charles replies, "I don't have a favorite anymore. It's the government's fault."

By the time the museum exhibit is over, I need a large glass of wine and a large shoe to beat Jacqueline with.

We meet up with Jacqueline and her date after the exhibit and make plans to go get something to eat. Jacqueline and Kenneth head in one direction and Charles follows me.

"Where'd you park your car?"

He shakes his head. "I took the bus. Cars are bad for the environment."

On the inside, I scream.

"Can you excuse me? I need to run to the ladies room?" I ask.

"Sure. Just be sure to only use four sheets of toilet paper. Environmentalists say if we can cut back on our toilet paper usage, it would go a long way."

I don't reply as I walk to the bathroom. As soon as the door closes, I grab my cell phone.

"Hel-"

"Bathroom now!" I shouted before she could finish her greeting.

It only takes Jacqueline a few minutes before she walks in the bathroom all smiles. As soon as the door closes I check all of the stalls .We are all alone and I let out a loud scream.

"What's wrong, Na? Aren't you having a good time with Charles?"

I nearly choke Jacqueline with my bare hands. "Charles, is driving me crazy," I tell her. "And to think I waxed my kitty kat for this. I can't take another minute of his b.s."

"Maybe you're overreacting. It can't be that bad. Can it?"

"I'm going home,"I tell her.

"Wait, what am I supposed to tell the guys?"

"Tell them I got my period." Then I leave out the back way.

By the time I make it home, my feet are aching and my stomach is grumbling. I can't wait to get out of my clothes and into my bed. As soon as I walk off the elevator I notice a bed of red roses and a note attached to my door. I run to pick up the roses up and read the note.

I would love to take you out on a real date. Call me. 404-748-0890-Matthew

I pick up my cell to call Matthew and invite him to share some vanilla ice cream with me on the roof. He agrees. I put two scoops of ice cream in two separate cups, grab two spoons, and head for the roof. Matthew walks out on the rooftop.

"Hello again, stranger," he says with a broad smile.

"Hello, yourself," I reply with a smile.Matthew grabs two chairs and we sit at the nearest table. I pass him his cup of ice cream and a spoon.

"Thank you," he replies.

"You're welcome."

After two scoops and a brief brain freeze. Matthew asks, "So, how was the blind date?"

"Challenging to say the least."

"Always is."

When he's not looking, I steal a glance and take mental photos of him with my eyes. He catches me and says, "Do I pass?"

"Huh? What do you mean?"I ask, playing dumb.

"Am I all that you want?"

"Yes. I'm hoping there's more than meets the eye," I admit. I'm tired of fighting it. I'm going to just go for it.

"Stay tuned. It gets better."

"Are you happy?" He scoops more ice cream unto the spoon.

"I believe so. Are you?"

"I can actually say so."

"Hmm. What's missing? Love?"

"Yes. Is that so bad?" he replies with a furrowed brow.

I shake my head and reply, "Love is only a feeling nothing else to compare to."

Matthew clears his throat and says, "Interesting statement from such a beautiful creature."

"How so?"

He grabs my empty hand and says, "A heart absent of love isn't a heart at all."

I ease my hand away as his touch makes me nervous. "Very true," I manage to say.He rests his back on the chair and releases a sigh. After a brief silence Matthew asks, "Why are you alone?"

I shrug and look away shamefully. Matthew rises from his seat and walks over to me. He takes the spoon out of my hand and turns my chair in his direction. He squats down in front of me. He holds my hands and looks into my eyes. "I've always wanted to be your friend. Will you let me?"

"I-I don't know. I-"Matthew shushes me with his index finger against my lips. He stands and pulls me to my feet. His hands are holding mine. He looks down at me and says, "Jump."

"Huh?" I reply in confusion.

"It means for you to allow me to be your friend and possibly your lover."

I drop Matthews's hands and walk to the edge of the roof.

"Think about it." He turns to walk away.

"Wait!" I exclaim and run in his direction. I grab Matthew's hands and stare into those hypnotizing hazel eyes. I look into his eyes and say, "Okay. From strangers to friends and ultimately lovers."

"From strangers to friends and ultimately lovers," he repeats.We nod in agreement and Matthew lifts me up off my feet and seals our deal with a kiss.

I inhale and remind myself to live for the moment. Or as my mother would say, "Leap in my best stilettos." I don't know where I'm going with Matthew. I just know that I'm finally going to allow myself to enjoy the ride.

***M.C. Walker** is a down to earth, funny, sophisticated, and ambitious modern day young woman from the great city of Atlanta. Currently hard at work on her debut novel, Before The Lights Go Out, and many other projects, M.C. is always working hard and reaching her goals. You can find her at home on the web @ writermcwalker.blogspot.com.*

Just Call Me Honey

By Marcena Hooks

Five, four, three, two, one. She released slow breaths. As many times as she'd done this, she always questioned her nervousness. It was only sex. No commitments, no soul ties, and no love.

She inched closer to the door and looked at the room number: 669. That should be easy to remember, considering the acts she would perform behind the closed door.

Knock, knock. Two times was her code. Then she would slide the hotel key in the slot and wait for the low beep and green light. She always had the john leave her a key at the front desk. She didn't know why, but suspected it was because it gave her some sense of control.

With little effort, she slid the key into the slot, opened the door, and entered. White walls, floral paintings, and dim lighting greeted her. She cleared her throat and said, "Mr. Smith, I'm here."

She heard shuffling in the bathroom and then the knob turned. At first Honey noticed the towel wrapped around a manly waist and the trail of hair leading down. Her eyes moved up his chest and settled on his eyes.

"Hello, Miss Honey," the man said. He grabbed her hand and placed a light kiss there.

She snatched her hand away. She didn't like kissing. That was one of her rules. It made her connect with her male partners and she despised that. She just wanted to make her money and leave. That's it.

"Rule number one: no kissing," Honey reminded him.

He flashed a toothy grin. "I forgot. Let's get down to business." Mr. Smith proceeded toward the bed and dropped his towel. "Any more rules I should know about, like no touching?" He smiled.

"We'll stick with the first rule for now and see if you can master that." Honey set down her purse. The sooner she got started, the sooner she could finish.

"Okay, I'm up for the challenge."

Yeah, you're UP all right, Honey thought.

Honey began to undress as he turned on some music on his iPad. He began bobbing his head and humming as Marvin Gaye came through the speakers. Honey got in her zone – the place she mentally escaped to in order to make it through these nights.

"Come on, Sweet Thang. Daddy's ready for you."

Honey forced a smile, then proceeded to do what she did best.

***

"You are amazing and beautiful." Mr. Smith drooled as he eyed her naked body.

"Thanks," Honey replied as she slipped her dress back on. That was nothing new; they all said that.

"Can we meet again sometime?"

"You have the number to the agency. Just call when you're ready."

"No, I mean, like can I take you to dinner."

She continued dressing. She was used to this too. "Against the rules."

"Sure, I understand. Can I request you though?" He looked hopeful.

"It just depends on schedules and availability."

Honey slid on her boots and then held out her hand for her money.

He reached over and grabbed his wallet off the nightstand. "Here you go. I had a great time." He held her hand a little too long.

"I'm glad," Honey said. "Look us up again when you're ready."

With that, Honey scooted out the door so fast, she almost fell. She never looked back. She never did.

Walking back to the car, Honey thought back to how she got to this place in her life.

"I don't love you anymore." The words coming from her ex-fiancé, Chris, made Honey sick to her stomach. She had given her heart and life to that man and he'd repaid her by dumping her a month before their wedding.

"What do you mean you don't love me anymore? How can you say that, Chris?" she'd cried.

They were inside her apartment that night, and had just returned from dinner. There was no indication over the meal, in the car or otherwise to prepare Honey for what she heard next. Chris put his hands in his pants pockets and tried to avoid her pouty gaze. "Because I could no longer stand to string you along. I had to tell you before we walked down the aisle. I can't continue living the lie, Delaney."

She was known as Delaney then, before she started living this double life. Before she took this job as a call girl, she was known as the good girl. She was a student and had a decent job in retail. Her parents praised her for good grades and often told her how pretty she was.

"Delaney, I know you will continue to make us proud. You are a good girl and remember you are beautiful inside and out," her father used to always tell her.

She believed those words back then, but why didn't Chris agree?

She used to love kissing, and was not afraid of commitment. This was before all of Chris's lies. She began to think back on all those times she would call or text him with no response. Just an excuse once he finally did call back. On occasion when she would mention them going out, he would have to work late. And they had not been making love as often as they used to. He just became distant, and now it was so clear.

Delaney saw Chris's mouth moving but couldn't understand what he had the nerve to say. She forgot she had asked him a question. "Just shut the hell up and save it! I don't need to hear any more of your lies!" She backhanded him across the face. It stung her, too. He didn't even try to reach for her or console her in any way. He just stood there looking dumbfounded. She couldn't fathom why he was being so cold.

"I thought I would grow to love you," he said, rubbing his cheek. "I had to be married in order to get that church. You know most congregations want their pastors married. I did initially find you attractive, but it was like once we got together, you let yourself go too much. You let go of dreams, your looks, and it just seemed like you didn't care."

This time Delaney looked at him dumbfounded. *How could he?* Even if what he was saying was true, that didn't give him reason to be so hurtful. "So it never occurred to you before now, to mention any of this to me? Tell me your thoughts? Or better yet, tell me the truth?"

"Believe me, I wanted to, but I didn't want to offend you. I was wrong for assuming you would notice and just fix it. I thought you knew how to be a first lady."

"Damn right, you were wrong. Don't ever assume," she had told him.

That had been the last time they'd talked. All their years together and it was over just like that.

***

Honey had drifted off to sleep thinking about Chris. But this morning, as the sun peeked through her bedroom window, Mr. Smith popped back in her head. Honey pushed away thoughts of him as she climbed out of bed and made her way into the bathroom. She caught her reflection in the mirror and instantly, sadness crept up on her.

How did I get here? Why couldn't I stay Delaney Murphy?

Delaney was from a middle-class family. Her brother Donald, Jr. was 18 years her senior, so she grew up in the 80s with her nephew instead. He was only two years younger than Delaney and moved in with them when she was six. Michael and Delaney fought like siblings, but learned to love each other.

Honey's mom, Norma worked in manufacturing for over 30 years at the telephone company. She was now retired and waiting on Delaney to have some grand babies.

"Delaney, I want to see my grandchildren before I die, you know," her mother said almost every time they talked.

Donald Sr., Delaney's dad, was a retired military man. After serving 35 years in the U.S. Army, Sgt. Murphy devoted all of his free time to his horses. When Delaney was small, he took her horseback riding. Delaney remembered that first time, and how she didn't want to ride because she was afraid.

"Don't be scared, Laney. Horses can sense that, you know. Let them know you are in charge," her father said.

When she fell off the stud, she figured out really quick who was in charge. "I told you I didn't want to ride Daddy," she said through tears. "You made me anyway." She decided then that as soon as she got grown, she would do things her way.

Delaney was a straight-A student from elementary to high school with dreams of becoming a writer. She went to college and graduated, but when she lost her best friend in a car accident, her world went topsy-turvy. Delaney had been lonely ever since Latrice died. She had yet to find a friend, confidant, or buddy like Latrice.

Honey turned to sex as a way to filter her frustrations. Deep down it really bothered her, but she had bills to pay. She accrued a bunch of debt in college with credit cards and shopping splurges. Back then, Delaney didn't buy it if a designer's name wasn't attached. And now that her parents were retired, her money well had run dry.

One day when she was on the Internet looking for a job, Honey found two. One at Debonaire's, a men's specialty shop, and the other at Top Notch Agency. As a clerk at the shop, she could cover-up what she did at night to make her living. At Debonaire's she was Delaney, but at Top Notch, everyone knew her as Honey. She came up with the name because of her skin's soft-golden brown hue. Honey hadn't expected to stay in the call girl business for long. She just needed to get out of debt, pay some bills in advance, and build a nest egg, since her wedding-that-didn't-happen had wiped out her savings. But she'd been surprisingly good at pleasing men, and in a matter of weeks, had become one of the agency's most requested dates.

If only the people that knew Delaney could see Honey now.

Honey snapped out of memories of the past. She needed to focus on the present. And the present called for her to pack a bag because in just under six hours, she'd be on a plane, to take her business on the road.

***

"Passengers and flight attendants, please prepare for takeoff."

Sure, Honey had been on a plane before, but she still got bubble guts each time one took off. In a few minutes, she would have her drink and then she could relax. She may even get some reading and writing done since this flight was about four hours long.

The flight attendant had approached Honey, but she had drifted off to sleep. A nudge from her passenger woke her up. She jumped and had to look around to remember where she was.

"I took the liberty of ordering you a Bloody Mary. You seemed a bit nervous." His rich baritone voice forced her to face him.

She blinked and said, "Thank you, I think."

The guy just smiled and opened his bag of pretzels.

Honey grabbed her cup because she was suddenly very thirsty.

The Bloody Mary felt refreshing going down her throat. She finished off the drink, then laid back to try and enjoy the rest of the ride.

Once she'd arrived at her hotel and gotten settled in, Honey realized that she had a few hours to spare. She was staying in the hotel across the street from where she'd meet her client. She stretched out on the couch in her suite and pulled out her journal. Most people swore by using laptops, but Honey loved writing long hand. Before she knew it, she had written five pages and felt she had tapped into her first love again.

Satisfied with what she had written, she began to get ready for work. Honey packed mace, spare underwear, and deodorant. She looked around the room to make sure she hadn't forgotten anything and left.

She crossed the street and entered the client's hotel. Honey pulled out her phone and glanced again at the profile picture.

"I can do this," she muttered. Then she began her countdown as she approached the room. She gave her signature knock, then dropped the key in the lock. But before the green light beeped, the door swung open.

"After a long flight, I've been waiting for this," he said.

Then they just stared at each other.

"You've got to be kidding me," Honey managed to say. On the plane, she had seen him reading his Bible and taking notes. She even heard the gospel tunes coming through the ear buds of his headphones. He had gotten her a drink. How could this be?

"I must say, I am a bit surprised too," he replied, then finally added, "Well, do you still want to come in?"

Honey nodded, then stepped past him and into the room.

"So let me get this straight to make sure I'm not trippin'. You, James Williams, really did call our agency for services?" The profile picture she just looked at must have been an older photo. He looked decent, but in person, he looked as good as sin.

He nodded. "You do intend to follow through on those services?"

"That's what I came here for. But, circumstances are complicated now."

"Aren't these arrangements confidential? I mean, it's usually the first time you meet the person, right?"

Honey nodded. "We don't know each other like that, but it's just a bit of a surprise that's all. If you are still willing, I must comply." She echoed one of the contractual statements, but inside she still felt a little strange. This was a bit eerie, but she remembered that work trumped her feelings.

James walked toward her and said, "I just want to make sure you are comfortable with it."

Surprisingly, Honey didn't feel as bold like she did the other times, but she forced herself to go through it. "I'm fine, really."

"Good," he replied. "Very, very good."

***

Honey couldn't understand why she broke all the rules with this man. She woke up and thought she was dreaming. She looked over at James, who was still snoring. His arms were sticking out of the crisp, white sheets and she felt drawn to poke him in the biceps. She eased out of the bed and started looking for her clothes.

"Do you have to go?" he asked, coming out of his sleep.

"I do," she replied. She turned to stare at him, then she didn't know what made her say, "Are you a preacher?"

He looked taken aback by her question.

"Why does that matter?" he replied.

"It just does." But his non-answer was her answer. "Why would you even use this service? Isn't that against all your so-called morals or something?"

Since Latrice died and Chris hurt her so badly, Honey wasn't into the Lord or the church. Yes, she prayed on occasion, but she was too conflicted and felt God had failed her. And if this man was a preacher, well, it was way past time to jet out of there!

"I have morals," he said, "but I feel that you do, too. You didn't seem completely comfortable when we made love."

Honey tried to smile. "Maybe you weren't all that."

"Oh, I know better than that," he said, sitting up.

She caught herself. It was her job to always make the client feel like The Man, so why was she letting her guard down.

"Sorry. . . I was just, I don't know, I was just trying to understand," Honey found herself saying.

"Well, I have been hurt in the church and right now, I am probably running away from God," James replied. "Maybe I'm waiting on Him to give me another chance. And I just happen to enjoy sex."

His eyes. This man had the most beautiful eyes. And right about now, they were sucking her in. Making her feel things she shouldn't be feeling for a client.

"Excuse me, I have to go." Honey jumped up, grabbed her money off the dresser, and headed toward the door.

"Honey, wait! I'll answer your question." He took a deep sigh. "I am a happily divorced minister who has stepped down from the pulpit. My ex-wife left me six years ago because of my high sex drive. Of course I didn't see it as a problem then, but I do now. Preachers are human and we love sex just like the next man. I still sin and make mistakes, but God is working on me. I realize I have to get my relationship right with Him before I can have one with anyone else."

Honey stared at him. She immediately thought of Chris and looked at James to see if she could find any similarities. He seemed truthful, but then again, so had Chris in the beginning.

"Well good luck to you," Honey said as she headed toward the door.

He jumped up, and before she knew it, he pulled her to him and kissed her. Hard. And her heart immediately began to betray her.

"I am glad my last time was with you, Honey. I hope I can see you again sometime," James said before she could even gather her composure.

She told him thank you and gave her normal spiel for the agency. Then she replayed his words in her head. *His last time?* What in the world did that mean? Honey quickly left. She didn't need to stick around and find out what he meant by that.

***

Why can't I get his kisses off my mind?

Honey had been asking herself that question for months. She'd had several clients since James, but no one had compared. No one had made her want to kiss.

"Don't forget the truck brought in that new merchandise." The sound of her boss, Tom's voice snapped her out of her thoughts. "Our customers are going to love these new shirts." He took one out and examined the French cuffs. "I can't wait to buy mine and have my initials monogrammed on them. What do you think, Delaney?"

Delaney had been folding the same shirts for the past thirty minutes. She was surprised Tom hadn't said anything.

"Yes, those are nice," she said, answering Tom. "But putting your initials on them is a different story." She smiled, knowing Tom would be the one to do it. He was a sharp dresser and that's why he was the manager. She appreciated his sense of style and often told him so.

"Thanks. Well, look, can you go grab one of the boxes because I really want to put those new ties on display?"

Honey nodded, then made her way to the back of the store to grab more boxes. When she came back toward the front, she heard Tom talking to a customer. Her mouth dropped open the moment she saw him.

"Wow, if this isn't fate, I don't know what is."

Tom noticed the exchange between the two of them and grinned. "Well, why don't I let you handle this client," Tom said, as he patted James on the back. "Delaney here is our best salesperson. She'll take good care of you."

"I know she will," James said with a sly smile. "So is it Honey or Delaney?" He asked once Tom was out of earshot.

She put her finger up to her lips and said, "Please hush before you blow my cover! No one here knows me by that name." she stepped closer. "My real name is Delaney. I work here during the day. Everyone here knows me by Delaney while everyone at the agency knows me by Honey. I plan to keep it that way. Understand?"

"Yes, I get it. I know what it feels like to live a double life. I've been there, but I was always uncomfortable with it. I got tired of lying and running. Are you tired of it yet?" He let the question hang in the air as he began looking at suit jackets.

He held up a jacket, motioning that he'd like to try it on. As Honey helped him slid it on in front of the mirror, he said, "You know, God is a God of second chances."

It was strange that he would say that. Her mother had just told her that last week when she was trying to convince her to return to her roots in the church.

"Okay, Preacher Man. That suit looks nice on you," she said, trying to change the subject. "Will you let me wrap that up for you?"

He studied himself in the mirror, then said, "Actually, I think I will take it."

She smiled as he started removing the jacket. She'd make a nice little commission off this sale.

James looked down at her nametag. "You have a beautiful name."

"Thank you." Honey rang him up and after handing him his receipt said, "Can I get anything else for you?"

James took the bag. "Yes, as a matter of fact, you can. I have a proposition for you, Delaney. How about we stop the running and lying? How about we give up our double lives and work on our relationships with God together? What I am saying is that I want to date you exclusively and get to know you. What do you think?"

Honey hadn't dated in years. Her lifestyle as an escort had only temporarily filled the void.

He must've sensed her apprehension. He stepped closer and lowered his voice. "God does everything by design," he continued. "I used an out of town escort service because I was trying to hide what I was doing. I'd rather pay to fly someone in, than to let it get out what I was doing. I'd prayed for God to give me a reason to stop. He did. You. I was supposed to sit by you on the plane. You were supposed to be the one they sent to my room. And I was supposed to end up here in this store, bumping into you. Now, that I have connected with you again, I don't ever want to let you go."

Honey was dumbfounded. He'd said everything she felt. "But, you don't even know me."

He let out a small laugh. “We’ve shared the most intimate parts of one another. I think we can take some time to get to know one another. I want a real date.”

That made her laugh, too. She knew exactly what he was saying too. Because she was ready for a real date as well.

“Why not, James?” she found herself saying. “You’re right. Maybe we deserve some true happiness. Let’s just try.”

With that he took her hand and placed a gentle kiss there. “I look forward to it.” He looked down at her.

“Me too,” she said.

Delaney was finally ready to date again and this time she had some new rules: Yes to kissing, yes to a commitment, and perhaps, even yes to love.

Marcena Hooks is a graduate student working on her MFA in Creative Writing at Antioch University, Los Angeles. She is an aspiring writer who plans to work as an author after graduation. Marcena is also a married, stay-at-home mom with two children. She can be reached by email: marcenac@yahoo.com and on Twitter: @Marcenahooks.

Holiday Party

By Loureva Slade

"Did I tell you how amazing you look tonight?" Greg asked as our car approached the valet stand positioned under a street lamp directly in front of Rhonda's massive home.

I blushed and smiled at my handsome husband. Even after a year of dating and five years of marriage, his smooth voice, dark chocolate skin, and deep dimples still gave me butterflies.

"Yes, but you can tell me again," I said, batting my faux lashes.

Greg grinned naughtily and looked me in my eyes. I melted, as usual.

"Kelly, you are the most beautiful woman I have ever laid eyes on." He kissed me on my ear and rubbed my belly.

"Thank you, baby," I said as I placed my clutch in my lap.

My window was rolled down just a little and I could hear Snoop's "Santa Claus Goes Straight to the Ghetto" blaring from Rhonda's house. The number of cars that lined the street and the bodies I could see moving to the beat through her front window let me know that the party was already in full swing.

The valet pulled on my door handle and helped me out of our silver Volkswagen Passat. Greg rushed around to my side and gently held my hand as we walked toward Rhonda's front door. There wasn't a trace of fog, which was unusual considering the time of year and our proximity to LAX.

I was six months pregnant and my body still wasn't used to the extra weight. Standing, sitting, walking, laying, and just about everything else was extremely uncomfortable. I tried to make it look easy and even though I had found a cute pair of ballerina shoes to match my outfit, I'm sure I looked as awkward as I felt.

"You look fine," Greg assured me, as if he could tell what I was thinking.

“Thanks,” I said and smoothed my “little black dress.” I had worn it many times before my pregnancy and was happy that the flared waist allowed me to fit it easily even now.

Rhonda opened her front door before we rang the bell. She was fabulous, as always. Her jet-black hair was parted down the center and lay perfectly mid-stomach. She wore a tight red A-line dress with a black belt and three-inch black heels. She had on a Santa hat with her name stitched across the front. Bright red lipstick accentuated her pouty lips and her gold accessories brought the look together.

Rhonda and Greg had been friends since childhood. He introduced me to her shortly after we started dating, and although the two of us hadn’t grown to be the best of friends, we did talk occasionally and hung out in party settings at least twice a year. I admired her style. She was confident, connected, and well respected. She had an easy way of making you feel like royalty whenever you were in her presence. I liked that.

“My two favorite people,” she said as she pulled Greg and me in for a group hug that lasted a little too long. Her slurred words highlighted the spirits on her breath. Her glassy dark-brown eyes were a sure sign of an interesting night.

“Thank you for having us,” Greg said and kissed her on the cheek.

"I'll take your coats," she said and sloppily hung them in the entry closet.

I glanced around the room. Rhonda was quite the party planner. From the decorations and the h'ors deurves to the music and the guests, Rhonda never disappointed. She had cleared her great room and dining room of most of their furniture, creating one huge dance floor that extended through the French doors and onto her patio. The space smelled of fresh pine, and red, white, and silver decorations were sprinkled throughout. It was breathtaking. There were already about 50 guests present and every one of them, with the exception of us, was dancing.

"Let's dance, babe," Greg said as he pulled me onto the dance floor.

"Enjoy," I heard Rhonda call after us.

The DJ played Mariah's "All I Want for Christmas is You" and Greg and I proceeded to do what we did best.

I always liked to see who would be at Rhonda's gatherings. Her travels and career as a film producer kept her in touch with some rather entertaining people. She had a way of mixing A-list Hollywood types with middle school administrators like Greg and me. No one ever seemed uncomfortable and egos never seemed to be an issue. Her parties promised good times and laughs for all.

This year, reality star Milo Briggs was rubbing elbows with Christian Whitaker, supporting actor in the highest grossing Black movie of all time. Christian obviously had no interest in what Milo was talking about, but he nodded and eyed the hostess who was overtly flirting behind Milo's back.

Shawn Hines, BET News Anchor, had his eye on the same pretty little waitress that Christian was eyeing. I leaned over and asked Greg who he thought would woo the girl. Greg gave it to Christian hands down.

"The news is too boring for someone like her," Greg teased.

We both laughed, but of course I had to speak up for her. She looked like a smart young lady who would rather be a main squeeze than just one of many. For that reason, I believed she would choose brains over beauty.

As we danced, we occasionally leaned in to share scoop about the party goers around us. I noticed Rhonda gazing in our direction a couple times. I put both thumbs up and smiled to let her know we were having a good time. As soon as the disc jockey played "This Christmas," Greg looked over my shoulder and his face lit up with excitement.

"Aw, babe, look. I see my boy, Theo. I haven't seen him in a minute."

I turned and spotted Theo, a head above everyone else. He smiled as he walked in our direction. Although I had never actually met him in person, he looked exactly the same as he did on all the pictures of him that Greg had shown me.

Greg had told me on many occasions how Theo had taken him under his wing and treated him like family when he was a freshman at Howard. Theo joined the Marines immediately after he graduated and although he and Greg still emailed one another, they hadn't actually seen each other since college.

I stepped to the side as they greeted each other with a handshake that ended with the "Kid 'n Play." I couldn't help but laugh.

"Greg, my man! Long time!"

"Yeah, man. I see you finally decided to just cut it all off," Greg teased.

"What can I say? The ladies love a bald head."

They laughed and then his buddy glanced in my direction and said, "Who is this pretty lady and what is she doing with you?"

I blushed.

"Back, back!" Greg joked. "This is my wife, Kelly. Kelly, this is my boy Theo."

"I've heard a lot about you, Theo. It's nice to *finally* put a face with the name."

He extended his hand and politely said, "It's a pleasure to meet you. And don't believe *anything* you've heard. I was a kid back then."

"I've only heard good things," I smiled, returning his positive vibes.

While Greg and Theo caught up, I excused myself and perused the room. I noticed that the hostess was cozying up to Christian, who appeared confident she would leave with him tonight. Greg had been right.

"Hey, Kelly," I heard Rhonda's voice over my shoulder as she approached me.

I turned and smiled.

"Girl, you look like you are having way too much fun," I said with a chuckle.

"Not at all," she said seriously. "Can we talk?" Her words were more garbled than they had been when we first arrived. It hadn't even been an hour.

"Sure," I said.

"Come on."

She grabbed my hand and escorted me to the patio. There were tents and plush seating set up along the perimeter of the yard. The pool on the far side was lit with red lights. The palmettos and shrubbery that lined her backyard were decorated with red and white Christmas bulbs. Rhonda and I walked past dancing guests to the tent at the end of the yard and we sat down.

"You've done it again!" I smiled. "Great party."

Her eyes were glassy and I could tell that she hadn't heard a word I said.

"You look pretty," she said with a loud sigh.

"Thank you. I feel like a whale," I said quite frankly and laughed.

"No. You look beautiful," she slurred and shook her head..

"Thank you."

"I'm jealous."

"No way!" I laughed. There was absolutely no way she was jealous of me on my best day, and especially not with the watermelon I was carrying around in my stomach. "You know I look like a cow."

"Not at all," she said as she broke down and sobbed.

I didn't quite know what to do, so I rubbed her back and then pulled her into a quick tight embrace.

"What's wrong?"

She didn't respond. I couldn't imagine what was so horrible that it was worth her messing up her gorgeous face at *her* own party. Whatever it was, I just hoped I'd be able to console her.

The disc jockey mixed in Run DMC's "Christmas in Hollis" and a wave of energy erupted on the dance floor. Guests hollered, "Oh snap," and hands flew in the air as heads bobbed to the beat. This was my song and as difficult as it was, I kept the largest part of my attention on Rhonda.

"It shoulda been me," she finally said.

I rubbed her shoulder. I didn't quite know what she was referring to, but I was happy that she felt comfortable enough with me to cry in front of me. This was a first.

"With Greg," she continued.

I held my breath and waited for her to finish her sentence. It took me a few seconds to realize that she already had.

"What do you mean?" I asked.

"Did Greg ever tell you that I was supposed to have his baby?" she asked.

No. I hadn't heard that at all. I dropped my hand onto my lap.

"What do you mean?" I asked again, my mind racing.

"Greg and I dated in college. He even proposed to me, but I said no. I should be the one he's married to. I should be the one having his child."

"Let me get this straight. You and Greg—"

"Yes," she cut me off.

"But he told me that you guys have always been *just* friends."

She didn't respond.

I didn't know what to say or do. I felt betrayed. I was quite positive all the emotions I felt were visible at that very moment.

I didn't say another word. I left her sitting there and headed to the restroom to splash water on my face.

I felt my body temperature rise and I fanned back tears with my hand. I couldn't believe what she'd just said.

I thought back to the time I'd asked Greg if they'd ever dated.

"No," he'd said.

"Why not? She's gorgeous."

"She's not my type," he had replied firmly.

That had been hard to believe. I mean, Rhonda had to have been one of *the* most attractive women *I* had ever met. She had dark chocolate skin and the most entrancing dark brown eyes. I could only wish for a body as well-proportioned as hers.

I had pressed Greg to explain why she wasn't his type. He assured me that he was a man of substance and there were things about Rhonda I didn't know. He swore that although he cared about her as a friend, it stopped there.

He'd said just what I wanted to hear. I didn't want to breathe life in a place where Greg assured me there'd been none and so I left it alone.

Now here I was, in the bathroom, confused, hurt, and upset. What else had Greg lied about? If he couldn't be honest about his past relationship with Rhonda, could I believe that he had been honest about anything else? I wanted to scream. I had to talk with Greg to see whether there was any truth to the story.

I opened the bathroom door and headed in the direction where I had left Theo and Greg. I could feel the baby kicking as I walked and I rubbed my stomach to soothe her.

"I need to talk to you," I said as I approached and interrupted Greg, who was still engrossed in conversation with Theo.

He turned and looked at me—his face an amalgam of shock, confusion, and concern.

"Is everything alright? Have you been crying?" Greg asked as he stood and gently held my shoulders. He attempted to kiss me on the forehead, but I stepped back before he could. From the corner of my eye I could see Theo pull out his cell phone and *pretend* to answer a text message.

"Let's get out of here," I said.

"Alright if you insist," he said and turned to tell Theo he would catch up with him later.

"Let me say bye to Rhonda," he said to me.

"Let's just go," I said resolutely.

Greg looked taken aback. I could tell by the rapid movement of his eyes that he was searching my face for understanding.

"All right. After you," Greg finally said.

I marched toward the front door and grabbed my coat from the closet.

The cold air hit and chilled my face as soon as I stepped outside. A layer of fog was nestled at our shins. Greg handed the valet the ticket for our car and when he ran off to fetch it, Greg reached for my hand and said, "Babe, I sure wish you would tell me what's got you so upset."

"You lied to me, Greg. I can't believe you would lie to me."

"What are you talking about?"

"What do you think I'm talking about? What all have you lied to me about?"

I stared him in his guilty eyes—eyes that had always seemed so authentic to me. I was disgusted.

"I have always been completely honest with you."

"The fact that you are lying to me right now pisses me off even more, Greg."

Greg lifted his hand. "Baby, look, I think your hormones…"

"Don't touch me. And don't you dare blame my hormones for me being upset because you lied about you and Rhonda."

Greg's whole demeanor changed. He shifted nervously.

"It's not what you think," he said.

"Well explain to me what it is because in my estimation, you blatantly lied. I asked you whether the two of you dated…and you *never* mentioned that she once carried your child."

"I'm not sure what she told you, but it wasn't like that. And she NEVER carried my child."

"I can't stand anymore lies, so unless you plan to be completely honest with me, I don't even want to hear it."

The valet pulled up and ran around to open my door. I angrily got in and slammed my door before he could close it for me. Greg handed him a few dollars and thanked him before getting in and pulling off.

Greg made a few turns before we ended up at the scenic overlook in Culver City. This had been one of our favorite places to sit and talk since our dating days. He drove up the winding road in silence and parked the car.

The skies that were so clear earlier in the night were now occupied by a thick layer of fog. The fog made the view seem non-existent.

Greg cracked the windows, turned off the motor, and faced me. I had never seen his face so full of dread.

"Look. Rhonda and I dated for a week when we were freshmen in college. It was actually less than a week."

"You told me that you were just friends—that you had never been romantic."

"We have *never* been romantic," he said.

I rolled my eyes and faced the window. "But the two of you were in a relationship? I can't imagine you not being romantic with her," I said.

"Yes. We were friends and we thought we'd give a relationship a shot, but we decided we were much better as friends. It took us less than a week to realize that."

"Did you guys kiss during this 'week'?"

He paused for a moment, his face a ball of loathing. "Yes," he said, "But never before or after those few days we were in a relationship."

"So did you get her pregnant?"

"No. I hadn't ever been with anyone in that way. Right after we started talking Rhonda told me she was pregnant. When she told me I was the father, I knew it was impossible since we had never been together, and I also knew that although I loved her like a friend, there was no way I could be in a serious relationship with her."

"Where's the baby?"

"Kelly, I don't know if she ever *was* pregnant," he said and shook his head. "I never saw a baby. And we never talked about it," Greg said.

"She said you proposed to her."

"Not true," he answered firmly.

"Why did you keep her around as a friend after she lied to you? I just don't understand that."

Greg took a deep breath and looked at me with sad eyes. "The thing I never told you about Rhonda is that she had a very rough upbringing. You know I lived right next door to her and we talked about everything growing up. She told me that her mother hated her and her stepfather beat the crap out of her every day. You should've seen some of the bruises he left on her. It was horrible. I felt bad for her. And I guess knowing what she had been through made it hard for me to turn my back on her. Before we tried the whole relationship thing we were friends—best friends. I didn't want to let go of our friendship."

I felt a lump in my throat and breathing became difficult. I turned the key in the ignition and rolled my window down a little more.

"Why didn't you ever tell me any of this?" I asked as I turned the car back off.

"Kelly, I don't know," he sighed. Most people are dishonest about *something* when they first start talking to someone."

"I was completely honest with you about *everything*," I reminded him as I cut my eyes in his direction.

"You're right. Look. I'm sorry. I never meant to hurt you. I was only trying to protect you. You had nothing to worry about with Rhonda. She was really just my *friend*. I guess I thought if I told you about our less than a week relationship when we first started talking, you might want me to end my friendship with her."

"You're absolutely right about that," I said, and rolled my eyes. "I feel so stupid. Everybody told me that I was a fool for thinking the two of you had never been together, but I just knew you would never lie to me."

"I wanted to tell you, but it got harder as time passed. I'm sorry, babe," he said and reached for my hand.

I pulled it away.

"Do you know how many "friends" I gave up for you, Greg? All of them," I reminded him. "You were worth it to me."

Neither of us spoke for a while. I looked out my window and wiped away an occasional tear.

Just then, his cell phone went off. He sent the call to voicemail. My cell phone rang next. I pulled it out of my clutch and saw Rhonda's face on the screen. I sent her to voicemail. My phone rang again. I turned the ringer off and put it back in my purse. Greg's phone rang next. He sent the call to voicemail and turned his ringer off as well. I glanced in his direction, rolled my eyes, and then looked back out the window.

"Look, Kelly. I'm sorry I lied to you. That was selfish of me. It was wrong," he said.

I kept my gaze out my window.

"I will do whatever it takes to make it up to you."

I responded with silence.

What could he do to make this up to me? For start, Rhonda would have to be taken out of our equation. That was for sure. I liked her, but I couldn't imagine being in her presence after tonight. She was intoxicated at the party, yes, but I believe people say exactly what they mean when they are. Then when they sober up they feel remorseful and try to convince the people they hurt while intoxicated that they didn't mean anything they said. She meant to hurt me and she was in love with my husband. Two things that meant she had to go permanently.

"So here's what has to happen," I finally said. "First of all, you already know that you maintaining a friendship with Rhonda after tonight is out of the question. We will both talk with her tomorrow and make that clear."

He nodded and said, "All right."

"That easy?"

"Yes, baby. You are worth more to me than anything and anyone else in this world," he said. His eyes pleaded for me to believe him.

I looked down at my hands and continued. "Second, I need you to reassure me that I can trust you and I don't know how you can do that. I know it's going to take some time though because right now I'm feeling like the whole six years we've been together has been built on a foundation of your dishonesty."

"Baby, that hurts. I haven't lied about anything else."

"That sounds good, Greg," I said and looked up to make eye contact, "but yesterday morning you would have told me you had never lied to me about anything at all only for tonight to happen."

Greg dropped his head.

"The third thing that's going to have to happen from this moment on is that you never make a decision to 'protect' me that involves withholding information or flat out lying to me. I'm a big girl, Greg. I can handle it."

Greg looked up and arrested my eyes with his. He reached for my hand. This time, I didn't pull away.

"I'm so sorry, Kelly. I love you more than anything in this world and I promise I will *never* be dishonest with you again."

I exhaled for the first time in a long time. I absolutely believed him.

The space around us felt completely different than it had ever felt before. It felt—pure. I was happy to know the complete truth about Greg's relationship with Rhonda—the truth that I myself had chosen to overlook for so long.

In a sense, I was just as much to blame for lying to myself as he was for lying to me. I loved Greg enough to ignore the tug in my heart that let me know there was more to his story with Rhonda six years ago when I first felt it. I loved him so much that whenever thoughts about his possible past with Rhonda ran across my mind, I ignored them too. And if I was completely honest, there was nothing else that he had ever told me that sat as uneasily with me as his "friendship" with Rhonda. Greg was a good man. And I loved him.

"You'd better not," I said finally answering him, and I leaned my head against the headrest.

I closed my eyes and exhaled again. It felt so good to breathe in an atmosphere of truth. Of course I still felt the residual effects of the emotional rollercoaster I'd been on tonight, but now it was time to open myself to the freedom that forgiveness and healing brings. And the love that Greg and I shared was completely worth it all.

***Loureva Slade** is an up-and-coming author who has written pieces for newsletters, blogs, magazines, and anthologies. The Los Angeles native is a proud co-founder Of C.A.L.I. Girl Newsletter (Christian and Loving It), which is an inspirational publication for Christian young women. Connect with her on social media and visit her website, www.LourevaSlade.com.*

If you enjoyed The Dating Game,
Check out this excerpt from

Touched By An Angel

By Victoria Christopher Murray and

Princess F.L. Gooden

Chapter One

With the bare tips of my fingers, I lifted the red thong from my husband's suitcase, slowly, deliberately as if it were a pit viper. My lips parted into a wide O as I stared at the lace underwear, panties that I'd never seen before.

It wasn't like I was searching for trouble; in the twenty-three years of my marriage to Sheldon, there had never been anything close to drama in our relationship, especially not this kind. The two of us were solid, the kind of couple that Ashford and Simpson sang about back in the day when as a teenager, I dreamed about the man who would take my hand after my father walked me down the aisle. That man had been Sheldon Hudson – and he'd kept every single one of the vows we'd shared on our wedding day.

At least that's what I'd always thought.

I took a deep breath, just to make sure that I was still alive.

Why am I still holding onto these? I wondered.

But even as I had that thought, I could not release the death grip the tips of my fingers had on the panties. In my mind, I imagined the woman who owned this strip of material and I could almost see myself – twenty years younger. I could hear myself – with a high-pitched tone that belonged to someone who had not yet fully stepped into womanhood. And worse – I could see Sheldon – grinning as the tramp sauntered toward him wearing nothing more than these five inches of silk and lace. And maybe a pair of matching stilettos.

I snatched myself from that nightmare and shook my head. How in the world had I ended up here? After all, it wasn't like I was sneaking around, rummaging through my husband's bag as if I was a wife with no trust. No, I was doing what I'd always done when Sheldon returned home from a business trip.

Like all the other times, the car service had dropped him off in front of the house less than an hour ago and he had dragged himself and his bag across the trace of snow that sprinkled the path to the front door of our Capitol Hill townhouse. His eyes were blood-shot with exhaustion from the red-eye flight he'd taken from Los Angeles.

But even though he was tired, he'd kissed me with every bit of energy he had left and I followed him as he dragged his suitcase up the spiral staircase to the second level of our home.

Inside our master suite, Sheldon had dropped his luggage at the foot of our bed, tossed his briefcase and cell phone onto the bed, then staggered into the bathroom.

While he relaxed under the double heads in our steam shower, I had eagerly unzipped his bag in search of my gift. Years ago, he'd given up hiding my surprise – now, he laid it on top for me to uncover quickly. From perfume to pearls, he always brought home something that put a smile on my face and gratitude in my heart. And today, just days away from Christmas, I couldn't imagine what I would find.

And...well, I had never expected to find this!

The sound of the shower shutting off, snapped me from my shock and my head twisted toward the bathroom. Through the closed door, I heard Sheldon singing his favorite song.

I believe in you and me...

I believe that we will be...

In love eternally...

When the movie, *The Preacher's Wife* had hit the big screen, Sheldon had declared that this song was our song.

As he sang, I could tell he was rejuvenated and refreshed; inside the richness of his tenor, I heard his anticipation.

I did the only thing I could – I stood still and waited until the door opened and Sheldon stepped out. His damp skin glistened and his smile was just as bright. The towel tucked at his waist was loose as if he didn't plan for it to stay there long.

"Hey, baby." His greeting was filled with the lust that always came from being away from home for five days.

Still grasping it with just my fingertips, I held up the thong. "What is this?" I asked. I didn't even recognize my own voice – my tone was as deep as my husband's.

His smile rolled upside down and he squinted, trying to see what I held. "What's what?"

My heart pounded with a pain that made me want to fall to my knees. But, I pressed through it and held the underwear higher – straight in front of his face for his eyes to see what mine had seen.

His frown deepened. "What's that?" he asked again as if he didn't know.

I had hoped for more from the man who had promised that he would forsake all others. I had expected my upstanding husband to confess right away that he'd fallen and quickly beg for my forgiveness. Maybe then, there would have been a slither of a chance that I would forgive him and we could somehow find a way to move on.

But now, there was no chance of reconciliation. Not if he was going to play me like this. Not if he was going to lie and deny.

The words of my three-time-divorced best friend came to me now.

"Men cheat, and then they lie. That's what 'man' stands for - men-admit-nothing."

Theresa had lost her faith in men a long time ago, even though I constantly worked to get her to see that all men weren't the same. And, I always held up Sheldon as Exhibit One. But now it seemed like Theresa was the one who needed to be schooling me.

"Savannah, sweetheart." His voice was full of the same confusion that was etched deep in the lines on his face. "What *is* that? Why are you showing me those..."

"Don't you dare do that, Sheldon," my voice quivered as I interrupted him. "Don't you dare stand there and tell me that you have no idea what these are." I shook the cloth between my fingertips.

"I don't."

Raising my hand high, I tossed the satin and lace toward him; the thong hung for a moment in the air before landing at his toes. "Whose are those?" I screamed. "Who do those panties belong to?"

He held up his hands, shook his head. "I don't know what you're talking about."

"I'm talking about you bringing your whore's underwear into my home."

"What?" Now, his voice was as loud as mine.

"I'm talking about you cheating on me. How could you do this?" I cried.

"I don't know what..."

I didn't let him finish. "Don't deny it, Sheldon!" I screamed. "I found those in your bag; I'm not stupid, I know what those panties mean."

Now, he said nothing. And, it was the way he stood silent that made me snap. That made me rush to him with my fingers clutched into fists, ready to attack. But he grabbed my wrists before I could begin my assault.

"I can't believe you did this to me!" I said. "After all these years. After all the love that I've given to you. After *everything* that I've given to you." Fury gave me the strength to wrestle free from his grasp and I pounded my fists against his chest.

His eyes widened at my punches and he tried to push me away.

Stammering, he began, "I...I...I..."

The beginning of his confession came out in a gurgle. "I...," he said again before his legs shook, his knees bowed, he fell to the floor, the towel now completely free.

I stood there for a moment, confused. Was this really the way Sheldon was going to handle this? He was going to pretend that he fainted?

But then, it was the way he laid there, his eyes rolled back, his fingers clutching the skin on his chest.

Now, it was my eyes that widened and I dropped to the floor.

"Sheldon!" I sounded different now. Yes, I shouted, but my voice was filled with panic.

His mouth opened and his eyelids closed.

"Sheldon!" I pressed my fingertips against his neck, felt his pulse, then jumped from his side. Rushing to the nightstand, I grabbed the telephone.

"Help me, please," I exclaimed to the 9-1-1 operator. "My husband. He collapsed. I think he's had a heart attack!"

Made in the USA
San Bernardino, CA
16 November 2017